The Ajax File

by

M J WEBB

This novel is a work of fiction. Unless otherwise indicated, all the names, characters, places, events and incidents in this book are either the product of the author's imagination or used in a fictitious manner. Any resemblance to actual persons, living or dead, or actual events is purely coincidental.

No portion of this book may be reproduced in any form without permission from the publisher, except as permitted by copyright law. This book is licensed for your personal enjoyment only. If you would like to share this book with another person, please purchase an additional copy for each recipient.

Thank you for respecting the hard work of this author.

Copyright © 2025 M J Webb
All rights reserved.
ISBN: 9798307907207

ACKNOWLEDGMENTS

As always, I would like to thank my good friend, John Dunning (J.D.). I know I am fortunate indeed to have his support, input and advice. It is greatly appreciated.

I am also eternally thankful to Tanya Knapper for assisting on every one of my novels to date.

Finally, I'd like to thank all those who have offered a word of encouragement over the years, read and/or reviewed my work and took a chance on an indie author.

It means the world.

FOR MY FAMILY

*Dedicated to my good friend Tim Coultas.
A true gent taken too soon.*

Chapter 1

Miles Dalton glanced down at his father's old watch for the umpteenth time. The scratched TAG Heuer Carrera Chronograph on its well-worn NATO G10 strap reminded him of happier times and a contented smile *almost* made its way to his lips. Not quite though, because the six-thirty train into London was late again having arrived a full thirty minutes behind schedule. He doubted even the bequeathed heirloom could improve his mood today, already deflated as it was by recent events. The new job brought with it a significant pay uplift and relocation so it *should* have been cause for celebration, the fresh start he craved allowing him to turn the page on endless torrents of grief, which had threatened to overwhelm him of late. A few weeks in however and even his sorrow had been pushed out now, replaced by a severe sense of morning dread he couldn't quite shake. The new boss was the cause of most of his anxiety and she wouldn't take kindly to his tardiness. She'd been all smiles and laughter during the interview process but it had not taken long for her true colours to show afterwards. She was now a woman on a mission it seemed; to make his life hell. With a terminal case of bad attitude and even fouler breath. Smoked so much, she needed her own health warning. He had no idea why she disliked him so but Miles was beginning to suspect that he *wasn't* her preferred candidate for the role. The thought of facing her again aggravated the pit of his stomach once more. He closed his eyes and gave a heavy sigh, told himself that it was *only a job*. Still, it was time to face a few facts; his long-term prospects at the company were already looking pretty bleak, so maybe he should find something else and quit?

An attractive woman around his age brushed past his seat with a smile and Miles gazed straight down at the floor, as was his way. Lean and wiry, like an over-aged Harry Potter, the bespectacled twenty-five-year-old was not what you might call, a *people person*. No *ladies' man* either. Not adept at conversing with the opposite sex, he was in fact pretty useless around them in general. Repeated uprooting and a preference for the company of computers and gadgets had left him socially awkward in many aspects, so that he often appeared sullen or moody. It didn't help that in himself he felt deeply unfulfilled, bursting with energy of a kind he could never fully describe or dispel. Manic *and* glum then. It was hardly a winning combination. His lifestyle did him no favours either. He attended the gym regularly at all hours and trained hard, kept himself in peak physical condition, though he never seemed to gain much muscle, probably due to his preference for cardio over weights. Miles would slip in his air pods and run like Forrest Gump. Often, he would remember to look down at the control panel on the treadmill only to discover he'd been sprinting at speed for over an hour or more. And at night, his vigour barely affected, he rarely slept or socialised like he knew he should. Instead, he gamed freely into the small hours with like-minded souls who were now just about his only true friends; a small and exclusive online group he'd termed rather boringly, The Nerds. As the self-appointed Chief Nerd, he was fuelled by copious amounts of energy drinks and the thrill of clan matches with players from all over the world. He was frequently only disturbed well after sunrise by the morning alarm. At most, he thrived on four hours sleep. By rights he *should* have been a walking zombie. Yes, Miles was a lengthy bike ride through a sandy desert, away from ideal boyfriend material. Too much like hard work for any prospective partner to take on. Not that he cared too much about that, for the only downside *he* could see to his chosen lifestyle at present, aside from the constant ridicule of some and the possible harm it was inflicting on his body and mind if the so-called experts were to be believed, was a persistent, unrelenting craving he had for... well, *more.*

If only he knew more of *what.*

It was an itch he couldn't quite scratch. All he knew for certain, was that *something* was missing from his life. And that he would feel permanently in limbo until the nagging omission was identified, preferably found. Miles was a Gandalph without a staff, a Winnie absent his Piglet, a knight minus a quest...

Outside of the speeding train, the daily routine continued and the mundane world he was forced to endure passed by in a blur, as it always did. His was a tedious existence governed by limitations and rules, with horrid bosses, false personas and zero cheats or do-overs. He was merely one more player added to the lists, a side-character, a bit-part entity making up the numbers. Such was his lot. It was enough to get you down so he resolved to move on in more ways than one. He'd deal with the Queen of Halitosis only when he had to. Cross that bridge the very second it loomed large on the horizon. Not a moment before.

Time to focus on something else. *Anything* else.

Miles was seated at the rear of the carriage by choice with his back to the connecting doors. This was his preferred vantage point as it afforded him an excellent view of his fellow passengers, essential for the activity he had in mind. *People-watching* had been something he'd believed rather dull until quite recently. Hadn't considered himself the type. Of late though, he'd tweaked and developed it into an art form.

Most of his fellow travellers had their heads down, eyes glued to a multitude of screens as normal, endlessly scrolling though their phones like zombies. Of the rest, some were reading newspapers or books, broadening their horizons. A few more were simply staring aimlessly out of the windows, pondering perhaps the concerns of the day ahead. He knew *that* feeling. He studied each stranger in turn, attempting to create an amusing backstory of his own which matched their look and demeanour, to pass the time. He began with the closest; an elderly couple seated opposite him. They were holding hands and smiling, like they were eternally grateful for every single second they could eke out of their time together, appeared to be on a shopping trip, or visiting relatives. *However*, today, in *Milesland*, they were *also* Olympic champions who had achieved near superstar status. The old man was more agile than he appeared. He'd taken gold in Table Tennis at the World Championships, won the 2023 European Open and came third in the Qatar Grand Prix earlier this year. A medical marvel who defied time with two new hips, no finer ping-ponger was there than *Fingers McGhee*, renowned for his amazing dexterity and forehand smash. His beautiful lady wife was a BMX rider unsurpassed in her field. In anyone else's fields too. *The Peddling Pensioner* was an internet sensation, the fastest thing on two wheels this side of Peckham, poster girl of the octogenarians, of all the bowls clubs and golf courses throughout the land. These senior citizen mega-celebrities Miles decided were on their way to sign a lucrative, big-money contract with Channel 4 Television, having been offered their very own talkshow entitled, *Ethel and Brian on Life.* Prime viewing, if that was your bag.

But what struck Miles most about Ethel and Brian, or whatever their real names were, as he stared in fascination and chuckled to himself, was how wholly content they obviously were in one another's company. Totally at peace. Oblivious to the outside world almost, to anything and everything beyond their perfect little bubble.

He couldn't help but envy them.

Tracey and Stacey from Arkansas, USA were social media stars too. Video bloggers, travelling the world committing a series of murders in the most bizarre and heinous ways, uploading it all onto the World Wide Web for their fans. The gruesome details bar none. Their channel had grown steadily over the last couple of years but following an appearance on a popular TV show, ratings had trebled.

'...And don't forget to hit like, subscribe and share. It really helps the bank balance,' they would say in unison at the end of every programme to the sound of tinned laughter. Awful stuff. *'Remember, gore lovers; if it ain't slime, it ain't crime!'* Then they'd wave at the camera both dressed in frilly lingerie, pink gloves and matching wellies, covered in blood and entrails. Fun times for the masses, or the sick of mind, depending upon your point of view.

Miles sniggered to himself again, only too aware that his twisted sense of humour was possibly getting worse. His attention immediately shifted to a man in his mid to late thirties wearing a navy-blue uniform of some description.

What's your story? he wondered.

He was just trying to make out the logo on his polo shirt when, at the opposite end of the carriage, the connecting door opened all of a sudden and a petrified, scruffy and dishevelled man came sprinting into view.

'Move! Get out of the way!' he yelled, as if his life depended on it, making his way quickly down the aisle and snapping Miles out of his daydream.

A host of heads instantly turned in unison.

What the hell is going on?! All kicking off on the morning commute? Miles asked himself. His brain kicked into overdrive. He hoped the guy wasn't some nutter on day release from the local madhouse, or a druggie about to cause a huge scene...

'Phut! ...Phut! Phut!'

Wrong on both counts it seemed.

The terrified runner practically fell onto Miles' arm and he winced having felt a sharp pain, before the guy hit the deck like a downed partridge blasted from the sky, not a yard from his feet. Two small holes were burned into the centre of the guy's back and pretty soon, an increasing flow of blood began to pool underneath him, spreading out onto the carriage floor.

'He's... He's been shot!' Miles automatically spat out loud like a simpleton, without realising what he was saying. 'No, not a terrorist attack, please?!'

His eyes were up and alert now, focussed, immediately scanning for the shooter.

Slowly, the other commuters also dialled into what had just happened. Many in the carriage began to murmur, then cry, then scream in abject terror. However, try as he might, Miles could see nothing of note ahead, only fleeing persons of all shapes and forms as he stared intently down the train, through the open door.

The high-pitch shrieks of horror continued unabated as many of the petrified passengers hurriedly moved out of the aisle, made for the safety of the next carriage. Then, a very brief, curious silence descended, almost as if all the commuters further away out of sight who could actually see the triggerman, had drawn in a collective breath at *exactly* the same time. Miles looked at the old man opposite in disbelief, seeking confirmation from the pensioner whose eyes had suddenly sprung into life too, signalling recognition, telling plainly of a soldierly past. The old boy nodded his head just once and turned quickly to shield his wife with his own body, a totally selfless act that was mightily impressive given the circumstances.

Miles Dalton was a computer geek who spent far too much of his life indoors. He was no stranger to firearms, however. His father had served in the military all his adult life, retired a major. Over his service career, he'd moved his family unit more times than most gypsies, but he'd always ensured that his boy knew all about weapons wherever they went, if nothing else.

Another near-hysterical cry sounded shattering the quiet. A teenage girl in ripped jeans and an oversized white hoodie sat on a nearby seat, her hair in bunches. She was staring in horror at something and made to stand up, but an overtly menacing, male figure loomed over her before she could and out of the basic instinct for survival, she closed her mouth and remained where she was.

Stood in the now half empty carriage, in the middle of the aisle, was the gunman who had for whatever reason mercilessly felled the petrified runaway laying at Miles' feet. Late thirties, tall but not overly so, solidly built without being over muscular, clad in black Timberland boots, dark jeans, a navy jacket, black gloves, a dark cap and wraparound sunglasses. His expressionless face scanned the scene. He'd moved like a big cat in the zoo. Gracefully, with a powerful, menacing gait which nevertheless covered the ground rapidly and efficiently, hardly any sound. A weapon was held in his right hand and pulled in close to his body, with the barrel angled upwards.

Everything was happening in double-quick time. And yet, Miles had captured all that detail from one sudden glance. What was going on? He ducked down instinctively but just couldn't help himself. He *had* to peek out again and he hissed through gritted teeth, fighting an irresistible urge to *do* something, even though he would normally be cowering in fear at this point.

Then, he saw it. His chance. The emergency break leaver. Without a moment's delay, he was up and yanked on it with all his might. The carriage lurched and shrieked as the break engaged and everyone was hurled forwards.

Miles shifted his gaze swiftly back towards the main danger, staring straight into the eyes of the still advancing shooter, horrified now that he might have angered him and he would seek to bring down more than just the one solitary target. Adrenalin was coursing through his body and his hands were shaking. He had no clue what he could, or should, do to help the other passengers, for he was in mortal peril himself now. He watched on in horror, as well as a pinch of relief it had to be said, as the man righted himself and continued moving forwards, his eyes fixed on the wounded victim alone. From a distance of only six feet away or so, he fired another round into the man's back and Miles gasped in shock and terror at witnessing such a cruel act.

The object of the merciless attack was still breathing, though only just. Short, sharp, violent wheezes as he clung on determinedly and precariously to life, beyond all reasoning.

'Phut!'

Another suppressed gunshot tore yet *another* hole in his back and the dark-clad stranger targeting him inched past Miles in a callous, drawn-out manner, aiming his weapon straight at his doomed target's head.

Something deep within the mild-mannered dork snapped at this point and his rage swelled to hitherto unknown levels, all fear forgotten or dismissed. The assailant was now very close, distracted by the desire and need to complete his kill. Miles realised that this presented him with a tiny window of opportunity in which to act. Without fully understanding why, without rational thought of any kind, he exploded out of his seat with phenomenal speed and before he realised what he was doing, he had grabbed the suppressor on the gun and twisted the pistol in the guy's hand violently to the right, so that his fingers were trapped in the trigger guard, attempting to employ a disarming tactic he had been taught years ago as a teenager by his karate instructor.

Miles noted with satisfaction that the gunman yelled out in pain, cursing loudly in a distinctly South American accent. The firearm fell to the floor and the young man kicked it away, under some nearby seats. Unperturbed though, the immediate reaction of his new adversary was swift and violent, and a flying left elbow connected powerfully with Miles' jaw. His vision flashed white then began to close down. A left fist came hurtling down upon him at the same time. He saw it blurred at the last moment and tried to tuck in his chin, but it was no use. The punch was delivered with full force and landed with a loud *crack*.

Miles' legs buckled. He was going down. Maybe, going hand-to-hand with a professional killer, wasn't one of his better ideas?

The haymaker was followed swiftly by a front kick. It was sent with such force that it would have booted down any locked door and it was more than enough to lift Miles off his feet. He reeled backwards, his lungs devoid of air. Detached from reality briefly, he simply stared out ahead of him at a haze, unable to react in any way. His senses were muted and all feeling had deserted his body now.

Somewhere off in the distance he heard the tell-tale, **'Bang!'** of another round going off. Louder this time. The killer had dispatched his target with a final, deliberate headshot, whilst Miles was out of it. He'd been carrying a secondary weapon that he had drawn from an ankle holster.

The job done, the murderer then spun on his heels and disappeared out of the carriage like a ghost.

Totally and completely disorientated, Miles took a short while to regain his composure, all the time fully expecting another powerful assault to be launched. It never came, however, and an absolutely absurd silence descended on the carriage again, taking him by surprise, as all those who had remained nearby seemed too afraid to move, or even speak.

He sat himself upright. His head was swimming. His jaw ached like hell and his insides throbbed. The stillness ended abruptly when the old man nearest to Miles moved over to him.

'Here, you alright mate?' he asked, with an unmistakable cockney twang.

Miles wasn't sure and shook his head to clear his vision. He could think only of the victim at this point though and waved him away, turned to render what help he could.

The sight that greeted him would haunt his nightmares for the remainder of his days.

The luckless fugitive was still as still can be, lying face down. He was dressed in faded blue jeans bearing the grime and filth of constant wear. Grubby, white trainers adorned his feet and his dark green sweatshirt was filthy, ripped and torn in places. The area of his back was holed four times. The entry wounds were already oozing a little blood and a huge puddle of the red stuff now covered the aisle floor. It was spreading outwards quickly, running under the seating. Miles could glimpse only a small portion of the guy's face, which was carpeted in a good few days' worth of stubble. He lay with his head to the side, almost as if he were looking over his left shoulder. The final shot had cracked his head like a melon, displaced part of the skull. And what lay underneath was even worse. The exit wound had torn out a large chunk of flesh just under the right cheek bone. Despite this, and with all sign of life gone, Miles knew enough to know that he had to make *certain* the guy was dead. He reached down and with some difficulty turned him over. Then, he bent forwards to place his fingers on his carotid artery and checked for a pulse.

As he did, Miles caught sight of the victim's face for the very first time in all of the commotion and his lungs deflated aggressively and rapidly for a second time. The air within vanished so explosively, that he almost fell over. His entire body, including his mind, felt as though it had been zapped with a thousand volts of electricity.

His instinctive response was not caused by the actions of others, as before, but by the *enormous* shock of a totally unexpected discovery. For lying before him was the body of a complete stranger he had never met. Wholly unknown. A man around his age, whose face, at first glance, was *identical* in every minute detail to his own!

Chapter 2

Weird didn't seem to do it any justice at all. The whole thing was totally bizarre and had Miles completely freaked out. It was like he was staring into some ghastly, magically-possessed mirror in which everything was distorted and confused. As if a hostile entity had reached inside of him, its long fingers and sharpened claws twisting his intestines so hard and fast, that a sudden and violent bout of vomiting had leaped right to the very summit of his immediate to-do list. He fought hard to gather himself and pushed down the urge with some difficulty, then realised that for some reason his right arm was hurting like hell which redirected his thoughts. The gunshot victim must have hit him with his elbow or something as he brushed past. He rubbed it hard and fast but that only seemed to make it worse. In no time at all it began to feel quite strange, like his funny bone had been aggravated and moved a few inches. He shook the offending limb several times to rid himself of the pins and needles sensation and looked out of the window. The train had screeched to a halt just shy of Hitchin station, around forty miles north of London. Many of the passengers were beginning to dismount the stationary carriages and were sprinting smartly away from the scene of the crime, running along the grass embankments on either side of the track towards the nearby platform. Most presumably had no knowledge of what had actually happened to halt their journey but aware that a serious incident of some kind was in progress, they were understandably not keen to hang around.

Inside Miles' carriage however, the scene was different. Not a single soul stirred within, everyone rooted to the spot. Until, that is, watched in horror and fascination by silent witnesses too petrified or stupefied to move, the young would-be hero slowly reached out towards the motionless corpse, cleared a little hair away from his face. A touching gesture, but one of captivation too. Only a few moments ago, this lookalike he did not know had been an energetic and vibrant being. Even now, after suffering such a violent end, the deceased's facial features were *still* not disfigured enough to hide the remarkable resemblance. Miles stared intensely at him, examining his features. Then he noticed that the stranger had a small scar on his left cheek. He hadn't registered it before. He wore no spectacles either. That was something at least and he clung on to those small distinctions like a comfort blanket, as if they distanced him somehow from the gruesome event. Beyond those two minor differences though, they were so incredibly alike that within moments, Miles became utterly convinced that he was by some unexplained wonder in the presence of his own twin brother.

Only trouble was, Miles Dalton *had* no twin brother. Not to the best of his knowledge. He was an only child, raised in what he believed until recently was a decent, loving family. Until the army had informed him of his father's suicide that is. And his mother's subsequent vanishing act not long afterwards. Both events had all but destroyed Miles and he still hadn't fully recovered, not by a long shot. His father had retired and then promptly killed himself just eight weeks later, abandoning his family to fend for themselves. It happened a full five months ago now but it was a tragedy that came out of the blue and the pain of it was still visceral and raw. His mother had reacted swiftly and decisively. Some had said irrationally. She'd immediately returned home to England with her only son and cut all ties with anyone from her past. Pretty soon afterwards, they were severed with Miles too. She became a stranger to him and then disappeared without a trace.

Grief does funny things to people. At least, that's what he was told, by more nameless faces than he cared to remember. But his life had imploded for reasons he could not fathom and he just wasn't listening to them, retreated into his own private world of gaming and exercise.

Those thoughts flashed by in an instant. He'd had it tough of late, that was for sure. Was still emerging on the other side of it, punch drunk. Despite the recent upheaval and tragedy though, his parents would *surely* have informed him if he had a sibling, wouldn't they? After all, they'd had over *twenty years* in which to come clean. The completely ludicrous notion that an identical brother existed out there some place, one he knew nothing about, that those he loved and trusted had hidden such a momentous revelation from him, was completely *absurd*. So much so, that he almost dismissed the whole, crazy idea out of hand.

However, even in his current state, his rational thought processes were in tact just enough for him to quickly confront the facts. He may have *wished* to ignore the obvious but the irrefutable proof was lying right before him. The blood-soaked similarity was a grotesque image he knew would never leave him. How do people move on from seeing something so unspeakably brutal? A warrior like his father *could* perhaps, but he wasn't that sort. Wasn't cut from the same cloth. And what upset him most as he mulled things over rapidly in his scrambled brain was the fact that those motionless, insipid eyes were now clearly fixed on *him*. Even in death, *he* was the object of their gaze. The creepiness of that revelation really freaked him out and he pushed down the lids gently so they were concealed, for he knew those eyes well. Mirror images of his own, created from the same gene pool. They *had* to be. Same with the nose, lips, chin, cheekbones… *everything*.

Nothing on this whole, wide planet could have disturbed him more. An avalanche of questions for which he had no answers fogged his mind and added to his distress. Fatigue came in waves and the sickness returned. His pulse had rocketed to epic levels due to the unprecedented shooting, as well as his failed attempt to prevent it and subsequent beating. Despite his relative youth, his body burned fiercely in objection to the explosive burst of energy deployed in order to fend off the killer. The very capable mystery assassin from the other side of the world who had so efficiently hunted down and slayed…

Well, *who* exactly?

Who *was* this chap before him who wore his face? And why was he gunned down in such a fashion? There was no way this incident was any kind of coincidence so what the hell was going on?

Miles wanted to look away but the more his mind began to calm and he tried to make sense of what was happening, the more he was drawn back to the bullet-holed corpse, pulled by some invisible power he could not fathom. He leaned in for another, closer examination, watched all the time by several curious onlookers, some of whom began leaving their own seats warily to join him in the aisle.

Something caught his eye. A miniature EpiPen about half the size as normal was clutched in the deceased's left fist, protruding slightly so that a tiny needle was just about visible.

Miles immediately clutched at his stinging arm and gasped in panic again at the disconcerting sight. Had he been attacked himself, injected by this stranger? Was that why his arm stung so badly? And if he had, injected with *what?!*

A mobile phone began to ring.

Those around him halted their advance and Miles was wrenched away from his fears in an instant. The noise was emanating from the dead man's pocket. Miles wasn't thinking straight at this point, his mind whirring way too fast for shrewdness or perfect judgement, so all deference to the normal rules of evidence gathering or crime scene preservation, most of which he had learned through watching a multitude of crime shows on T.V., was tossed out of the window. His morbid fascination and intense curiosity had the better of him now and he reached forward, retrieved the small phone quickly from the dead guy's jeans and opened it up.

He stared down at the display with a great deal of surprise and disbelief, having expected it to be locked or password protected. It wasn't and the caller's name was Jenny. Well, that was the contact details that flashed up on the screen anyway. He swiped to answer and placed the phone to his ear. An almost hysterical, animated scream cried out at him immediately, before he even had chance to speak.

'Jase! Thank God! What the...?! Why haven't you been answering? Where have you been?! I've been dialling for ages, pig sick with worry. What's going on?! Where are...?'

'Stop! Please, stop?' he answered, interrupting her rant, which sounded as if it had only just begun. 'You have to listen to what I'm about to say... Mmmn... you may want to sit down for this... I'm sorry to be the bearer of bad news but as you may have gathered, this isn't Jase.'

There was a second or two of stunned silence in reply. Then, 'What do you mean? Who *is* this? Why do you have Jason's phone? Put him on for me, I need to...' she responded, forcefully.

'Err... *Jenny*, is it? No, I... My name is Miles. And you're not listening to me. I apologise again, but that won't be happening. I *can't* you see, he's...'

'*Can't?* Why not? Why *can't* you? Now just you listen here, I have to speak to...!'

Another soundless pause as comprehension dawned on the female caller. It was followed by a brief hush ladened fully with soft sounds of genuine angst and pain. Then, a few sorrowful, searching enquiries, and an obvious, tangible sense of guilt.

'No! I *knew* it. They've gotten to him, haven't they? He's dead, isn't he?' she implored.

The lack of any reply to her questions in the subsequent moments was enough to confirm her fears. Sometimes, silence plays out louder than a megaphone.

'I... I *knew* something was seriously wrong this time. I should have... I just don't know what I could have...? Yah! I can't think straight. I hadn't heard from him in a good while and yet he rang me out of the blue? I thought we were past all that. He must have been at his wits end, to ring *me*... Oh, Jase, what have you done?'

Though her voice was gentle and quiet now, Miles could still hear her sorrow clearly, her heartache and distress. Jason, if that was his real name, had apparently meant an awful lot to this lady, for a multitude of falling tears resonated in every single word she uttered. He remained quiet out of respect, looking up at the strangers around him and shrugging, uncertain how best to respond to her in such extreme and difficult circumstances.

Then, without warning, something immediately stirred within the female caller named Jenny and she speedily sniffed her cares aside, much to Miles' amazement. It was as if a switch had been thrown inside of her and she'd been instantly thrust back into the present. She wasn't grieving any longer, wasn't recalling events or reminiscing, but concentrating hard on the shocking crime committed against her friend, as well as her immediate priorities.

'Right... Think, Jen! Jase is gone. What does that mean? You have to pull yourself together. Okay, we...' she began, talking to herself.

She ceased talking abruptly and to Miles she suddenly stated, '*You* have to get out of there! You have no time. I'll mourn him when you are safe. Whatever your name is, I *strongly* suggest that you listen to me now and listen well! Your life depends on doing *exactly* as I say and in record time, do you hear me? Are *you* listening?! Forget *everything* else, all that has happened, and focus on my words. *Move! Run!* I don't know you and you don't know me, but we have to trust each other now. You *must* get out of there, sharpish. I must sound like a mad woman but… Look, I know very little, but if *you're* what Jase was seeking, or if you have in your possession whatever he was fixated on, they *will* return to finish what they have begun! *They will kill you! So run now!*' she yelled at him down the phone, so loud that it was like a canon exploding next to his head.

The supremely forceful instruction was abundantly clear in its meaning and intent. Nevertheless, Miles Dalton had been through quite an ordeal of his own that morning and in his current fragile state of mind, he was in no mood to be ordered about by someone he did not know. Or to go anywhere.

'I *can't* simply leg it. I'm sorry, I don't know you from Adam, as you quite rightly point out. Think I'm just going to believe what you say? You could be in league with whoever did this. If I bolt now, it will only make things worse for me in the long run, surely? Think of the optics. I'll look guilty as hell. Why should I go anywhere anyway? I've done nothing wrong here. I tried my best to save him. You say these murderers will get me? Why? Why would they do that? I'm not the one they want. I'm a key witness to a homicide I suppose, saw the guy who killed him close up, but that's about it. Does that place me in danger? Possibly. But a man has died here and I have to stay and talk to the police. Give a statement.'

In his muddled state of mind, it did not occur to him to mention the uncanny resemblance. In hindsight he probably should have but, in the moment, the urgency of the warning given temporarily trumped that minor detail.

'…No, I'll be far safer with the coppers,' he added.

Jenny's tone changed dramatically once more. It became even harder, morphing into a fiery cocktail of extreme exasperation and fury. She was *desperate* to make him see sense, all too aware that a decision to act had to be made immediately.

'Aargh! I was *talking* of the coppers as well, you idiot! *They* will kill you too! I'm trying to save your skin is all! I don't have much information to give you as I said, but I promise that we'll meet up soon and I'll tell you everything I know, *if* you make it out of there alive. No police though! If I see the law, I'm gone, and you won't see me for dust. *Take the phone and get moving!* It won't be locked. Jase never did that, despite me nagging him to… *Why are you still there?!* You're dicing with death. All I can divulge to help you now, to persuade you of my good intentions, is that you can't trust *anybody*. And I mean nobody. I may be your only hope. Jase only spoke to me for a few minutes, he was being followed at the time and making no sense for most of it, top-secret, hush-hush stuff, but the one thing he *did* say that I remember vividly was that those who were after him absolutely *owned* the police. Had them tucked neatly in their pocket, or on a short leash. They were bigger and far more deadly than the boys in blue, or so he said. Told me that straight out, as if it were burning his tongue somehow.'

'But…!' began Miles in protest, semi-convinced now but still unable to decide what he should do given the gravity of the decision and possible consequences of getting it wrong.

'Oh for…! Okay, enough of the pleading. Now it's *you* who isn't listening to *me*. I'm out of here. My conscious is clear and at least I tried. Have it your own way but if you *do* stay on that train, you're a stiff, already sized up for your coffin. It was nice knowing you, almost. Get yourself killed too, just like Jase. Only, do me a favour and destroy that phone before they take you? Get rid of anything which links him to me. All messages, and the call log.'

She hung up on him then without another word, leaving Miles stunned and caught squarely between a rock and a hard place. Should he stay or should he go? He had mere moments to make up his mind whether to remain with the body as he knew he should, or ignore every instinct he had, take the mysterious girl's troubling and stern advice.

As the small crowd of passengers around him inched a little closer, for some reason he did not quite fully comprehend, he suddenly rose swiftly and bellowed threateningly at them, 'Stop where you are! And be quiet, all of you! Nobody move!'

His unexpectedly hostile action was completely out of character. It also produced a near hysterical response from several young girls, who began to scream again.

'No! Quiet!!!' he roared, quickly restoring the silence. 'You have this all wrong! I'm no threat to you, or anybody. This thing here, the killing of this man, it has absolutely *nothing* to do with me, I swear it! Tell the police that for me, please? I can't stay here though. I can't take that risk.'

Miles made for the exit clutching his arm but stopped before he was half way there.

The gun!

He searched around under the seats for the discarded weapon, located it quickly and then bolted out of there at high speed. He slid it into his belt, in the small of his back, slowed as he reached the crowd on the platform, mingled with the masses at their tempo so as not to stand out. Within minutes, he was making his way to the final barrier, leaving behind him quite the commotion as security and police officers arrived and immediately swarmed the building, and ultimately the train.

A slight queue had formed at the turnstile guarding the exit to the station. A rather youthful policeman was attempting, on his own and with limited success, to close it to foot traffic. Many of the disgruntled commuters though, fearful of arriving at work late again after having been delayed, were rather rudely and forcefully pushing through the cordon he was trying to establish. Miles joined them without a second thought and after jostling his way past the beleaguered and miserable officer, he stepped out onto the street into glorious sunshine, his eyes taking a second or two to adjust to the brightness.

An immense sensation of relief flooded his entire body and he began walking away to his left, though he had no idea where he was at this point and where that direction might actually take him. He looked all around nervously at his new surroundings, fearful of attack. His only thought was to place as much distance as he could between him and the crime scene. He fumbled for the phone in his pocket to ensure he still had it, willing it to ring. Then realised almost immediately with dismay that he had left his *own* mobile on the train, and he cursed aloud. He'd risen from his seat so fast when he saw the shooter's weapon pointing at the man's head and it hadn't entered his mind after that. How could he have been so foolish? Still, what was done, was done. He had the victim's device after all.

There were people everywhere on the street, most having escaped the aftermath at the station and probable detention as witnesses, or just arriving to catch a service which would not now run. Across the road, on the opposite pavement, tracking his every move as they waited impatiently to cross, two huge and brutish, military-looking men in their early forties were matching his pace stride for stride, with eyes of extreme menace and undoubted purpose.

Chapter 3

Miles quickened his pace and threaded his way past a steady stream of pedestrians fleeing the incident at the station. As well as many stationary individuals who were attempting to contact employers and families on their phones to discuss what had happened, let them know they were safe, or give notice they would be delayed. Others were deliberating the alarming events in small groups with their fellow travellers. All were barring his path and slowing his escape. Due to Jenny's blunt and forceful warning he continued to glance fretfully over his shoulder. The two intimidating males were behind him now, though still some distance away, standing out so noticeably in the crowd that it was almost laughable. His heart skipped a beat. Whoever they were, they were most definitely shadowing his every move as their eyes never left him and they had crossed the road way too swiftly for disinterested locals. Then, they noticeably increased their speed. Within seconds, both began running as best they could, weaving in and out of foot traffic, cutting their way through those in their path at an alarming rate. Miles tried to react by lengthening his stride but the gap was closing fast no matter what he did and pretty soon he stepped out onto the road and burst into a flat-out sprint in order to get away. Which was matched easily by his resolute pursuers. On one of his many anxious looks to the rear, Miles caught sight of the lead guy reaching inside his jacket, pulling out a gun. Sweat trickled down his brow as the large stranger immediately fired once into the air. A warning shot to disperse the throng between them. Men and women dived to the ground as a result, or spilled out onto the road, narrowly avoiding the oncoming traffic which screeched to a halt, bystanders and drivers preferring to take their chances with a ton of speeding metal, rather than face a gunman firing a loaded pistol.

Screams, shouts and cries shattered the suburban hush and a second shot was despatched towards Miles, despite the shooter running flat out and the multitude of innocent people in his way. Miles weaved like a madman and yet he was *still* almost hit. He heard the bullet whistle past so near to him, that he knew instantly he had just come perilously close to death. Who *was* this looney tune, to be able to shoot so accurately on the run using a pistol, without halting to take aim?! He hadn't hesitated, or blinked at all. Didn't appear to give a damn for the very real probability of inflicting collateral damage.

As if to underline the extreme threat he faced, yet another gunshot sounded. It was followed almost immediately by a dull thud and stifled cry and Miles was horrified and sickened when a lady just ahead of him dropped to the ground. Her face was a perfect depiction of shock as she was struck squarely in the chest by a bullet with his name on it. He could not, *dare not*, stop to help her and he raged inside. He desperately wanted to but he knew better than that and he continued his frantic flight, searching urgently for options now. *Any* options at all.

There were precious few. He began wildly scouring the immediate vicinity in his anxiety. A tiny alleyway appeared abruptly on his left as if by magic. If only he could make it that far, he had a chance of disrupting their clear line of sight. He had no idea where it led but if he continued running in a straight line like this, making it easy for them, he felt sure he was a dead man for these mysterious villains chasing him now, were quite obviously of a different calibre to anybody he knew. Anyone he'd heard of in fact. Highly competent marksmen.

Which made them *what* exactly?
What have I gotten myself involved in?!

He could scarcely believe what was happening to him. He was a computer geek who lived a life so dull that he was an object of ridicule for most. He wasn't a spy or a soldier. Nothing special about him. As far as he was concerned, unless his digits were dancing merrily on a keyboard or gadget, he hadn't a courageous bone in his body. He was just an ordinary guy with a bank balance in cardiac arrest. Joe Average. Had literally nothing of note. *Was* nothing in fact. He was certainly not worth a bullet. If only he could persuade his current pursuers of that. Unfortunately, however, neither of these armed and hostile goons appeared to want to engage him in conversation right now. So, he darted through the gap in the fence and disappeared from sight, scarpered about as fast as his young legs would carry him.

Miles was pleased and relieved to find that the alley and pathway led out onto an open cul-de-sac, with numerous properties arranged in a sort of horseshoe design. Those hunting him down were still a little way behind but gaining gradually. He was not confident he could evade their pursuit so he decided quickly that hiding would be his best option. He selected a house halfway into the street and made his way around the side of the building before being seen. Sprinted to the rear and prayed that nobody was home as any response now to the noise he made would most certainly give the game away. Then, he would be trapped. He vaulted the gate without delay and was thankful to discover no dog yapping at the intrusion. His luck was in and he hoped for all the world that it would last. He headed straight for the centre of four, large leylandii trees which bordered the back fence, pushed his way forcefully through into the darkness and hid behind the largest trunk and dense foliage, out of sight. There, he waited silently and attempted to calm his rapidly beating heart and breathing, which was so ragged at this point that he thought for certain he would be heard and discovered.

A succession of rapid footsteps announced the arrival on scene of his new foe almost immediately. They stopped on the other side of the gate, the racket they made so loud that it was clear they had converged on that property to join forces and share information. Was that some weird coincidence though, or had they zeroed in on his whereabouts somehow?

It soon became apparent from their tone that he had lost them completely. All purpose to their actions tumbled like a house of cards and they remained stationary for a time, talking. At first, Miles could hardly hear what was being said due to the sound of his own respiration drowning them out. He held his breath and pretty soon he could just about catch everything.

Only trouble was, his understanding of Russian dialects wasn't just rusty, it was non-existent. Though, this startling new revelation *did* raise his eyebrows somewhat.

This is all messed up. An American or Latino at the station. And now a couple of Russians or Ukrainians or something?! Why are they here? And why do they want me dead?

From the furious edge in his voice, it sounded very much as if the Russki with the mightily deep growl was in command, asking his subordinate where their elusive prey had disappeared to. He sounded irate, as if someone had just murdered his daughter. His companion though, whose speech was only slightly higher, didn't appear to have a clue, thankfully. A few more words were spat out between them, which were evidently several choice expletives expressed in their mother tongue, followed by an enormously loud roar of anger and exasperation from number one. Then several short and sharp, barked orders, before they moved off together speedily and returned the way they came.

It was yet another close call for Miles but he reckoned he was safe enough for the time being. Just to make certain however, he remained in hiding a little while longer and used the time to think things through.

The one inescapable conclusion he arrived at, came to him blindingly fast.

Act in haste, repent forever… I'm deep in a pile of poo!

The murder on the train was one thing, a headline act of complete butchery which would no doubt shock the entire nation, as brazen as the most overt of contract killings. A declaration of war almost. *But* these new hoodlums here, these Russians or whatever they were, they had *deliberately* discharged their firearms on a crowded street. Once again in broad daylight and surely under the gaze of several cameras or phones? This time maiming or killing a passerby, an innocent, unarmed civilian bystander. No warning was hollered at Miles before they opened up. No attempt was made to talk to him at all, or stop him without using lethal force. *Zero* hesitation in their actions, which were most certainly designed to kill at all cost, for they did not even try to search him, or bring him in for questioning, as the cops say…

No, they had only one intent here. One solitary aim. Something inside of Miles turned his stomach at that thought and made its way straight to his knees, so that he almost collapsed.

What did it all say about who they were? Who they worked for? The limits they were prepared to go to in order to achieve their goals? Which were *what*, exactly? Why was his death so vital to them, that they risked so much exposure? And had they waged war against him with no constraints, no limits whatsoever? Who *does* that?! On whose behalf? Were they connected to the killer on the train at all…?

He had questions galore, but no amount of time spent deliberating them seemed to help, possibly due to shock. Miles wasn't sure of *anything* right now. Other than the fact that *he* was the sole object of their hunt, he was clueless. On his own.

One thought leaped out at him. The notion that they might want something he possessed, as this *Jenny* had mentioned, was no longer on the table. He could discount that theory at least. You don't *kill* the golden goose. You don't shoot on sight. Not if you want *all* of the eggs he has. Those you can't see too. You talk to him first, only choosing to end his life when you know for certain he does not have them hidden away somewhere… And yet those hunting him down most certainly wanted him planted six feet under, or the final journey of vapour from a chimney.

He was going around in circles and getting nowhere. Questions would have to wait for answers. He'd get them though.

Time passed as he decided on his next course of action. It was peaceful in the garden. The birds were happily chirping away and he really did not want to move. Nevertheless, he knew he *had* to. He needed to find somewhere he could think straight without worrying about being caught and executed. Maybe, contact the only person who could possibly shed a little light on everything; the mysterious Jenny. She'd sounded a little deranged on the phone at first, granted. Still, in the very brief time since they had spoken, *all* of her warnings had proven to be right on point. The nightmare scenario she had predicted for him had quickly become his reality. He had to give her that at least. And she didn't *have* to warn him. She *could* have hung up immediately and cast him loose, left him to fend for himself, as others had done.

Why didn't she do that? Something else he really didn't know to add to the pile.

She was a complete mystery alright, but one he felt he had to at least try to unravel. Besides, who else could he turn to now? Who else could he trust? He'd probably be all over the news by dinnertime. He had a few friends and family in the form of cousins living in the area but he didn't want to risk dragging anyone else into a potentially life-threatening situation, at least until he knew something of what or whom he was dealing with. He turned silently and raised himself up to peer over the rear garden fence. The house backed onto the railway line not far from the station. The train was out of sight and the two grass verges he could see, leading away in the opposite direction, were both clear. In a flash, he had climbed over the fence and was running stealthily along the embankment, hugging the few trees around and the undergrowth for cover. After a while he reached a pedestrian bridge and decided to see where it led. Another short walkway opened out onto a shopping area and a huge supermarket car park. Beyond that, lay a small arcade. He strode purposefully towards the entrance, hoping to find a place to lay low for a while as he made the call, but his peripheral vision somehow alerted him to the presence of yet more danger.

It came in the form of an insanely attractive Asian woman in her late twenties. She was gorgeous, dressed like a movie star. She was also quite blatantly dangerous, evidently on the hunt, and now pointing his way. Then, she drew a weapon of some kind and marched majestically towards him like a femme fatale.

'Oh, don't give me this James Bond stuff!' he huffed, frustrated at his incessant poor fortune and immediately breaking into yet another mad dash.

Once more he was running for his life, immensely grateful now for all those hours spent pounding the streets and the treadmill at his local gym. A Chinese-looking guy on the other side of the road joined the chase. The Asian duo were undoubtedly partners, determined and very fit, easily matching his pace. Though neither was gaining nor falling back at this point, Miles had no way of knowing if he could outlast them and it was a matter of stamina now. He knew that *his* was outstanding but the stakes were too incredibly high to bet his life on it and without doubt, the first to falter in this race would probably *not* be going home alive.

They soon entered a built-up area with few places to hide. The hunters were now so close that they would easily observe any rash attempt to deceive them. Miles spied a small High Street ahead and foolishly began to believe that the increased crowds would mean safety. He should have learnt by now.

His error in judgement was confirmed when the man behind him fired off a round which struck a stationary car he was passing. It shattered the rear window with a deafening din and narrowly avoided showering him with glass, confirming their murderous intent. Out of another instinct for survival, Miles found an extra gear he did not know he had from somewhere and increased his speed, began to extend the gap. Before long, he'd turned a corner and was temporarily out of sight. He seized his chance and darted into a nearby café. The terrified staff and customers gasped in horror and moved out of his way, frightened no doubt by the frantic-looking, sweating stranger with bulging eyes. He sped straight through to the rear areas, grabbing a coat and cap from a stand on the way. Beyond the kitchen lay a small rear door and garden courtyard, with bins lined up against a wall. He used them to vault the bricked barrier but instead of continuing his flight, he doubled back, took out his gun and waited for the pair to follow him, intending to end their pursuit once and for all.

After a minute or so of silence lying in wait, it became apparent that they had given up the pursuit and he tucked his weapon away, sucked in a deep breath of fresh air. Only then did he fully begin to appreciate what had occurred. It was as if somebody had struck him right between the eyes with a brick. He replayed the entire morning in his mind on fast forward, then promptly expelled the contents of his stomach onto the ground.

Eventually, both his mind and body were clear of gunk.

I must have upset the entire world! he thought.

Miles wiped his mouth dry and stood up straight. He had no plan to speak of but the urge to keep moving was strong. He wracked his brains for inspiration and saw a taxi driver returning to his cab a few houses away, having dropped off his latest fare and helped them in with their luggage through the rear entrance.

Good lad. He'll do.

'Hey! Hey, mate!' Miles called out to him, trying to appear nonchalant and not like a man who had a giant target painted all over his back.

'Who me? 'Sup? What can I do you for?' answered the cabbie with a cheeky grin.

The jovial nature was a given in these parts it seemed for all those who served the public. The excess beer belly and shirt hanging out of his trousers, which was adorned with several coffee or gravy stains, was the mother of all cliches too.

'You free?' he asked.

The driver gazed around at his empty cab and smirked at him incredulously, as if he were his old schoolteacher. 'Sharp one you are, eh? Nothing escapes you, does it Einstein? Ha, ha… Just joshing with ya, kid. Guess so. Hop in,' he stated.

Miles accepted the invitation gratefully. He fastened the seatbelt as the driver eyed him via the rearview mirror.

'So? You gonna spill or what? I ain't no clairvoyant, ya know. Or is it a secret, where we're going to?'

Extreme weariness washed over Miles like a tidal wave all of a sudden as the young man succumbed to an unexpected overload of adrenalin. He rubbed his aching arm as he thought for a second or two, considered his options.

There weren't many that came to mind. He felt like death warmed up now, sickly, clammy and weak, though he did not know why and didn't dare go home. He wasn't exactly certain of where he was either. He recalled the journey on the train and quickly did the maths. They were travelling south when the killer struck, had just under an hour or so before arriving in London. Maybe fifty minutes, he reckoned. That placed him close to any one of several towns and cities and geography was never his strong point. He threw caution to the wind and made his choice.

'Alright, just needed a second or two to get my bearings. Do you know Cambridge at all?'

The cab driver tilted his head to the side as if he was offended. 'Yeah, course I do. What you take me for? It'll cost ya though.'

'That's not a problem. Just so long as we can hit a cashpoint. You take me to the city centre and I'll see you right.'

'I... I usually tell the young'uns like you to pay up front, but you look like a trustworthy sort. Okay, no probs,' said the cabbie. 'Err, you alright by the way? You're not looking too chipper. Done in, if you ask me. Like someone's just stomped all over your grave too.'

'Who, me? Nah, I'm fine. Thanks for the concern but just concentrate on the road. I decided to go for a little run whilst out for a walk. Bit off more than I can chew, I think. That'll teach me. Feeling it a little, that's all.'

'Ah. Say no more. Mugs game that is; this fitness lark. I mean, cop a load o' me. I'm your prime specimen right 'ere. Hunk of the month. Four pints a day, a pie or a kebab to follow and I'm as fit as a fiddle. Ha, ha...'

Miles smiled back at him. He liked this guy. He made himself as comfortable as he could on the rear seat and for the first time since the opening shot had been fired that morning, he started to relax a little.

Chapter 4

Detective Chief Inspector Edward Farley took the call on his mobile as he fought his way through the London traffic on his usual route to the station. He was briefed on events by the duty officer and listened intently to as much detail as he could before immediately stating that despite the crime taking place outside of London, it was close enough and serious enough to possibly be terror-related, so *he* would be assuming command of the investigation. He knew that would be a contentious call. He then ordered his subordinate on the other end of the line to inform the relevant parties of that fact, once they had alerted his new partner, Detective Sergeant Samantha Lennox. The phone rang out on the speaker in his car once again a few minutes later, by which time he had pulled onto a petrol station car park in anticipation and was mulling things over.

'Sam?' he asked, without affording her the opportunity to speak.

'Oh-oh, this doesn't sound good. Yes, boss?'

'No, it's not I suppose. Sorry for the early hour. Didn't wake you, did I?'

'Me? That'll be the day. Early riser I am. Already been for a four miler, actually. I was just about to leave the house. I take it we have something new?'

'Up and at 'em sort, eh? Good. Yes. You'll like this one. Could be the start of something big. The vultures will be circling by now but I've pre-empted their response and said that we'll take it. Squatter's rights from here. I'll deal with any blowback as and when. It's ours so look sharp. A few rather large noses are going to be put out of joint so I need you on top form. It's something meaty to get your teeth into at least. Not bad, coming so early in your career. Be a chance for you to impress me... Listen up, put any plans you might have on hold, Sam. I wouldn't expect to see too much of your home or family over the next few days or so. Maybe weeks. It'll be all hands lashed to the oars on this one.'

He could hear the satisfaction in her voice as she replied, 'Understood. Fine with me, gaffa. What's happened?'

'Not much. Only an as yet unidentified shooter offing someone on a crowded commuter train. Several shots fired, just short of London. One known fatality so far. Killer's in the wind. There's reports of more gunfire and a casualty outside the station too, near a busy road. Tons of witnesses and probable footage. I'll swing by and pick you up, give you more of what I know in the car. It's causing havoc already, as you may appreciate, with the line being closed, so we'll have to work fast with a fire up our ass. The team will all be receiving calls about now and they'll meet us there. Your home address is in my satnav so I'll be with you in around twenty minutes or so.'

'Sounds good. See you soon.'

Sam Lennox placed the phone back on its cradle. She stared at the half dozen or so empty Johnnie Walker bottles strewn around her kitchen and lounge, as well as the disgusting remnants of numerous days' worth of takeaways in various containers. She really had to begin taking better care of herself, had promised her mother as much when she'd popped round for an unannounced visit last week. *Inspection* more like. Sam reminded herself again that it was only because she cared and felt pangs of guilt, the same as she always did. Once more, she determined to act and sort her life out.

She grabbed a huge bin liner and bagged up the empties, threw them out in the trash in double quick time. Then paused outside for reflection. *Another* near sleepless night. It was getting to be a habit; waking up in pools of sweat with the world's worst headache and a throat like sandpaper. Things were definitely deteriorating. She had been warned they would. Though she was none the worse for it as far as her energy levels were concerned. She craved the long hours and intense action a large investigation like this would bring. It was *exactly* what she needed, to keep herself busy. Inaction meant time to dwell on things. A potential killer far more deadly than any criminal or terrorist she might face.

Her hand was shaking. She took a pack of Marlboro Red from her suit pants, placed a cigarette between her lips and lit it with her Zippo. Inhaled deeply and blew the smoke up into the morning sky. Slowly, that familiar sensation of the first cigarette of the day made its presence known and a wave of relaxation washed over her.

The whole place cleaned, she waited in complete silence for her new DCI to arrive, in the hallway, foot tapping with impatience, stood well away from the half-open bottle of Johnnie Walker twelve-year-old she knew still lurked in her kitchen cupboard which was calling her name. She began sweating slightly. A common occurrence. The shakes returned. Also, a regular event.

Sam knew perfectly well why all of these symptoms still plagued her. She was just about the only one who did. One or two switched-on colleagues clearly suspected something was off, given the way she was with them at times, but now that she had managed to blag a clean bill of health from the quacks, the psychiatrists, there was not much anybody else could do. She'd won that particular fight against all the odds, been declared fit for duty. End of.

Perhaps, she *should* have joined the Royal Academy of Dramatic Art, rather than the police force?

Doctors be damned. She'd had her fill of their kind, would never allow herself to be labelled again. After all, in the mind of Samantha Lennox, *she* was one of the fortunate ones. A survivor. She owed it to those not so fortunate to make something of her life. And she had no right at all to bitch about the way things were.

DCI Edward Farley was a forty-six-year-old, twenty-year veteran of the Metropolitan Police Force, London born and bred. A graduate of Cambridge University, for the past five years he had held a top position in the prestigious Homicide and Major Crime Command (SCO1) and was considered one of its finest detectives. SCO1 was one of several units who could be assigned to investigate top level, organised crime. A fatal shooting on a packed passenger train most certainly fell under their remit, though local police and others were expected to challenge that decision vehemently. Farley was a tough, no-nonsense commander who did not suffer fools gladly. He could be brash and arrogant at times, demanding and insensitive, but he was also a ruthless and determined workaholic who lived for the job. A man who had earned the complete respect of all of his colleagues. He'd joined the force straight from Cambridge on a fast-track promotion scheme and had enjoyed a stellar career to date, putting away many of the capitol's major career criminals. He reported straight to high command; the current Metropolitan Police Commissioner, Elizabeth Barker and her staff, as well as senior civil servants from Whitehall on occasion and several high-ranking politicians. He was usually dressed in fine, designer suits which fitted him perfectly, his short brown hair always immaculate. Many considered him handsome in a rugged Jack Reacher type of way, but a failed marriage and a string of girlfriends spoke of an abject car wreck of a private life.

Farley usually worked alone but his newly-acquired partner, Detective Sergeant Samantha Lennox, known to all as Sam, had been thrust upon him by the top brass just three weeks prior in an almost completely unheard of cross-hierarchal move he had been given absolutely no choice about. He'd been instructed in the way he was expected to behave as far as she was concerned and that was that.

Fast-tracked also and clearly being groomed for stardom, Sam's path to the lofty and sought-after position in the elite unit had contrasted sharply with his. With *anyone's* in fact. A very fit, mildly attractive singleton in her mid-thirties of mixed race with shoulder length, wavy brown hair and deep brown eyes, she had joined the Army Intelligence Corps as an officer straight out of Sandhurst. She specialised in covert reconnaissance and surveillance and her service career took her to places far and wide, including two tours of Afghanistan. The second of which culminated in an intense firefight and a life-changing, serious wound ultimately leading to her discharge. To soften the blow, the powers that be offered Sam an unheard-of transfer into the Met Police, comprising of a minimum two years on the beat as a constable, followed by entry onto an accelerated promotion scheme, numerous strings having been pulled by someone unknown who sat very high in the current government. This poorly kept secret was by now pretty much common knowledge in the rank and file, the source of much irritation and conflict among her peers.

Thus, Lennox had a new role to learn and fresh battles to wage, to go alongside the Military Cross she had earned on active service. She was untrusted and, in some cases, despised. It was hard for her to reconcile but the war hero had quickly come to realise that she had to prove herself all over again.

Despite his initial annoyance and misgivings, DCI Farley had so far been rather surprised and more than a little impressed by his capable new protégé. She could be both edgy and intense but he'd liked what he had seen. Sam was bright, enthusiastic and keen, without being annoying and asking too many silly questions. The deluge of enquiries or comments she *did* voice, were usually all relevant and inciteful. She was professional and courteous when in the presence of company and clearly respected his experience and rank. He did not want to like her. But neither was he overly concerned with popular opinion or the rumour mill. Nor what others thought of him. With the decent head on her shoulders that she had displayed so far, time would tell if Sam would *earn* the prestigious role she had been gifted and win over her colleagues. However, the early signs were exceedingly promising and Farley knew *exactly* where his money would go. He had already decided to give her a fair crack of the whip therefore and he brought her up to speed as best he could on the journey to Hitchin station, as promised.

Immediately upon arrival, Farley and Lennox made straight through the cordon and summoned all senior staff and involved parties to an immediate briefing, including those first on scene. A crowd of around twenty-five professionals gathered around them within minutes.

'Morning everyone,' began the DCI, throwing his considerable voice out to as many as he could, 'no time to waste. Get what you need and quickly. The carriage will be moved as soon as you are done and the line re-opened. We're looking for a suitable location so we can continue examining every inch of it. I need a sitrep and I need it now. Give it to me fast and hard. Let's start with what we know?'

The blend of colleagues and complete strangers around him looked at each other briefly before the officer in charge of the firearms team piped up nice and loud. He was ex-military too, Farley could tell. His uniform was immaculate and he carried himself as if he were on the parade ground, all confident and assured, with the resolve of someone who had seen his fair share of action. Possibly combat.

Lennox was impressed that she could see her outline reflected clearly in the polish on his boots. Wondered how long he'd been bulling them.

'The techy types will give you the full work-up, guv. All the specifics like. I need no Oxford brainiac type to tell me that this was a hit though. A targeted elimination. It's as plain as day. There was minimal attempt to avoid detection. No waiting for a better advantage or clearer shot for *this* guy. No, the very moment the victim was spotted, he was *slotted*. There's a great deal of accuracy here too. Scored a tight grouping firing on the run at high speed, at a moving target with a suppressed pistol. That's not easy. You have to be a top-notch shooter, or desperate, to even try it. Plus, they had collaterals standing in their way, moving about, distractions. Even so, he was as calm as you like, according to witnesses, took the time to deliver a headshot to ensure matey boy snuffed it and...'

'And yet our mystery stranger intervened?' Farley added, finishing his sentence for him and nodding his head slightly. 'Yes, I have to agree with everything you have said, at present. On the information I have.'

'They... Forgive me, sir, he took one hell of a risk, our unknown helper,' ventured Sam Lennox. 'Whoever he was, this gunman was most certainly on a mission of some sort. We don't know why, or who sent him, but bloodlust would have been high in that moment. Adrenalin running through his veins like wildfire. Red mist in his eyes. It does crazy things to you. All this would have been affecting both his judgement and vision. I don't care if he *appeared* outwardly calm, I've been there. The whole landscape narrows down in that moment to just you and your immediate priority. Your target or assignment. Tunnel vision kicks in. They will have been focussed on the kill, on the victim, to the exclusion of everything else. And they will have used lethal force against *anyone* getting in their way... Despite this, our young hero tries his best to save a complete stranger? Now *that's* living on the edge. Assuming they were not known to each other, of course, which nobody here has refuted so far. We could have done with his phone. One of the passengers swiped it though I hear… Why would he risk his own life in those circumstances? And *why*, after doing so, did he have it on his toes?'

DCI Farley grinned at her approvingly, then turned his head back to the group. 'Fine questions. Take note everyone. We'll hopefully discover all of that in due course. I want to know everything that happened here from start to finish and in detail. What do we have on the killer so far?'

The Scenes of Crime Officer was a middle-aged woman of limited height in gold-rimmed glasses. She still wore her protective clothing and spoke with a clear, distinctly Scottish accent.

'Aye, well, we've only just finished our preliminaries. We'll know more after the postmortem. We did take several bullet casings from the carriage which were almost certainly fired by the perpetrator. It's a Winchester, nine-millimetre, nickel-plated brass. Probably a 124-grain jacket hollow point, maybe a +P loading too, judging by the wound cavitation on the victim. I'm saying trained professional also. It ties in with what we've been told by those present. The deceased took two rounds to his back from relatively close range. Then a *third* and *fourth* from almost point blank. These missed major obstruction in the way of bone so exited his front and have been recovered. Ballistics will therefore ID the weapon if it's on file, but I doubt that it is. This doesn't feel like your typical gangland shooting, more like…'

She trailed off, lost in thought. After a moment, she resumed.

'…The second shot is likely to have killed him. Its trajectory looks as though it would have pierced the heart. Which is consistent with the amount of blood loss. Our victim was probably already on his way out before the Good Samaritan showed up, though he had no way of knowing it at the time of course. The killer was taking no chances too.

There's also a .380 Auto casing we've recovered, probably another hollow point due to the small entrance hole and large exit wound damage. Almost certainly a case of insurance. He was seen to retrieve a short, square, stubby gun from his right ankle, possibly a Glock 42 or something similar. Our shooter was wearing gloves, so likely no fingerprints. If he *is* a pro like I think he is, I doubt that we'll get any off the casings either.'

'Why not?' somebody from the crowd asked.

'Because, I'm betting he also wore gloves when loading his bullets into the magazine. People like this don't make schoolboy errors.'

There was a hush for a few moments as it all sank in.

'We also found this.'

The SOCO held up another evidence bag with what looked like an EpiPen inside.

'So, what, our victim was diabetic?' the chief firearms officer offered.

'Not so. Whilst on the surface this looks like an ordinary auto-injector pen, the kind *used* by diabetics, this is no EpiPen I've ever seen. It's... well, something else.'

Sam took the bag from her and studied it for a moment. 'This is military,' she said, before handing it back. 'Seen them in Afghanistan. Pilots and special forces types use drugs like Modafinil, to keep them alert and on their feet. I've seen stuff like that administered in gear like this.'

'This just gets weirder and weirder,' Farley stated.

'Yeah. A pro and yet such a blatant act, almost as if they wanted to be caught?' the SOCO responded.

'Maybe, our murderer knows full well that even if he *is* caught, he can't be prosecuted?' said Sam Lennox, which raised more than a few eyebrows. 'In that case, they wouldn't give a damn about being seen, would they?'

A ripple of conversation spread among the group, indicating a growing unease.

'Look at what we know so far. The timing and witnesses did not faze them. High end ammunition and military grade medication?' she added.

'It's possible, but we know nothing right now, so let's not speculate. I don't want to assume anything,' replied DCI Farley, firmly. 'This could just as easily turn out to be a gang hit over some new designer drug hitting the streets, dressed up to make it look sophisticated.'

'It's a poser, isn't it?' answered the SOCO. 'Now, the *victim* in this case is even more weird. His identification is likely to prove troubling also, to say the least. Though, several sources stated he bore a remarkable resemblance to our rabbit.'

Farley gave her a stare of disgust, before adding, 'Go on. *Why* is it going to be tough?'

'Oh, it's all there for us. I have evidence coming out of my ears. Things people just don't carry around in normal circumstances. Driving license and passport. Our Vic may have been planning to leave the country I suppose? I *can* tell you that the real problem only surfaced once I had a good look at his documents. They're all fake.'

'Are you certain?' said Lennox, her mind beginning to whirr and her hand automatically fiddling with the Zippo in her trouser pocket.

'Yep. Take it from me. They're as dodgy as... Well, really dodgy. I've seen more than enough forged papers in my time. The name on them is for a, *David Jones*. That isn't his real name, I'm sure. He's another mystery to solve.'

'That's just excellent!' rasped DCI Farley, exasperated. 'This case has a will of its own. Facts appear to be few so we work with what we have and *find* the rest. I want a significant break in this enquiry and I want it yesterday! Fingerprints, CCTV, work ups and histories, criminal record checks, ballistics, statements, PM report and I want to know what's in that pen! I need it all from you in record time. You're all working round the clock on this one, or our superiors will know about it. Cancel whatever plans you had and keep your phones on you at all times. Contact myself or Sam here with anything you find, at any hour and without delay. Do you all understand me?'

Everyone nodded their immediate acquiescence and a murmur of, 'Yes, gov,' echoed around the group.

'Then, that will have to do for now. Thank you all and get on with it. We have a killer and a fugitive to catch!'

Once they had all dispersed, Sam Lennox turned to her vastly more experienced superior. She spoke in a hushed tone so that nobody else could hear.

'Are you always that hard on your team, boss?'

'Hard? You call that, hard?' he replied, surprised. 'I wasn't expecting that kind of observation to come from the lips of a veteran like you. I'm a pussycat. You must have dealt with a lot worse than me. Besides, it was needed, I think. I really don't like what I'm seeing here, Sam. It smells off, as if it is going to smack of some kind of secret bull anytime soon. I just know that we are going to be paid several visits from shady characters in nice suits. The kind who usually divulge nothing, but demand *everything*.'

'Hmmn... You may be right. If we *are*, I'll probably have worked with most of them. In a former life.'

'Really? Excellent. That's about the only good news I've heard today. If they come at us then, they are all yours to take care of. Liaison duties, we'll call it. Just keep them all away from me.'

'You got it. Now that we're alone, what do your first instincts tell you about this crime?' she asked. 'I'm eager to learn and they say you're the best. Why was he killed do you think?'

'Don't do that. Don't try to butter me up. I'm far from the best, believe me, and it's beneath you. Flattery won't work, so cut it out... No way to know for sure as yet. Too early to say. Though, they're right, it doesn't feel like the usual gangland stuff. He's scruffy and dishevelled, as if he's been on the streets, or on the run. That means probable enemies. Trouble of some sort. No backup to front it. Few of our gangbangers are big enough to upset the Americans or their cousins though. He was chased down, that much is clear. Possibly to retrieve something he had on him. Did our fella take it away without the others seeing? Did the killer miss the pen? Was that it? Or was it on his phone say? A picture, message, video…? If the object was to capture him and make him talk, they would have waited for a better opportunity and brought more people, delayed until an exit option became available, not slot him on a train full of witnesses. Makes no sense. And this thing about them appearing so similar. That has me really intrigued. Were they related, or did they know each other?'

'You weren't kidding about this case. So many unknowns. It might prove to be massive. If the murderer *is* a foreign asset, operating so blatantly on British soil, that makes things a whole new level of complicated, doesn't it?'

Farley rubbed his chin and sighed. 'You have no idea, Sam. And if he's a domestic gun for hire?'

'That's not ideal either. Far from it in fact. We'll be superseded by the chain of command, told what to do, how high to jump and when. They'll order us to back off while others get to play and take over, won't they?'

'You catch on fast. For sure. They'll need control. Though, they can *tell* me until they are blue in the face. Doesn't necessarily follow that I'm going to *listen* to them.'

Chapter 5

Owen James was also alerted to a new assignment by a call on his mobile. Though, it was actually the *third* call to be more precise which had finally succeeded in rousing him from a blissful sleep. The first two efforts had barely registered, sounding for an absolute age before the unknown caller eventually rang off, only to keep trying and trying like an annoying, persistent hound nibbling away at his ear. Owen lay on a deluxe, oversized bed in his spacious, converted warehouse apartment which was situated in the prestigious Docklands area of London. He was surrounded by the trappings of a wealthy, lavish lifestyle. His home was worth well over a million pounds and Owen had paid cash, a fact of which he was extremely proud. Money flowed like wine for James, the proceeds of several *off the books* contracts he conducted for shell companies undertaking the unofficial, totally deniable, dirty work of the British government. What the military in the U.K. at least termed, *Green Ops*. Better known as the *blacker* variety to most of the rest of the outside world. He was the product of an upper-class upbringing and top private schools, a graduate of Bath University who had served as an officer in the Royal Marines with some distinction. Until, that is, just over four years ago, a chance encounter with a former Special Boat Service comrade, which inevitably involved copious amounts of liquor, led a few weeks later to an unsanctioned, completely illegal raid into the territory of a supposed ally. A knee-trembling soiree for which he was more than handsomely rewarded when he eventually arrived home. Four of his comrades were not so lucky. When one door closes in that specialist environment however, another one opens and great success was met with an unforeseen, on-the-spot job opportunity. He'd accepted the extended offer instantly, for this was the chance for advancement, excitement and untold riches that Owen James hankered for. A brand-new career to be forged for the stagnating captain. He secured his release from the Marines and hadn't looked back since.

Fast forward to the present and Owen James had made it to the very top of his profession. The tough mercenary and assassin was now immensely rich, set for life in fact, the *go-to* man for various wealthy clients including government ministers, industrial moguls, several shady unofficially-sanctioned criminal enterprises, and multiple foreign nationals. Owen wasn't fussy who he worked for just so long as the pay was good. He did everything from private security to contract killings and kidnapping. He moved effortlessly in high society courtesy of his upper-class background, which proved a major draw for clients as it meant he could move in closer proximity to high-class targets than the average ex-squaddie or sniper. Attack from within. His reputation had soared with each successful venture and the majority of elite contracts these days were now coming his way on a regular basis, with most commanding huge sums.

It was already midday but the curtains were drawn and the room was dark. Owen didn't care. The damned phone chimed yet again. It was becoming abundantly clear that the persistent caller wasn't going away anytime soon.

Couldn't they take a hint?!

Eventually, Owen had heard enough. He reluctantly crawled out of bed with his eyes half closed, strode fully naked across to the drapes and opened them a little to let some light into the room so he could see. Then he shuffled over to his couch, picked up the blasted noisemaker and squinted angrily through tiny eye slits at the display, in order to identify the ill-advised culprit. Possibly, to add them to the growing list he kept of all those awaiting termination free of charge.

He cursed under his breath, severely irritated. The killing idea was a no go. The *fool* trying to contact him in the most annoying manner turned out to be the one guy in the whole, wide world who was one hundred per cent safe from his wrath. The only man he could never envisage killing. Deciding quickly that he had no choice but to take the call, he shrugged his shoulders a little and turned to face the bed. A strip of sunlight lit up one half and in the shaded area, there lay a red-haired beauty queen whose name he could not quite recall. She grabbed a pillow, placed it over her head, pulled it down tight to block out the noise she knew was about to come her way. She had kept him awake most of the night with her almost insatiable desire for passionate, loud and energetic love-making. It was worth it though. Sleep was overrated anyway.

He liked this one. More than he ought perhaps. Though, like the others before her, not enough. Not when duty called. Not when there was coin to be made. He smiled gently as she wriggled and groaned in protest at being awakened and her bare behind slipped from under the silk sheets, adding to her ample charms and conjuring up a host of delightful images of the previous night's many adventures.

'Morning, sleepyhead. Afternoon, I mean. Just you stay right there, my beauty,' he stated softly. 'There's no need for you to get up just yet. I'll take this call and then I'll be right back with you.'

The apartment was open plan and Owen sauntered through to the kitchen area with the phone still ringing in his hand. He filled up the kettle and switched it on to boil, before finally swiping up and placing the mobile to his ear.

'Arro? Chinese raundry? Wo you wan?'

'Oi! Stop messing about! About time, you waster! Owen, you there, you numbskull? We have a job.'

It was the exact same former special forces soldier who had recruited him. Only now, he sat at the head of a powerful organisation; the largest agency in London supplying top-end soldiers of fortune. Those very few who commanded maximum dollar on every single outing. The guy was a self-made millionaire now, a sort of agent of death if you will. A purveyor of mayhem on speed dial. The kind of fella who could quite easily bring governments crashing down in a heartbeat, and still make it home in time for lunch. On a list of all the elite operators in the world you most certainly didn't want to cross, *this* player was right at the very top. He was king of any battlefield, chiefly because of what he could bring to the fight.

Owen though, had grown quite close in recent times to this legend. He enjoyed a unique banter with him born of shared military experience, which was at least partially reciprocated.

'Course it's me, ya knob! Where else would I be in my downtime, playing croquet? What little I get of it. You *are* familiar with that concept still, time off? And I do hope you're using the scrambler. Don't want any uninvited visitors... Come on then? Speak quickly, or not at all. I have a hot date on ice and I'm just about to deliver the thaw. *Again.*'

'Ew! Too much intel. So that's what you yutes are calling it these days? Of course, it was a lot simpler back in my day. Simply ply them with drink and Bob's your uncle. Yah! Enough reminiscing. You never change, do ya? You've just hit forty, Jamo. Most men your age would be slowing up by now, finding a nice foxy lady to settle down with, have a few rugrats an' the like. But not you, eh? Not, *Owen James...* Ah well, each to their own. I suppose it's good for business anyway, that you have no ties. No distractions. Though, I certainly don't need that image in my head of you thawing anything, thank you very much...'

'Nuff smalltalk. Pay attention. And don't worry, we're quite safe. Got some new gear which takes care of everything. I have another task that requires your expertise. And before you start going off on one, I know it's a quick turnaround this time, but you were requested specifically by name. It's as big as they come, for a lone operator. You'll get plenty of offers on the back of this too, if successful. And the client is willing to pay you *double* your usual fee.'

That gained Owen's attention alright. He was already by far the dearest to commission in the field, so his eyes were open fully now. 'Double, eh? That's seriously impressive, mate. Do go on.'

'Thought that might take your mind off whatever bit of skirt you're with this week. Stick with me and I'll make you a God. It's a solitary hit. Nothing more. One kill. Only, you'll need to do the legwork on this one, track down the mark. He's scarpered see,' the voice added. 'Should you engage, you'll have every support we can provide on call, as usual. Back-up is available in force as and when required, though your mobility will be an issue.'

Owen's suspicious nature rose to the fore. 'Why are you telling me all this? You know I work solo. I have never requested help on any mission that I have completed for you so far?'

A momentary silence on the line confirmed the caller was considering how best to phrase his reply.

'Well?' prompted Owen, when he made no sound after a few seconds. 'Talk to me. We've known each other long enough to dispense with the usual crap. Out with it. What's the issue?'

'Fair enough. I owe you that much. You, err, may not be the only one in the game. Others are already in play I'm told, released from the traps by an overeager client. *Not* my doing. They have a head start on you. Expect an extremely hostile response once they learn you are on target also. You can blame the rep you've forged for that. Some of the current top five are engaged. They will want to see the job done, collect the bounty, so this has the potential to get messy if it's not done right. It's a race to the finish line against some of the best. Hence the increased fee.'

James gave a short sigh as he deliberated what was on offer. He knew deep down that he'd say yes. He just wanted to make his old comrade sweat a little. Was enjoying having him dangling in suspense. Eventually, he stated, 'I see. This is highly irregular. If it *does* go sideways, I'll be stranded in a turkey shoot and you won't be able to reach me in time. You won't place a Rapid Reaction Force on permanent standby, not for me. Risky. I'll face those odds but I want triple!'

'Ha! Is that so? That's pretty steep my lad, even for you. I'll swing it though. Okay, *done*. Anything else?' came the immediate response, indicating that his associate had expected such a demand and prepared for it, which again made Owen smile.

'Yeah. You can inform the gutless wonders behind this, that triple pay is just for the hit. That will buy them a kill. I'll make certain he disappears never to resurface or bother them again. If they want anything more than a corpse however - capture, interrogation or anything untidy like that - it'll cost 'em even more.'

'I got you. Shouldn't arise but seems reasonable, given the possible intrusion. The client may be *gutless* as you put it, but they have empowered me to act on their behalf in all matters. So, contract is extended and accepted I take it?'

'Seems like it to me. Pleasure doing business with you again... Now that that's over with, who am I gunning for this time?'

The veteran handler sounded far more congenial now that Owen James was confirmed as recruited and on board. Almost relieved in fact.

'Straight down to it. That's why I enjoy working with professionals like you. We made a great team in country, you and I. I sure showed you a thing or two about soldiering...

Young man in his early twenties. Goes by the name of *Miles Dalton*. No military background that we know of. Not for him anyway. His family is, or was, active. Not certain if they passed on any skills. He's a loner and a computer nut according to his file. Can't see where he would access any assistance from someone likely to cause you any grief. Latest intel puts him on his own. There's a purpose to his movements however, and we know that he took a call from a female. Maybe just a warning. We're working on it. We hear anything further, you'll know about it in almost realtime for we have birdies in the cage. So far, he has evaded all efforts to terminate him. Some of the others have already tried and came second.'

'Really? And he has no training, huh? Outstanding. I think I like him already. It's been a while since I enjoyed any real sport. I'll still kill him though.'

'Quite. Now, listen, there's a few bruised egos out there so be careful as they may be trigger happy. Don't think they're used to the hare fighting back. It's not gone down too well. Nobody of your calibre was involved, I'm certain. You need to find him, Owen, and put him down. Last known whereabouts are sketchy, though we are advised he was heading for Cambridge.'

James began pouring himself a cup of coffee and trapped the phone between his chin and shoulder as he continued to speak. 'Cambridge? Nice city. Who does he know in Cambridge I wonder?'

'Nobody. At least, as far as we can tell. He's alone and scared, lad. He knows he's being targeted by now and he's probably not thinking straight. He won't last long if he employs any logic, for we will predict that. We're too good at what we do. His only hope is to keep us guessing, so expect some irrational thoughts and actions.'

'Understood. I suppose Cambridge is not far to go at least. Should be a quick job. In and out. Hey, isn't that what your mob was good at, back in the day?'

There was a slight pause on the other end of the line. No response once more.

'I was talking about your unit, not you yourself... Never mind. What's he done, this Miles Dalton, to warrant being top of their blacklist?' Owen asked.

'Now you're getting personal. Does it matter?'

James smirked a little at being caught out. 'Like a bloodhound you are. No, not in the slightest. It's a very expensive job, that's all. Sometimes, it's just nice to know who you have in your sights. Consider it done. I'll send over the confirmation via the usual channels as soon as the job is complete. Proof too. Send everything you can on the secure line... I guess that's about all for now. Thanks for nothing. I'll grab some stuff and leave for Cambridge in an hour or two.'

'An... An hour or two?! Nah, that's not good enough, chum. Why not now? And here's me calling you a pro. You're losing your touch. Or maybe arrogance is dulling your edge...? Right, if that's the best you can do. Let's hope the rest of the pack aren't any nearer to finding him. Then, you'll lose your big payday and I'll lose a bet. Be lucky... Oh, and say hi from me to whoever you have there under the covers with you... On second thought, I don't have a lot on at present. I *could* drive over there and look after her for you, keep her warm while you're away if you like?'

'Ha! Doubtful in the extreme. Seriously pal, really, *really* unlikely to happen. I mean, I *would* extend the offer on your behalf, of course I would. Given all we have shared together and what you have done for me. You're like a very much older, favourite uncle. However, it's just not the done thing, is it? Besides, your daughter has informed me in no uncertain terms that you and her are no longer talking these days?'

'Dickhead!'

Banter aside, Owen knew exactly what he had to do. Without any hint of an explanation, he dropped the girl's bag and dress onto her sleeping form and woke her up.

'Time to go, love. See yourself out.'

Owen heard the door close as he stepped into the shower. He was out and dressed in less than five minutes. He opened his wardrobe and selected his usual work attire; black Timberland Euro hiker boots, dark blue Armani jeans, a grey cotton T-shit and an Arc'teryx jacket, topped off with a baseball cap. He put on his Panerai Luminor Flyback and checked the time. Finally, he took a Benchmade Infidel knife out of the kitchen drawer. He pushed the switch and engaged the blade. Satisfied, he retracted it with a push of the button and stowed it in his right jacket pocket. He felt in the left for a pair of gloves, put them on, grabbed his car keys off the counter and headed out.

Owen rode the lift down to the private garage and hopped into his Audi RS5, gunned the engine. Within twenty minutes he was at his self-storage unit. The place was deserted at that time of day and he made his way inside, walked through a long grey corridor either side of which was a series of red roller shutter doors. Upon reaching his own unit, Owen checked that the tell was still in place at the edge of the door. It was. Nobody had been snooping around so he took out his key and rolled up the shutter. Quickly, he ducked inside and closed it behind him. He stood still for a moment and just listened. Nothing. Only then did he flick on the lights.

Half a dozen fluorescent tubes spluttered into life, casting a dingy, almost metallic, white light about the place. Owen's eyes adjusted and he quickly set to work. On either side of the storage space were a set of large, grey-metal cabinets and red-metal, five-drawer tool chests. Owen unlocked one of the metal cabinets and scanned over its contents. He had in his armoury an AKMS assault rifle with a 75 round drum magazine attached, a HK G3A4 battle rifle, a Remmington 700 in a McMillian chaise, an Accuracy International Arctic Warfare sniper rifle, a Czech CZ Bren 2 assault rifle and a Daniel Defence M4. He selected the M4. This model had a 14.5-inch barrel and was fitted with a surefire suppressor, along with a PEQ 15 and an M600 tactical light. The rifle was fitted with an EOTech 551 red dot sight and a G33 magnifier. It was topped off with a Blue Force gear sling. A thing of real beauty.

Owen removed the magazine, checked the rounds and re-inserted it. The stainless steel Duramag slid home with an audible click. He chambered a round and flicked the selector to semi-auto, before placing it back into safe. He turned on the EOTech sight and was greeted by the bright red, round reticule. He shouldered the weapon and scanned around the lock-up, moving it from object to object, flicked over the magnifier and suddenly the reticule had the 3x magnification the G33 provided. Lastly, he squeezed the pad on the foregrip and the M600 light flicked on. Perfect. Just how he had left it.

The M4 went into a large black holdall bag that sat on a workbench counter. Next out of the locker came the Accuracy International sniper rifle. It was chambered to 7.62 x 51mm and held ten rounds in a detachable box magazine. Owen removed the magazine, worked the bolt and squeezed the trigger. There was an audible snap as the firing pin flew home. It was fitted with a Schmidt & Bender 5-25 x 56 scope, a Harris 6-9 swivel bipod and a suppressor. He folded the stock, unscrewed the suppressor and placed the rifle in the bag.

Next, he moved smartly to a set of drawers and took out five thirty-round magazines for the M4 and two additional ones for the sniper rifle. These too went into the bag. He opened another drawer where he kept a selection of handguns. A SIG P226, a Glock 19, a Glock 18 fitted with a suppressor, a .22 suppressed Ruger, a CZ 75, a HK USP chambered in .45 ACP, a Walther PP, a Smith and Wesson Model 686 .357 magnum revolver with a six-inch barrel and a lovely stainless-steel finish. He took out the Glock 19, opened another drawer and fished out four magazines pre-loaded with bullets. Took up the suppressor, ejected the magazine, checked the chamber was clear and screwed it on. These also went into the bag, followed quickly by the Glock 18, this time with three 33-round extended magazines.

He lifted a pair of AN PVS15 night vison goggles and head strap from another drawer and powered them on. Satisfied they were in working order, he grabbed a spare battery and set these to one side. He found four German, DM51 hand grenades. *Might come in handy,* he smiled. Then a couple of AN-M14 thermite grenades also went into the bag. Lastly, he opened another cupboard and took out a Black Crye JPC plate carrier housing two level four ballistic plates.

All the kit disappeared into his hold-all within minutes. He lifted it with some effort and difficulty and as quickly as he had arrived, Owen James was gone.

Chapter 6

Miles sat back and enjoyed a moment of blissful solitude. He took another slow sip of his cappuccino. The soft, comfy chair in the furthest corner of the café felt like heaven. It also placed every customer, staff member and the entrance clearly inside his immediate field of vision, meaning any new threat would be identified quickly, thereby allowing him to take prompt evasive action. He had already identified the fastest route out of there; straight through the toilet area and a fire exit door he'd located before even sitting down. He was relying on instincts perhaps, but he also was a fast learner. Still nursing the shakes and sweats and dealing with a migraine, experiencing aches and pains in places he never thought possible, he'd been dropped off in Cambridge city centre by the taxi driver. They had stopped at the first cash machine they saw and Miles had maxed out his card allowance, paid the fare. He pocketed the rest of the cash just in case, only too aware that sooner rather than later, his bank account would be frozen. The very moment the cabbie was out of sight, Miles had doubled back quickly to a small teashop he'd spotted on the drive in. It lay in a quiet side street and was not perhaps in the greatest location for any small business looking to turn a profit. However, it was ideal for his present needs as it was far from likely CCTV coverage. The centre he knew would be crawling with cameras and he had to presume that he was now high on any police search lists. Foreign agencies too, likely to have access to supreme technology. Of course, accessing his bank account was another trail they could easily follow but he needed cash quickly and short of robbing a bank, he could think of no alternative.

How had he come to this? A fugitive on the run, in fear of his life?

He set down his mug with a heavy sigh and took out the phone. *Jason's* phone. The brother he did not know he had and would now never know. He brought up the recent call list and hit the redial option for the last known incoming number. It rang out five times before it was answered by the exact same female voice he had spoken to earlier on the train.

'At last! You took your own sweet time about it, didn't ya?' a cold, almost hostile Jenny stated accusingly. 'Are you going to speak, or leave me hangin'? Are you okay at least? Did you manage to avoid the police? Or worse?' she asked, responding to his stunned silence with a mini tirade and apparently extremely eager for news.

'Err... Slow down a little and let me speak. We haven't even met, you and I, so why do I feel like I'm being scolded? I'm not five, you know... I'm fine. And thanks for asking. It was a close call.'

'Hmmph! I suppose that's something at least. Where are you now?'

'Cambridge. Not quite sure why. Couldn't think where else to go.'

She did not reply at first as she thought things through, possibly deciding on her options. '...Good. Nope, that's fine. I like Cambridge and know it well. Look, I've been doing some thinking. This morning was off the charts. I feel like I'm in some kind of movie. Like I should run a mile and not look back. *But* I just can't. It's Jase. I'll do what I promised. I'm willing to meet up with you, if that's what you want? It can't be until tonight though, after dark.'

Miles was a little perturbed by that. He wasn't quite certain what he had expected to hear from her but the delay in receiving what information or help she could provide, was most certainly unwelcome. He gazed around at the half-deserted café and the street outside.

'Great. That leaves hours for me to kill. What am I supposed to do until then?' he asked.

'That sounds like a *you* problem... Don't mean to sound harsh, but I don't know you either. I know your name is Miles and that's it. I don't much care either way what you do, just so long as you keep a low profile and don't attract any more attention. Take my advice and stay well out of sight. No visits to popular areas. No phone calls. Stick to back streets. That sort of thing.'

He huffed at receiving what sounded like orders from a stranger whose mannerisms so far, bore a striking resemblance to his own mother's. At least, what he remembered of her growing up as a teen. And his newfound confidence in talking to someone of the opposite sex meant that he wasn't about to let it slip. Which still felt a little weird to be honest.

'You may not *mean* to sound harsh, Jenny, but actually you *did*. I... Ah, never mind. I suppose I would be the same in your position. I'm not very good at reaching out to people and I know I haven't earned your trust as yet, but I'm already one step ahead of you on the Invisible Man thing, if that eases your concerns any? The High Street is a no-go area, I promise. Okay then, where *do* we meet?'

'I know just the spot. There's a park next to the river. Jesus Green, they call it. It's off Chesterton Road. Has a silver bridge which spans the water. You can't miss it. I'll meet you under that bridge at exactly midnight.'

'Alright, if you say so. You're not going to turn into a pumpkin on me, are you? Sorry, but this is all way too cloak and dagger for my liking. Sort of thing I play online, but never experience for real. I left my comfort zone back on that train. I'm not sure I...'

'Not sure you *what*, Miles?! Sounds like you've gotta grow up a little. Leave this pity trip behind, if I'm going to help. Can't deal with it, you hear me? You think I'm loving all this?!' came a short and sharp rebuke. 'Take me as you like, I don't care. *I'm* the one reaching out here, trying to aid a fugitive. I'm risking everything. Sounds like I should forget the whole thing because you're not inspiring much confidence. Jason was my ex. We were close once, very close. I loved him to bits. Thought he was, *The One*. I was wrong. We were over long ago. Feelings fade when you've been woken from the dream and exposed to the truth. I have no idea what he was mixed up in at the end, or why he got himself killed. I've mulled it over time and again and come up with nothing. I'm prepared to help you in the only way I can though, for him. I'll talk to you and that's all I'll do. Out of respect for what we once had, for what he said and for his memory. *Then*, I walk!'

...Now, the less we speak on the phone, the better. We can save the introductions an' all until we're face to face. Be there on time! I'll wait for exactly ten minutes and that's your lot. After that, I'm out of there and you are *not* to contact me again, understand? It sounds very much as if you are an extremely dangerous person to know.'

Miles took another mouthful of his drink. Let it warm his throat and insides on the way down. It felt *good*. Though she came across as a little rude and combative, she wasn't saying anything he didn't know.

'Okay, Jenny, you're right, about everything. I'm nuclear now, I guess. I wouldn't blame you for running from the fallout. I never expected you to do *this* much, so thank you. Though, I can't help but wonder if we shouldn't just go to the police with it all?'

'Better. You're welcome. I'm a sucker for a good sob story. But the *Old Bill?* Are you *kidding* me? Don't you think Jase would have tried that, if it were a serious option? I've told you what he said. See you tonight. Or not at all.'

Miles spent the entire day thinking, deciding, resting and sleeping in an open doorway on a rundown retail park, out of sight. The only positive was the fact that the inactivity appeared to ease some of his symptoms a little. The headache eased in the fresh air and the aches weren't quite as severe, though his arm still throbbed and as yet, he still hadn't recovered his appetite. He arrived at the park early, secured a decent observation point not too far from the bridge and concealed himself in a bed of thick bushes. From there, he watched Jenny approach the meeting point right on time and was pleasantly surprised.

She was of medium height, around five foot six, slim and attractive with long and straight, black hair. She wore a trenchcoat over plain black trousers, above low-heeled matching shoes. Her movements were slow and deliberate, cautious, eyes darting around in every direction looking for any sign of danger, or a tail. She stopped beneath the structure and looked at her watch, gazed around for a minute or so and then checked her phone, no doubt unhappy at his apparent no-show and searching for any messages he may have left. Time passed by as she waited impatiently. She was just about to leave when he emerged slowly from the shrubbery and walked casually up to greet her, satisfied now that she had not led him into a trap.

Jenny eyed Miles up and down in the same manner, sizing him up. The wonder and amazement as she stared at his face was striking, even in the near darkness.

'You're having a laugh!' she exclaimed, immediately taking his chin in her soft hands and turning his head sidewards for a better view.

She examined every inch of his face closely for a good minute, utterly astounded.

'That's...! No scar! Aha! You have no scar. You're the absolute spit of him in every other way mind, but for the glasses. Seriously, I've got chills just lookin' at you, like he's risen again somehow. I think I'm having a flashback or summin'. I would *never* have believed it, if my eyes weren't seeing it for real. How the...! Oh, *hell* but this is massive!

Why didn't you say anything on the phone, you clot?! *This*, right here,' she said, drawing a circle in the air around his head with her right hand, 'it changes *everything*. Puts a whole new perspective on things... So, what, you're his...? And he's your...? You have to... Wow! Just a minute there. Hang up the phone. I've just had a thought. It was *you!* No *wonder* he returned here. Jase was searching for *you!*'

'Hey! Slow yourself down, please? I know it's a shock but keep your voice low. Sound carries out here at night.'

Jenny closed her open mouth slowly, looked at him in complete disgust.

'There you go again. This isn't gonna work, Miles. I can feel it. We've no ground rules established. And we need some badly. Don't you shout at me, for one. It may have escaped your attention but *you* are the one deep in a world of... The one keeping secrets. His *twin?!* How could you fail to mention that?! I can go back to my life and forget all about you, and Jase. I'm not so certain *you* have that option? Nor anyone else to turn to? You *can't* have, or you wouldn't be here speaking with me.'

Miles recognised the truth when he heard it. He wasn't certain he'd said anything untoward as yet but he still softened his approach anyway. He exhaled slowly and put his hands up, signalling surrender.

'I'm sorry. I apologise, okay? I'm nervous. Anxious. Afraid of being caught. All over the place to be honest. I'm just trying to get my head around events which at present, have blown a fuse in my brain. You can leave if you'd like, but you're my only source of information so far and I need to hear this. Can we talk a little, please? That's why you came here, isn't it? Will you take a walk with me?'

She shook her head at him in defiance, then straight away seemed to have a change of heart. 'No... I mean, yes. We're too visible out here though, even at this hour. Mobile phones, cameras...? My motor's in the car park. It's not far away and it's much warmer. We can speak in there, where we can't be seen. That good enough for you?'

'Sure. Works for me.'

Once inside the car they sat in complete silence, each waiting for the other to begin. It was Miles who finally spoke first.

'I… I just wanted to thank you properly. For saving my life that is. I didn't want to leave that train under any circumstance, was rooted to the spot, but your words of warning convinced me otherwise and I've been hunted ever since. Don't know what might have happened if I'd stayed. So, it appears as though you were correct about the threats I face. I have no way of knowing where it comes from and how deep it goes, but if it's international as would seem to be the case, it's not a great leap to suggest they have infiltrated the police force. I would never have…'

'My pleasure. Though, your gratitude should really go to your…'

'Brother?' he ventured, still scarcely able to believe it himself.

Jenny noted the lost expression on the young man's face now and eyes tinged with sadness and regret.

'Yes, I suppose so,' she replied. '*Jason. He* was the one who started all of this. I gave him that scar you know. The one on his cheek. Threw an ashtray at him one night after he came back drunk from the pub and was a little too aggressive for my liking… No, he wasn't that sort normally. It only happened the once. How is it, that in all the time I knew him, he never even mentioned you?'

Miles wiped a bead of sweat from his brow. 'Here's the thing; I never even knew he existed, until this morning. I knew… I *know* nothing at all about him. I have to presume it was the same for him. He appeared before me for the briefest of moments on that train and now he is dead.'

'That's awful! You must be tearing your hair out. I can't begin to imagine what you're thinking. How you're feeling. I'd certainly want answers if I were you. Any information I could dredge up at all... Maybe, I should just relay what I know? Let's see. Jason phoned me yesterday. He was on the run from somebody as I said. I don't know who, before you ask. He was out of breath and making hardly any sense... Perhaps these incidents are linked? The same guy maybe? What can you say about his killer? What was he like?'

Jenny noted a faint reluctance to speak in Miles, to recall the details of the crime. It was a momentary hesitation which was only natural given the circumstances she supposed. Eventually though, his lips moved slightly and in a hushed voice, he explained.

'He... was like you'd expect I suppose. Jason Bourne type, in glasses and a cap. Packed one hell of a right hand. I managed to fight him off somehow but my head has been pounding ever since. When I hurt him, I'll never forget this, he cussed in an American accent of sorts,' Miles began.

'Really? You certain of that?'

'Yeah. I'd say a hint of Columbian, but can't be certain. I lived over there until recently. Though, I'm not sure what it all means. Maybe a hired professional, C.I.A. or similar?'

'*C.I.A.?!* That's a whole new level. Surely not? I don't know much, but my money is on the *similar*,' Jenny mused. 'Gotta be things we're missing here?'

'Probably. Most definitely. It's the hit of the century and it's not gonna be all that simple to solve. I was attacked again when leaving the station. Two of them that time.'

'What?! How? Who? Are you some kind of ninja or something? How did you survive?'

He sniggered a little, then immediately held his aching arm and ribs.

'Ha, ha… Hardly. I mean, I can handle myself better than most. Fought in a few competitions in my teens. Though, I used tried and tested tactics this time. I *ran* as fast as I could. Got out of there like The Flash, hid behind some trees.'

Jenny laughed along with him. Her blue eyes sparkled in the moonlight and he didn't want it to end, but eventually she stopped and he added, 'They were Russians I think. From around that region at least. And yes, before you ask, I'm sure. A short while later, I was fired on by a couple, a man and woman of Chinese origin, maybe Korean. Outran them too.'

'No?! That's the international thing you mentioned? I was going to ask…'

'It gets worse. All these people wanted me dead. No doubt in my mind. They *all* blazed away without a shred of warning. There was no attempt at dialogue in any form. They killed or wounded civilians like it was a war zone, and it was allowed.'

Jenny looked completely horrified. 'So, they weren't after anything you had on your person then. I take it you have considered the obvious? That they no doubt believed you were Jason. It wasn't *you* they were after. Wasn't *you* they were trying to kill, though they may be now. Even I would struggle to tell you apart, if I did not know about his scar. Have to get up close to see that. Place a pair of glasses on him and he's you. And vice versa. His death had not been reported then. Still hasn't, as far as I'm aware. He's not been named on mainstream media at least.'

'Is that delay so strange? I don't know. What was he like?' Miles asked.

'Jase? An asshole!' Jenny replied without hesitation, much to his surprise.

'Okay. Not… Not the answer I was expecting?'

'Maybe so, but it's the one you have. He had the entire world at his feet, if only he knew it.'

She took a cigarette from her bag and lit it up, wound the window down a little and blew out the smoke.

'We were a damned good thing, him and I. Could have been great together. But Jason wanted *more*. He could never say what was missing of course. A huge part of him never grew up. Still insisted on his time with, *The Lads*, his adrenalin kicks and parties.'

'How's that?'

'You know. Got into fights, petty crime, drugs on occasion... He wasn't all that educated and his friends left something to be desired. There wasn't a decent one among 'em. Even on the night we were engaged, I caught him snorting coke in the toilets. We were never going to work, not unless he matured. I told him as much, but it was a step too far and, in the end, I threw him out. He moved away to Hull not long after where he became a mechanic, though he was still using I'm told. He maintained contact on social media, the occasional text when he was drunk, spouting gibberish and professing his undying love. I hadn't heard from him for a year or so. That's when all this kicked off.'

'I'm sorry.'

'What *you* sorry for? It's not your fault, is it? We can't answer for the actions of others. I'm devastated to hear he's gone though. Really crushed. I have to question why he was on that train at all? He *hated* London with a passion. So why did he die travelling into the city just inches away from you, his twin?'

Miles coughed a few times and squirmed in his seat, wound down his window an inch or two, breathed in some air. 'I think we've established now that he was looking for me. It's way too much of a coincidence otherwise. As for *why*, I have no idea, but I think he injected me with something. I have to find out what. Did he send you anything else? Any e-mails or such? I've checked the call register on his phone and you're the only entry. He may have erased the rest.'

'Injected...? Holy cow! Don't think so. There's nothing on my mobile at least. I'm not certain about mail. I haven't been back to my flat in a week. I've been staying at a mate's house. She's just split up with her husband and needed a little support. That's why I couldn't meet you earlier. Travelling.'

'Okay. I think you'd better check it out. There may be more evidence sitting on your doormat. You go home. Let me know if you find anything. You can reach me on the...'

Miles stopped speaking as for some unknown reason his attention was drawn to two bright lights which had appeared in the rear-view mirror. No sooner had he noticed them, they disappeared.

'What's wrong?' Jenny asked.

He swivelled around sharply, caught sight of a car silhouetted against a nearby rise, a solitary man climbing out and looking straight in their direction, with some kind of long object in his hands.

'Headlights! Start the engine and gun her, quick!' he yelled. 'We have company!'

'But how...?!'

'Never mind that now. I know I'm right, *trust* me. *Do* it, if you want to live!'

Chapter 7

The speaker in the Audi RS5 crackled into life. The voice emitted was refined and distinctly upper-class. It sounded like the public address system at Eton, or a pre-war radio commentary of an England cricket match.

'You need to take the next left, old boy. Slow down a little. He's stationary now. In a green site just ahead. Looks like an ideal meeting point. A drive leads down to a car park. It should be empty this time of night. Theirs will be the only vehicle. This is the perfect opportunity to eliminate him. Remember, we want an ending. All yours from here.'

Owen James rolled the RS5 quietly onto a grass verge that overlooked the parking area and killed the lights. He reached into the passenger footwell and drew back a tartan travel blanket, took up the M4 he had laid on the seat and quickly attached a shell-catcher bag to the picatinny rail on top of the weapon. He exited the car swiftly and surveyed the scene ahead. No more than two hundred yards from his position a black, Volkswagen Golf GTI was sat motionless. He strode purposefully to the front of his vehicle, turned on the PEQ-15 night vison headset. The infrared beam stretched out into the night, invisible to anyone lacking similar equipment. He powered on the EOTech sight, flicked over the G33 magnifier and brought the rifle to his shoulder, ready to go to work.

Suddenly, he heard the unmistakeable sound of a car's engine sparking into life and realised with disbelief and fury that he'd been made. He rushed to get off a shot, flicking the safety to semi-auto and raising the M4, firing without delay. He knew he was sacrificing preparation and accuracy for speed but he was hoping to delay their departure by taking out a tyre, or to score a direct hit on the driver by estimating their position. A split second before he depressed the trigger though, the small and nimble Golf took off swiftly, careering straight over the grass verge and skidding and swerving everywhere, heading for the driveway and rear exit of the park, in totally the opposite direction.

Several hastily-sent rounds peppered the dirt and ground around the escaping vehicle, the first of which actually struck the boot with a loud bang. The remainder missed their target, though not by much and James fumed inside as his tiny missiles of death whistled past the vehicle at high velocity, by the smallest of margins. Before too long, the Golf had rounded a corner and he was effectively blind.

James cursed aloud, bemoaning his misfortune and timing.

He was also rather impressed. That was *some* driving. He'd been ultra quick to locate the target and rapid in the extreme in exiting his car. The time to the first round being despatched was therefore minimal. He doubted anyone else would have been quicker to spot and evade him. Still, this *Miles* he was attempting to slay had somehow managed to not only see the danger, but also locate the direction of the threat, reacted like an elite pro, employing emergency drills so effectively and decisively, that he had chosen more or less the *only* option open to him, or them, to survive. It was a mysterious and astounding development. Either sheer luck, or this new fugitive he had been informed had no background to speak of, somehow possessed *serious* talent.

Owen James didn't believe in gifted amateurs. That was for the films. Years of military service had drilled that fact into him where NIG's, or New Initiate Grunts, had proven mostly a liability in theatre. At least until they had actually tasted combat.

He would *not* underestimate this lad again.

The British hitman raced to his car and threw his equipment on the passenger seat, started her up and immediately gave chase, moving across the exact same grass and churning it up further as he raced for the exit. Within minutes, he was hurtling along the back streets of Cambridge and had the Golf in sight again.

The car ahead responded though and they both ran traffic lights and roundabouts at high speed, made every camera flash furiously as the deadly pursuit continued.

Jenny had punched the accelerator hard with her right foot the very instant Miles had yelled out his warning. Despite her shock, fear and misgivings, there was something about the geeky-looking weirdo in such circumstances which made him incredibly hard to ignore. Something innately trustworthy which inspired confidence somehow. As if he was the right person in command at the right time and knew *exactly* what he was doing. Zero hesitation or doubt. That just wasn't right. Not from the look of him and all he had said. She clearly had not been informed of all the facts. She heard the first of the bullets impact on the rear of her vehicle and all other thoughts vanished. She screamed in rage. The Golf was her pride and joy and even in her current state of extreme terror, she seethed at the thought of it being damaged, gripped the steering wheel even harder and concentrated on the task in hand. Several more bullets obliterated the grass ahead and the earth around them exploded as she threw the car from left to right to avoid being struck. A multitude of shots followed her every move but pretty soon the grass ended and the concrete drive it bordered veered sharply to the right. She was possessed now with resolve and determination and she slid the car into an almighty skid, righted it like a professional rally driver, found the exit and fled the park.

'Percy! They've shot up my Percy!' she cried out angrily, slapping the steering wheel several times.

'*Percy?* Really? You actually named your car?' said Miles, trying not to laugh as he gripped on to anything he could.

'Shut up! He was my Grandad. My hero... None of your business, anyhow. Who the *hell* have you upset now?! Who *was* that?!'

Miles frowned a little, his lips pressed in a straight line. 'I don't know. The way my day's gone, it could be anyone. I've...'

'Save it! We've got more trouble. I don't believe it. He's following us, and he's good. Seriously good. Fast. He's gaining on us,' she shouted, her voice now devoid of its pleasant softness.

Miles thought of drawing his pistol and returning fire but decided it would be useless at such a distance and he would hardly be able to keep the gun still, with the car thrashing about so. He also had limited ammunition and knew he may need to make every shot count.

'You're doing really well so far, just concentrate on driving. Very, very fast. Ignore every lesson you ever had and don't stop for anything. Take any shortcut you like. This guy came prepared, knew his stuff. No indecision again. The headlights were caned and he was out and on us in no time. Could be the French, or the Italians for all I know though. Or anybody else with a grudge. Surrender doesn't appear to be an option. Nothing for it but to try and get away. This motor of yours is ideal for tiny lanes, it's small and quick, so stick to the back roads and away from any larger ones where he can use his big engine. RS5 it looked like. Probably the 2.9 twin turbo. We'll corner better hopefully though, accelerate harder over short distances.'

'Err... Where did you come up with all that? Most guys would need to change their underwear after being fired upon. That from the games you play? And how are you keeping so calm?' Jenny asked, genuinely flabbergasted and still more than a little angry.

Miles drew in a deep breath before replying. 'I'm *not* calm. Far from it. Inside, my stomach is doing somersaults. I feel like I could throw up at any second, and that's not entirely due to your driving. Which is excellent by the way. I'm just trying to be helpful, given that our lives are on the line and you appear to be doing all of the work at present.'

Jenny grimaced as she checked the rearview mirror again. The Audi was so close now that she could see the outline of the driver in the streetlight. She yanked the wheel hard to the right and drifted the Golf into another back street, took a series of speed bumps at high speed so that Miles' head banged off the roof each time and he gripped the door handle to steady himself. The car righted itself after an insanely tight left and she glanced at him quickly.

'Well, you're growing on me. Keep those ideas coming. Don't worry about me. Always loved karting when I was younger and did a few track days. This is a dream come true.'

Miles raised his eyebrows, then looked back over his shoulder again and saw that even with Jenny's superhuman efforts, the unknown shooter was *still* closing the gap. This guy was something else. There was nothing for it but drastic action and Miles pulled the gun from his belt.

'Wow!' Jenny cried, seriously perturbed. 'Where did you get *that* from?! And why would you carry it around?!'

Miles knew how it would appear. 'No! It's not mine, I swear! I don't carry a gun. Look at me. Do I *look* like I mix it with these types? I took it from the guy who shot Jason on the train. Not sure why I picked it up. Just seemed like the thing to do at the time.'

He wound the electric window down fully and took another deep breath, letting it out slowly. 'We don't have much of a choice. Do exactly as I say. I want you to slow down a little. Only, gradually.'

'What?! Slow down…?!'

'Do it. Don't look so worried. Everything will be fine. When I tell you, hang the sharpest left you can and ease off the accelerator for a split second when we straighten up.'

The high-level mercenary on their tail had taken another phone call just as the pursuit began, answering it on his bluetoothed device via the car's speakers and microphone. His client had cut out the middle man now. They were clearly getting edgy, far more impatient than usual, already requesting a situation report from an operative they would not normally contact under any circumstance, for the less a gun for hire knew, the less they could divulge if taken alive. And they weren't generally the trustworthy sort.

'Mr. James, would you care to enlighten us all as to why he is moving still?' the upper-class voice demanded. 'Speak, damn you!' he added, when not immediately afforded a reply.

Owen shook his head a little in contempt. He came from a wealthy background himself but the sort of toffs in *this* group, were evidently from a whole new level of righteous pricks. The upper echelons who rose to real power courtesy of wealth and birthright. The aristocracy, well above most people's glass ceiling.

'You're breaking all protocol in even speaking to me! You'll have to excuse my manners,' he answered, throwing the RS5 around violently like he was racing at Le Mans. 'You see, I'm a trifle busy right at this moment, trying to enact your wishes. Not really appreciating the interruption. He catches on fast, your mark. Don't ask me how he made me so quick, because I haven't a clue. Two more seconds and I'd have lit up that ride like a candle, with him in it. I'm chasing him down as we speak. Not long now.'

'Yes, I can see that. Good. That's something at least. Is he alone?'

'Negative. He's in the passenger seat. There's a female driving. Must be the one who warned him. She's doing a fair job of it too.'

'Yes, yes, but we were assured that you are the best. You certainly are not cheap. These amateurs are not in your league so be quick about it and get the job done!'

James was fired up by that unnecessary remark, coming as it did from a suitjob who had probably not seen a day's action in his entire life. A day's proper work come to that. Most likely waited on hand and foot...

'I'm sorry? Would you care to switch places?' he responded, angrily. 'I've told you. It won't be much longer. I'm catching them and the end is near. Stay on the line if you'd like? Hear it for yourself?'

'Why thank you, Mr. James. Rest assured that we intend to do precisely as you suggest.'

The Audi was so near now that Owen James was reaching one-handed again for his weapon. Jenny was growing increasingly anxious. She kept flicking her eyes towards Miles, willing him to make the call. She was mightily relieved when, on the cusp of another left turn, this one slightly wider and therefore longer, he suddenly cried out, '*Now!*'

She heaved the steering wheel downwards and stepped on the brakes. The Golf shuddered and skidded sidewards, veered across the road and slowed rapidly, exposing the passenger side of the vehicle to the flying Audi. Miles raised his pistol and fired off four rounds in quick succession. The nine-millimetre projectiles peppered the RS5 smashing the windscreen, holing glass, metal and upholstery. One bullet hit the driver high on his chestplate as he dived down for cover, unharmed.

However, this sudden evasive action meant that the hitman, who had escaped death or serious injury by only a matter of inches, could not see clearly to steer the car and it careered at speed into several parked vehicles, eventually crashing to a violent halt courtesy of a concrete lamppost. The airbags deployed and Owen James was soon in a world of hurt. His muscles ached and throbbed and the wind had been knocked out of him. There was smoke and glass everywhere but despite his discomfort and shock, the tough ex-marine recovered quickly. He grabbed his weapon and goggles, along with his phone, and as a strange man stepped out of the nearest house to investigate the din, he pointed the gun straight at his head and demanded his car keys. His wife behind him rushed to find them and James unlocked a nearby Land Rover Discovery which had been parked on the opposite side of the street and was undamaged. He then loaded the holdall and escaped the scene as fast as he could in the Golf's general direction of travel, aware and furious that the couple he was pursuing had in all likelihood evaded him this night.

Once on the open road he spoke into the phone, having placed it on the dash on speaker.

'Still there? I take it you got all that?'

'Yes!' the voice responded, sounding distinctly unimpressed. 'Not a satisfactory outcome. We are severely disappointed to say the least. To be blunt, your reputation promised so much more. Perhaps we were mistaken, trusting such a task to a lone operator. Maybe we should open the floodgates?'

'Now, now, it's only a temporary blip. Don't twist your suspenders. And there was me thinking you already *had*. No need for an overreaction though. Bad luck is all.'

'We hope so. For your sake. Failure can be quite costly in your line of work I hear. And it's a buyer's market. They are heading out of the city. We suggest you get moving.'

'On it. Send any details you can. It's still a live contract and I remain active.'

Jenny and Miles had relaxed just a little but their hearts were still racing. Both were checking the mirrors constantly for any sign of pursuit but could see nothing untoward. Eventually, they began to accept that the extreme action of the surprise manoeuvre, which had flown into Miles' head from out of nowhere, had actually worked.

'I... I think we lost him.'

Miles smiled at the shock resounding in Jenny's voice and tried hard to swallow saliva that just wasn't there. He was sweating still and he was parched, his throat constricted.

'Looks like it,' he replied in a slightly hoarse voice, thankful beyond measure for their unexpected deliverance.

His new associate's head moved gradually from side to side. 'That was amazing!' she said. 'How did...? What made you think of it?'

'Just came to me. I fired numerous weapons on ranges after my dad moved us to the States. Wasn't much else to do on some of the bases. Watched way too many old cop shows too. Dad bought me a DVD boxset of *The Professionals* that I very nearly wore out. It was his favourite and Lewis Collins was his hero. The James Bond that never was, he said. Something must have rubbed off.'

'You're a real dark horse and no mistake. You look like you grew up in Hogwarts. As if you couldn't punch your way out of a paper bag. Only, you have traits inside of you which...'

'Not sure how I feel about that. I'm not usually this talkative around girls though, so you're probably right. We can't all be sweet-talking hunks. Anyway, didn't *Ron the Ginga* end up snagging the girl in the end?'

Jenny giggled a little. 'Ha, ha.... He certainly did. Touche. You know your stuff. I'm sorry if I hurt your ego. It was meant as a compliment, believe me. It's troubling how they found you so fast, don't you think? Were you already being watched do you reckon?'

'No! I told you; I know *nothing* about any of this. If they *were* keeping tabs on me, I certainly didn't know it. Until this morning, I hadn't a care in the world. Well, that's not strictly true. But nothing connected to whatever is going on here. I'm an ordinary guy caught up in something *not* of my making,' Miles protested.

'Alright, I believe you. Then, we've *both* had it now. We don't know for certain how long that guy was watching us, nor what he has in the way of photos etc. Or, if he had company, who he was in contact with... Oh for...! I ran tons of red lights back there, there'll be cameras... They have my registration number. They'll most probably know my bra size and what I ate for breakfast come morning... Jase was correct, wasn't he? *Everything* he alluded to. It all has to be true. We've served ourselves up on a platter to them. They'll have my home address!'

She was panicking and hyperventilating now, so Miles tried his best to calm her. He was horrified at the thought that he had dragged Jenny into such a complete mess. That he could very soon be responsible for her demise. He felt awful, in more ways than one. And enormously guilty.

'I'm so sorry. I never meant for this to go so far. I only wanted to talk to you and then I was going it alone. You weren't supposed to...'

'Wait!' she interrupted him, abruptly. 'It's the *phone!* You took Jason's phone. They found him and killed him easily enough, on a crowded train. That *must* be how they are tracking you. How they tracked him. Throw it out of the window right now. And your own. I'll have to toss mine too.'

Miles did as instructed. 'That's it. I only have the one. I left mine on the train.'

Jenny indicated to her rear pocket and lifted her behind gently off the seat, as she continued concentrating on the road. He reached over and retrieved her mobile, threw it out of the passenger window also.

'So that's that then. We'll buy some pay as you go ones when we're able. Burners that can't be traced,' Jenny added. 'What?' she asked, noticing that he was staring at her in awe. 'You're wondering why I'm not freaking out, aren't you? I am too. Neither of us can change what has happened though. The damage is extensive, but it's done. Wasn't your fault, or mine. Gotta deal with it. And our destinies now appeared to be linked... Oh, you meant, the phone thing? I watch cop shows too.'

Miles folded his arms across his chest and stared out at the open road.

'What a day! I feel violated. At some point, I'll sit down quietly and reflect on all of this over a nice cold beer, hope it makes sense, for I'm at a complete and total loss. I feel like I'm living somebody else's nightmare... Hey, you do realise, of course, that this *also* means we will have to ditch this car?'

That elicited a gasp of horror from his new partner.

'No! Not Percy?!'

'I'm afraid so. I can see that is going to break your heart but there's nothing else we can do. What an absolute melt I've been. I've really done a number on you, haven't I? You can vanish I suppose, for these guys mean business and are killing for fun. If we follow your logic though, they have no way of knowing what I have given you, or told you. Whether you are involved in any way and to what extent... I don't know what I'm saying but it's all messed up and the only thing I know for certain, is that you may be squarely in harm's way because of me. I'd like to rectify that if I can. I think information is key. We *have* to understand why all of this has happened. My proposal of before still holds, though it wasn't much of a plan I grant you. We need to get to your place as quickly as we can, before they can figure out our next move and set up surveillance, or lay another trap. Get in, check for clues, get out. As quick as you like. Are you in?'

'Okay, if you say so,' Jenny replied, clutching the steering wheel even harder as a solitary tear formed in her eye.

Then, she brightened a little and turned to him briefly.
'I think I have an idea.'

Chapter 8

DCI Edward Farley set up an incident room at local police headquarters. It was pushing two in the morning before he decided to call a final meeting and do a round-up of the day's events. Everyone had worked flat-out for at least seventeen hours or so and most of his team were shattered. The uncompromising workaholic had begrudgingly accepted this fact and called a halt to proceedings, though he wanted to air openly all they had learned that day before finishing for the night. Pertinent facts and ideas could still surface even at this late hour and Farley had the bit between his teeth. He stood in front of several large notice boards covered in an assortment of images and scribble and an admin assistant sat ready to type into a database an accurate record of the conversation. He watched the rank-and-file trudge wearily into the room from the various side offices they had been assigned.

'Alright, settle down and grab a seat,' Farley began, as the disgruntled crew started muttering among themselves. 'I know you've had a long day but the quicker you plonk your backsides down, the sooner you'll knock off for the night... There, that's better. Firstly, thanks for a thoroughly decent day's work. It is expected of course, but it's also appreciated. I'm reliably informed that I drive you too hard...' A chorus of good-natured whistles and cheers filled the air as Farley shot a quick glance over at Sam Lennox, who cherried up a little. 'Yes, well, that may be so, but it is only because I *care*. Not about you lot, obviously. Couldn't give a toss about you. No, about serving the British public who pay our wages. About taking monsters like these off the streets so that the decent folk can sleep soundly at night. This was a heinous crime. Cold-bloodied murder. It is only by some miracle that others were not caught in the crossfire. Remember that fact. We may not be so lucky next time.'

He raised a glass of water to his lips and took a sip. 'So, I want you all paying attention despite the late hour. Who's going to start? Sam?'

There was an audible groan and more than one derisory comment muttered under breath. DS Lennox was staring down at her hand. It was no longer shaking. She was a little taken aback to be thrust into the spotlight so soon but ignored the adverse reaction and reacted coolly, professionally, pointed to the boards.

'Thanks, boss. I suppose a quick recap would help? Our deceased from the train was carrying false I.D. That would *normally* be a stumbling block. However, luckily for us, he's been a naughty boy in the past and has a criminal record. Did a four month stretch for affray in Wandsworth. We've identified him as one, *Jason Murphy.* Twenty-five, small-time petty criminal and product of the foster care system. As far as felons go, he's nothing to write home about. Lived locally up until a year or so ago by all accounts, when he moved away to Hull and became a grease monkey. At least, that's what those who know him said in the door-to-door enquiries. Confirmed later by his old Probation Officer. Jason Murphy apparently has no known family and no siblings.'

'Only, we know better than that, don't we?' DCI Farley interjected. 'We know for certain now that he has, or rather *had*, a twin brother out there. Apart from the many statements, the cameras show two passengers identical in every way. They are related. Question is, did he know this? Was Jason on that train by design, searching for his twin? You'd think he'd know of his existence at the very least. However, onlookers also confirm that that does *not* appear to be the case. The one we are saying is Jason's brother, reacted with extreme shock at seeing the likeness.'

Sam Lennox nodded and decided to jump back in. 'Ballistics report came back, guv. SOCO was spot on. It was a Winchester, 124-grain jacket hollow point. A google search confirmed these are widely available in the States. Not seen them before in any U.K. shootings though. Polygonal rifling is indicative of a Glock. Based on the round being a 9mm it was probably a model 19, or 17. Those, we *have* seen plenty of. Onlookers state the shooter was using a suppressor too. He fires three times, scoring two hits, downing our victim, probably killing him, or near as damn it. He then puts another two into his back, gets into a scuffle with our runner, takes him out using non-lethal force and draws a backup from his ankle. Hits the Vic again, this time from point blank range to the back of the head. SOCO was correct once more. A .380. Again, Polygonal rifling, so a Glock. Probably a Model 42. Not a favoured weapon here in the U.K.'

Lennox took a drink. '…So, *who* is the twin? The one who got away? Why was he on that train and why was his brother murdered in front of him? Hold that thought, I'll come back to it in a minute.'

The entire room turned to the questions section on the notice boards, following Sam's lead.

'Moving on,' she continued. 'Back to the shooter. This one is troubling. We're no further in identifying him I'm afraid. Not much to go on, other than what I've just said and statements that he was possibly from somewhere in South America. He was thought to be acting alone, but CCTV from the train station has him meeting up with a female associate, just after the murder of Jason Murphy. She's around five feet five, tanned or mixed race, possibly Hispanic, with short black hair wearing blue jeans and a white shirt. They exit rapidly and disappear from sight. It's not good camera coverage out there in the sticks so we're in the dark a little. We're trawling through what footage we can find but we're not hopeful. They seem to be avoiding any electronic eyes.

That's why we think they're pros. That, plus the hit itself and the gear he used.'

Farley piped up once more. 'I want that set as a top priority. We need to know who these murdering thugs are, who they work for, and how they took out somebody in broad daylight and got away with it in our backyard. Facial recognition scored no hits so we'll be trawling similar reports or incidents, trying passport control etc.'

A ripple of acknowledgement swept the room. More than one person also checked their watch and yawned, just to get their message across to the DCI and his new pet DS.

'Finally,' Sam Lennox continued, unperturbed, 'the fugitive. Our selfless identical hero who tried in vain to save his own brother, even though it doesn't appear as if he knew that yet. We had zero luck in identifying him to begin with. He has no record and his prints were not on file. The ones we lifted at the scene were therefore useless, as far as I.D. purposes go. Nothing to compare them to. He left a phone behind according to passengers, but one of those thieving gits had it away in the confusion. *Then*, Judy here,' Lennox pointed to a junior detective sitting not far from her, 'had a brainwave. She realised that we have the body of his brother in our custody, that they would share DNA. We were granted special dispensation to check medical records. After much persuasion and a bottle of scotch or two, we finally received a hit ten minutes ago. We are able to share with you all now, that our runner, whose life is most certainly in *extreme* danger, is a U.K. national named, *Miles Dalton*.'

The whole team began scribbling his details down on notepads.

'Again, there's nothing special about him as far as we can tell. He's the only son of Major James Dalton, latterly of the Royal Medical Corps. *He* took his own life whilst working in the United States a little over five months ago. His mother is Sarah Dalton. Miles and her appear to have moved back to blighty immediately afterwards. Though, Miles is now on his own. At least, he lives alone and within days of touching down on these shores and finding a flat, it is said that his mother disappeared. We've spoken to his landlord just now, woke him up and he was surprisingly forthcoming. She has not visited or been seen in a good while. He hasn't talked of her and we can't track her down. Enquiries are ongoing. The tickets were bought in two totally separate locations, so no link there to our supposed brothers.'

About Miles, the landlord said he keeps to himself. Games well into the night most days. These are his words but he is said to be a, *bit of a drip*. We're taking that at face value until we learn otherwise. A photo is on the board, but it's grainy as it's been blown up. It was sent in by the landlord who attended a garden party with Miles four weeks ago, from his phone. We'll access the best of the CCTV at the station, passport control and his driving license through the DVLA tomorrow, see if we can't obtain a better one.'

A hand raised slowly and DCI Farley pointed to the culprit, allowing him to speak.

The experienced sergeant in question stated, 'Sorry guv, but are we connecting these dots? What I mean is, do we think the suicide of the father and disappearance of the mother, as well as the murder of someone thought to be their son, are all related?'

'Gripper, you and me are way too long in the tooth to believe otherwise. Or to bank on it. Nothing is ruled out or in at this stage, though something is rotten here. It stinks to high heaven. So, you'll work with Sam on that angle and do some more digging. Find me a bone.'

'Will do, skip.'

DCI Farley turned once more to Sam Lennox. 'Continue, please Sam?'

More groans from the crowd and murmurs of, 'Teacher's pet.'

'Okay, I'll be quick, I promise. Shortly after he fled the scene of the crime, Miles Dalton was ambushed outside Hitchin station by two large males. They were described as late thirties, early forties, short military style hair. Again, they are unidentified at this stage and very much at large. They discharged a firearm, reportedly at Miles, but unfortunately hit a lady who was walking to the station. The two gunmen were last seen running after Miles. The woman regrettably succumbed to her injuries and died in hospital a few hours later. A, *Mary Thomas*, single mother of three, may she rest in peace. Wrong place, wrong time.'

'Some days you're better off staying in bed,' said one of the analysts, to a chorus of solemn but unanimous humming.

'Oh really?' fired Sam back at him, having heard enough baiting, her tolerance exhausted. 'And that is your expert take on things, is it? Your *professional* analysis? What chance did she have to stay under the covers with three little ones to look after?! Probably working two jobs as well! I know it's late but I'd be grateful if you kept your opinions to…!'

'Alright, Sam, that'll do,' said Farley. 'He meant nothing by it. We're all tired here and tempers are short. Move on. Let's find these scum and give her the justice she deserves.'

Sam breathed in deeply and calmed herself, looked the analyst in his eye. 'Yes, sorry, boss. Apologies. Though, you're paid well because you have a keen mind. *Use* it.'

Turning to the group again she added, 'The gunmen then gave pursuit. Only, our guy Miles, appears to have outwitted them, because they were spotted doubling back alone a little while later and no body has been found. No blood. Local bobbies state that a shot was also fired near a small shopping centre not far away around that time. It's too much of a coincidence to be ignored and the timeline fits. All these people were hunting Miles Dalton and/or his twin brother. The last two were reported to be of Asian origin.'

'It's global!' the old sergeant blurted out instinctively. 'I don't wish to speak out of turn sarge, but he's not making many friends, is he? What's he done to upset all these factions? And there's a pattern here; two-man, err person, teams? These are no amateurs. They're organised and professional. Just like the hitter on the train. Drugs, I reckon. Gotta be drugs,' Grippa added. 'That pen thing an' all... Triads, Columbians, Mafia or such...'

'Quiet!' Farley snapped. 'Sam?'

'I was getting to that. No joy on the auto-injector our end. We've asked for help from Porton Down. Might be drugs. Might be a nerve agent for all we know.'

'Jesus Christ!' Farley cut in. 'Not another Novichok incident!'

A collective murmur of extreme concern followed.

'If it *was*, sir, we'd already be showing symptoms of exposure by now,' Lennox pointed out.

'Yes. After all, we've trapsed it around in this station all afternoon.'

'Besides, CBRN staff did a sweep of the train and our victim. They came up with nothing,' Sam added.

The relief in the room was palpable.

'We'll know more when his bloodwork comes back but for now it's safe to assume he wasn't poisoned.'

'Thank heavens for that,' Farley stated. 'There's more questions and facts there that need checking and answering. If they *are* kill teams, why are they here and who sent them? And before you all retire to your pits, Sam has more, hot off the press.'

Lennox rose to her feet and walked over to the largest of the notice boards.

'Now, we know that Miles Dalton spoke to a female caller on the train. Multiple sources confirm this. On the deceased's mobile. Which he pocketed by the way. We've tried registered numbers but it's untraceable. She appears to have warned him about something and we believe *that* is why he ran. Passengers insist he stated he had nothing to do with the crime. Certainly, the decision makes no sense otherwise. He would have been far safer remaining on board, for we were already alerted and on our way. One guy stated he thought he heard Miles call her, *Jenny*. We can't be certain, but listen to this; we've been monitoring all systems, all incident reports nationwide since this incident occurred. Our colleagues at Cambridge took a call in their control room not too long ago. At around quarter to one this morning, multiple gunshots from what sounded like an automatic weapon were fired in the area of Jesus Green Park, off Chesterton Road. A lot of rounds. Possibly an entire magazine. That's unusual enough in itself, but the target we have ascertained was a black Volkswagen Golf GTI, registration number Delta, Tango, Seven Three, Oscar, Bravo, Golf. This *same* vehicle travelled away from the park at high speed, naturally. It was chased rapidly by a white Audi RS5, registration number Golf, Whiskey, One One, Foxtrot, Uniform, Victor. The photos are on the board. As you can probably tell, local speed and traffic cams managed to capture all occupants. Our colleagues in Cambridge rushed these to us under emergency protocol, given the circumstances. The passenger in the VW Golf is Miles Dalton. No doubt about it. We've compared what we have and there is little room for error. The female is a Londoner, traced through vehicle ownership records as a *Jennifer Pearce*. Twenty-six, single, lives alone in Barnet. No criminal record or footprint on our systems. This is another top priority; to find Miss Pearce. And to dig into her background and finances etc. In fact, we need to locate the pair of them as a matter of utmost urgency. Details have been despatched to all forces.'

Sam Lennox paused there to ensure everyone took in what she was saying, waited for the writing to stop and satisfied herself that she had regained their full attention.

'...The interesting part. The driver of the Audi is pictured clearly. Having actioned what can only be described as another attempted hit, one might have expected him to be wearing some kind of balaclava. But no. Doesn't help us one jot though, unless any of you know him personally? Again, he's not on our systems. Has he been wiped? The car is expensive, but it is not registered in this country at all. How does that happen? How is he driving around and nothing is being reported? Who *is* this ghost? We're circulating his picture and trying facial recognition again, cross-referencing with our friends abroad, though once more we are not hopeful. It is almost certain given reports coming in that whoever he is, he was well-armed and deployed on ideal ground to assassinate our fugitive. We are assuming therefore that he is trained to military standards and *extremely* dangerous.'

DCI Farley joined Sam at the notice board. 'Okay, that's enough for tonight. Well, this morning. You're all up to speed now. Go away and get whatever rest you can. Dream nice little dreams and keep a notepad and pen within reach. You never know what might come to you in the land of nod. Sleep here if you want to, save the fuel. There's a reason most of us are single and this is it. Or best friends with divorce lawyers. I'll arrange for breakfast and drinks for those who do. I want you all bright-eyed and bushy-tailed tomorrow morning, chomping at the bit either way.'

Farley's team required no second invitation to leave and the room cleared quickly, leaving the experienced detective alone with his new sergeant. Both turned and stared at the boards without speaking for a few minutes, until the DCI eventually broke the silence.

'We're moving forwards, Sam, just not fast enough for my liking. It's inch by inch at the moment and this thing's a race, as it always is. We're playing catch up. I'm not happy. Not certain we can save these people. They have the entire world after them it seems. Heck, I'm not even sure that they *deserve* saving. I don't know how they came to be involved in all of this, but who angers top pros like these? Who crosses them? Footsoldiers for someone who does not care at all who sees them, who they hurt? Jason was murdered and for what? Miles, Jenny too for all we know, have joined their hit list. I have to find out why. What they have or know!'

'*We* have to, sir,' Sam corrected him. 'You're not in this alone. I haven't a clue at this moment in time but we'll get to the truth. It's what we do.'

'Yes, that's the spirit. Let's put a name to all those faces and flush them out into the open. I don't appreciate others playing with firearms on my patch. It's downright impertinent. I'll stop at nothing to bring them to justice.'

For the first time since her army days, Sam Lennox felt something stir inside of her. A spark, a fire in her belly that she thought she'd lost forever. It was like the homecoming of a lifelong friend.

'I'm with you all the way, sir. I'll back you no matter what. *Whatever* it takes... You know, I *am* firearms trained. I believe it's time we kitted up and got in amongst them? We'll need eyes and ears on the ground on this one, if we're to react speedily and stop it turning into a bloodbath. Reactionary forces ready to strike at a moment's notice, if we're to catch these guys in the act.'

'Agreed. And wipe that smile from your face, sergeant. These are extreme times and measures. This is *not* the norm... Starting tomorrow, you and I are armed and mobile.'

'Sir, I didn't mean that *you* should...' began Lennox.

'Shush! I don't care what you meant. You're right. I'll call in another DCI to command here, someone I trust. This thing has grown altogether. You can liaise with the team electronically or on the phone. I'll make certain that Trojan units are armed and on standby wherever we are, ready to back us up when the bullets start flying, or look as if they might. Good enough?'

Sam dipped her chin and grabbed her coat.

'Cushdy.'

'You're loving this, aren't you?' Farley asked, smirking a little.

'Who me? Honestly? Too right I am. I love policing, really I do. But *this* is what I signed up for.'

Chapter 9

Jenny's idea actually turned out to be a real humdinger. Under normal circumstances, Miles would have dismissed it out of hand as the crazy notion of a desperate fool. She struck him as an intelligent being however, not a fool at all. She was smart and forthright, sassy and quick on the uptake. Plus, she had already in the short time he'd known her displayed a good degree of courage and determination. All qualities he very much admired. With the added bonus that she was extremely easy on the eye. Though, it was blindingly obvious that she was so very far outside of his league, that nothing could ever develop between them. At this point, he was just happy that he could string a sentence together in her presence without folding into a gibbering wreck. That was a new development that counted as real progress in his book. The Nerds would scarcely believe him. *If* he made it back home in one piece to tell them about it. On her journey into the city from an unfamiliar direction, she had mistakenly taken a wrong turning off a dual carriageway and ended up by some rundown, vacant garages. They sat like a blot on a battered, brick and concrete landscape, edged a bleak and depressing council estate in front of which she had fretfully executed the fastest U-turn in history. Though, not before spotting a rough-looking group of youths and young adults who were generally dossing; killing the hours doing nothing in particular. They looked like trouble with a capital 'T', bandanas and low-flying jeans everywhere, as well as plenty of spliffs, hard liquor, even harder drugs and copious amounts of knives. It was the kind of scene and people Jenny generally avoided at all cost. Now, however, she was re-tracing her journey in reverse attempting to find them.

She easily located the same side street, pulled the Volkswagen Golf up short of the garages and the remnants of the gang, the others having dispersed due to the late hour which left twelve or so still hanging about. Aggressive verses of hardcore rap blared out of their stereo so loud, that they could hear it in their car from quite a distance away even with the windows up, which was presumably much to the annoyance of the locals. Though, *they* were probably too afraid of retaliation to complain. Two old cars had their parking lights turned on illuminating the area just enough for those in the small gathering to see clearly what they were doing.

'Wait here,' said Miles as he cranked his door open, once again acting with a confidence that seemed to rise out of nowhere. 'Keep the engine running and be ready to floor it if needed. If I begin retreating sharpish, we won't be hanging around.'

Miles patted the pistol in the small of his back to ensure it was still there. He had only five bullets remaining, which was a tad concerning. He strode out into the night like a gunslinger leaving the saloon one last time about to stare death down, approached the mean-looking crowd like he meant business, no fear at all on show. Not far away, a huge muscular man in his early twenties with a prominent gold tooth out front spotted his advance. He rose to challenge him, pulling out the largest Rambo-style knife Miles had ever seen. Clearly in command of the mixed rabble, his face twisted in anger and venom at what he obviously perceived was an unwanted intrusion and challenge. This was *his* turf and he was evidently under the impression that everyone in the area knew as much.

'Hold up! Dat's far enough! Thffffpppt, would you look at this wasteman!' the guy scowled, sucking his front teeth with contempt. The music was turned off abruptly and several of the hulk's peers moved smartly to back him up, drawing their knives too, staring at Miles as if he was already a dead man walking. Weighing up if they'd be fast enough to take him *and* his driver.

'Evening, fellas. No need for all that. I don't want trouble. I just want to talk,' stated Miles uneasily, eyeing the weapons in their hands and ready to reach for the hitman's gun.

The large male in the centre was still doing all of the talking. He sucked his teeth again in derision and waved the blade in his fist menacingly from side to side, as if slashing some imaginary foe.

'You mad, cuz?! Brain damaged or summin'? That it? You's crazy, or av you a deff wish? Ain' nobody front man like dis. I own dis place! You lookin' to score, or meet ya maker? Chat ya shit an on ya way, or I's a wet you up blood right 'ere and now! Big time!'

As the others ahead of him inched forwards, Miles continued to plead his case.

'Look, as I said, just hear me out. I have a proposition for you. A deal you won't want to miss. There's pure profit to be made here so it's in your interest to listen, I promise you.'

The knifemen all ceased moving and looked to their leader for a decision, who raised his head just once.

'So, spill already.'

Miles lowered his hands slowly. He gazed beyond the guys who had challenged him to their cars. Then back to the main man.

'Nice rides,' he stated. 'A little old now though. There's only so much you can pimp them up, right? How would you like to swap one of those has-been machines, for a brand-new Golf GTI? That one over there to be precise.'

Money talks. The universal language. Gold tooth was interested now in what he had to say. His eyebrows raised a little in surprise and his tone seemed lighter.

'For real?' he asked.

'Straight up. I'm in a bind and I need to act quick. We can do this thing right now, and then we'll leave you alone. What do you say?'

The menacing brute looked briefly at his footsoldiers, calculating the odds which were firmly stacked in his favour. He cracked his knuckles and an evil glint appeared in his eye. Confidence began to flow through him then with an obvious gush.

'Nah. You offer nuffin', yute. I'm thinkin' mans should just jack you up right here, take your whip an' stiff you good. Ditch ya corpses. Why we need graft so ard, when it's offered up all nice and free like dat?'

He raised his blade again and his gang moved quickly towards Miles, each hoping to be the one to draw first blood, thereby gaining some kudos, maybe rise in the ranks.

Myles sighed heavily in disappointment. 'I was hoping you had some brains,' he muttered and pulled out the gun, pointed it straight at the gold tooth.

A collective growl sounded from the others, then a booming, derisory howl broke out almost at once.

'Mwah, ha, ha... Look at dis batty bwoy 'ere, with his smallman water pistol. Tinks 'im a gangster...'

'Phut!'

The stereo system shattered into pieces as a round from Myles' suppressed pistol struck home. Jenny was watching on nervously in the car as Miles was almost set upon. She placed it into gear and raced to a stop just behind him. A shared gasp of alarm then echoed from the group as they all took a step backwards and the blades rapidly disappeared from sight. Little use in a gunfight. They knew when they were beat and the way this dude was acting, as if he was high or something, nobody was risking taking a bullet this night. Again, the big guy spoke, only *this* time it was with caution, and a little begrudging respect.

'Easy, Fam! Put de strap away, yeah? Ain' nobody gotta die here. We's um do bare deals... Terra! Get my man your whip!' he ordered another member of the pack.

'Err... Yeah, safe,' came the timid reply and a small guy at the back moved to one of the parked cars.

'Good,' said Miles. 'This conversation is over. Here's what's going to happen. We're going to take off and we won't be heading back this way anytime soon. Those cars put together aren't worth half of what this Golf is. It needs a repair on the boot which should be simple enough but there's a lot of coin to be made here, if you're sensible and keep your mouth shut. *We* won't be saying a thing about this night, trust me. You're doing us a favour. You'll need to change the plates before you ride in it, as we've angered the police by running some lights. It's stolen too so maybe a spray job, but that should mean nothing to the likes of you I'm guessing? Am I right? You have the contacts to clone it?'

'Yeah. Five-O ain no big 'ting,' answered the guy with the bling in his mouth.

'Thought so. I'm an excellent judge of character. Then let's get this done and we're smoke in your rearview mirror.'

'I's right. You *mental* bro, you know dat?'

'So I've been told. Get a shift on.'

Myles waved his pistol to add some urgency to his command. He kept the gun trained on the gang as Terra reversed an old pimped-up BMW 3 series close to where he was standing. Jenny turned off the ignition to the Golf and said goodbye to Percy with a tear in her eye. She threw the keys on the ground near the garage and slid into the driver's seat of the BMW. Gave a thumb's up after checking the fuel gage, altered the chair and mirrors.

'Let's go!' she shouted, when she was ready.

Miles made to climb in the passenger side but he was halted by a parting threat from the gang leader.

'Mandem! Hold up! Appreciate da wheels an' all, but I's not forget dat face. If I'm see you 'gain, it's on! You's ain' nuttin' without de strap, ya feel me?!' he barked, trying desperately to save face among his peers.

Myles felt a surge of something surprising run through his entire body. He turned to gold tooth and raised the pistol, pointing it directly into his face. Then he suddenly blurted out loudly, 'BRRRAAPP, BRRRAAPP!'

He chuckled to himself as Goldy flinched like a schoolboy. Then, calmly, he backed off and slipped into the beamer's passenger seat. As cooly as he could, he stated, 'And if *I* ever see *you* again, I'll put you in the forever box!'

Jenny drove away as swiftly as she could, headed for her flat in Barnet, one of the most northerly boroughs of London. 'OMG!' she cried, as they left the estate. 'That was... incredible!'

Myles' head swelled with pride, though he was just as astonished as her by his own actions. 'Yeah,' he mused, 'got a bit hairy for a moment. Don't get me wrong, I was shaking inside. I'd never dream of pulling off something like that, with a gun, and you as backup. I don't... Ugh, I feel really rough now,' he stated, as he shifted in his seat trying to make himself comfortable.

Jenny reached across and felt his forehead with the back of her left hand. 'You're burning up. Check my bag, there should be some paracetamol in there.'

Myles took out four tablets and looked around for something to drink but came up empty-handed, so had to force them down dry. He checked the glovebox. All he found was some weed in a zip lock bag and some rolling papers. He threw them out of the window.

'I need to shut my eyes for a while,' he said. 'Wake me if I go to sleep before we arrive.'

They reached Jenny's apartment not long afterwards as the roads were quiet at that time in the morning and they met no traffic.

'Wow!' exclaimed Miles, as they drove past slowly and then pulled up a little way from the luxury complex. 'Property prices around here must be through the roof. You're doing alright for yourself. Rich parents, is it?' he asked, genuinely impressed and meaning no offence.

He'd given it anyway and Jenny looked over at him in disgust. 'Why would you assume that?! I've worked very hard for all I have, thank you very much! Decent job, actually. Research work for a pharmaceutical company that pay well. Hard graft and plenty of overtime too. So, you can keep your insinuations to yourself. I just hope I still have that job when we're through. A criminal record won't go down too well with my employers. Neither will jail time or… getting killed.'

The entire area was checked thoroughly to ensure they were not being watched and there was no hostile presence in the vicinity. When satisfied they were safe and alone, Jenny opened the front door quickly and they stepped inside. She scooped up the post on the mat and thrust it into Miles' arms, then raced away to grab a few essentials. Within minutes she had freshened up and returned with a bag rammed with clothes, make-up and toiletries.

Miles made his way to the kitchen and drank a couple of glasses of water as he examined the bundle of letters. He was parched.

'Found what we're looking for?' Jenny asked, noting that he'd cast aside all but one aside.

'Yep, think so.'

'Great. Let's get out of here then.'

Miles drove the car to give Jenny a break. She directed him to a nearby multi-storey car park and headed for the lowest level underground, reserved for residents only and therefore quite packed. The BMW was reversed into one of the few remaining spaces, in-between two parked cars, and he killed the lights. Perfect hiding place. All was eerily quiet and dark as Jenny then took out her phone, held it low with the torch on and read the address on the letter, offered it to Miles.

'No, that's not right somehow. It's addressed to you. Think you should read it. Only, would you mind reading it out loud please?' he stated, pushing her hand away gently.

'But he's your... Okay, if that's what you want.'

She ripped open the envelope and peered inside.

'No enclosures. Just a scrappy bit of paper with his scrawny scribble on both sides. Typical Jase. He was never one for writing much.'

'Yeah well, he probably had a lot on his mind at the time and was in a bit of a hurry. I think we'll forgive him. Go ahead.'

Miles squirmed uncomfortably. He'd definitely caught something.

Jenny coughed a little to clear her throat then read it verbatim in an emotional tone which evidenced noticeably her pain and sorrow. 'Here goes...

Jen, I have to be quick. I tried ringing the flat but no reply. I lost my phone the other day. It has your mobile contact details so I couldn't message you in the usual way. I got the pen out just in case I don't find it. I'll go over to Steve's when I can. I'm sure he has your number. I'll bell you soon so this might be overkill. You'll understand why (I hope) once I explain.

I know I did you wrong and I'm sorry. It was all on me. I can't turn back time now but I'm in trouble deep, of the worst kind believe me. I need your help.

I'm on my way back to London. Don't know how long it will take because I have to be smart about this. Can't afford to be sloppy and make mistakes. Too much riding on it. I'll need a place to crash though?

Before you say yes, I need to tell you straight that it may place you in danger. I would never want that but I have nowhere else to turn. A few nights ago two Italian geezers showed up in our local pub. Never seen them before. I'd had a few beers and they jumped me and pulled knives, over nothing at all I swear! I did nothing wrong this time, on my honour. I wasn't high or anything, and I owed them no money. If it hadn't been for a gang of my mates, I'd be lying in a morgue somewhere. We used bottles and anything we could lay our hands on, gave them both a good kickin'.

Anyway, I've been on the run ever since. Not from the police mind! This is beyond them. You have no concerns there if I do stay. They won't be knocking on your door.

Reason for my London trip? Besides getting away and coming to see you of course (lol). Get this - I have a brother Jen! Can you believe that?! A brother I knew nothing about. And I'm told he knows nothing about me too. I have to find him. It's the only thing I care about now. Can't go to his house because I think they'll be watching it. Watching him maybe.

Who's they? I'm not explaining very well.

Look, I know I'm a loser. I destroyed something special and live with it every day. Can't turn back time but I can do the right thing by him. I have his name and address. Can't phone him I've been told because I can't trust the phones.

How do I know all this? I had a visit from an older lady I did not know. The day before the scuffle in the pub. I kinda didn't believe her about the threats, or I would have left sooner. Turns out, he's my twin! Identical! Ha! Your worst nightmare come true – there's two of me!

This woman says she has lots to tell but we have to be together to hear it.

She told me we're being hunted because of something to do with our dad. I don't think even she knows the whole story though. She didn't want to stay too long for obvious reasons, but she showed me a short clip on her phone from a video she had for me on a USB drive. Wouldn't let me keep it in case it fell into the wrong hands. It was of my dad talking. Yes, she told me stuff about my dad! My real father! Worked with him, I think. I'm trying to be quick...

My brother's name is Miles Dalton. Remember that name! I'm going to try to follow him and if it's safe, I'll talk to him and... I don't know, explain what I can? Warn him? Maybe bring him back to yours, or Hull? Wait for her to contact us again I suppose. Or take off somewhere together. To save his life.

What else can I say?

Oh, yes, I remember some of my father's words on that video but can't put it all down here. Except this - just in case something happens to me, Miles needs to know this (I've written the address I have for him on the inside of the envelope). Our father (strange being able to say that) kept referring to a holiday they once had together. Wouldn't let it go. Kept on saying that it was a really cherished memory, the special time they had at Sandringham Gardens. I wouldn't put it in this note but for the fact that he was so over the top about it, saying Miles should remember and treasure that day - Might be something important.

Have to shoot now. Hopefully I'll see you soon. If so, you can screw this up and we'll have a good laugh at how silly I've been. Looking forward to having a brother. Looking forward to seeing you again also. Hope you haven't moved on and settled down, or I may need to find a motel.

Don't let me down, Jen. Love, Jase. X

Jenny wiped away the tears from her eyes after she'd finished reading aloud and handed the letter across to Miles.

It was a lot to take in and emotions were high so a period of quiet reflection was ended only when he ventured in a sympathetic tone, 'You okay?'

She responded with an impromptu display of raw feelings and didn't hold back.

'Not really, no. I feel like I've been run over, scraped up off the street and thrown into a cement mixer. It's all too much to take. I'm angry, confused, scared, lost... all of the above and more. I'm a fugitive from the law and heaven knows who else. *Me!* I've never had so much as a parking ticket. Safety's my middle name. I don't even do the lottery. All I had was in that car and that flat, and now I'm tearing around the country in a stolen vehicle, a single bag to my name, trusting my life to some guy I hardly know. I've lost Percy and whatever happens from here, be it prison or worse, if I live through it, the aftermath of what has already happened so far means I'll likely lose everything I have strived so hard to obtain; my job, home, lifestyle, mates, freedom... And that's the *best*-case scenario! So no, Miles, I am *not, okay!*'

He looked down at the letter and said nothing.

'Oh yes,' she added, still more than a little vexed. 'To top it all, as if all I have just stated wasn't enough, just about the only guy I've ever truly loved has been gunned down like an animal!'

Miles had no words of comfort. He knew nothing he could say would suffice. He felt awkward and inadequate again, the way he commonly felt around women he liked before he ventured onto that train; tongue-tied and brainless. He took the phone and shined the light over the page once more, read the contents over again whilst Jenny composed herself, his own eyes moistening as the combination of the writing on the page, the thought of his dead brother, and Jenny's own words really hit home.

Chapter 10

Jenny had settled and recovered her composure. She was still overwhelmed with all that had happened, upset and emotional, uncertain how to feel about everything, including Miles. Her peaceful existence had been shattered and for what? The death of an ex-lover she'd already gotten over and the life of a complete unknown she cared nothing for. It hardly seemed worth it. Nevertheless, she was embroiled in this thing now right up to her neck, could see no way out. The police would already know of her involvement for sure. Not to mention any criminal factions trying to get to Miles, or his brother. These were sophisticated groups and she *had* to be on their radar too. Yep, whichever way she sliced it, she was in real peril. So, the only thing that appeared to make any sense was to do everything she could to stay alive and fight to clear her name. *Anything* she could. To discover the motives of whoever was behind the murder, those now hunting them down. To try to scupper their plans in some way and take whatever they might learn during the course of their amateur sleuthing to some higher authority. At a time and place they might *actually* be listened to and believed. Then plead ignorance and outright stupidity as a defence strategy, hope for the best. To do all *that*, she had to stick close to Miles, for their fates appeared entwined and the mild-mannered geek was just about her only hope of salvation.

'I think that's the longest letter Jase ever wrote. I have soooo many questions now,' she stated, surprising him with her sudden declaration when he was himself lost in thought.

'I know. Me too,' he answered.

She snatched the letter back, kept glancing at it time and again as she talked, her voice now back to normal, without the full-on emotion of earlier and the understandable anger.

'I've calmed, so I can be more objective. Jase was an absolute idiot to get himself killed like that. I mean, he could be a knucklehead in general, but he didn't deserve to end his days this way. I always thought he'd go out like a rockstar surrounded by women, booze and drugs, not taken out by some villain and shot from behind. He was into stuff he shouldn't have been but it was never anything heavy. He was no master criminal anyway. Deep down inside he was a really good guy... You must realise by now, given the contents of that note, that he was trying to protect you? Kinda puts a whole new outlook on things, doesn't it? A moron of the first order maybe, but a braver guy than any of *us* knew. Aware he was being followed, subjected to threats and violence, but *still* determined to find his brother and warn him. Who do you suppose attacked him in that pub?'

'Italian agents possibly? Mafia? Plenty of Italians in this country too and some of those are heavy duty. I can't be sure of anything though. I'm new to this investigating lark but from all I've seen, it's not good to make assumptions. Perhaps, the *why* is a more important question than the who? *Why* did they attack him? Though, I don't know that one either. It's our first real clue, however; Jason said it himself, that it's something to do with my father and his work. Exactly which part of it, I'll guess we'll never know.'

Jenny shifted about in her seat to face him. Weariness was written all over her face but there was a part of her which refused to give in to it. 'Not good enough. I'm completely wrecked. I could sleep for a week. But we need to thrash this out and every second we waste could be crucial, allowing them the chance to find us. So, let's give it a go right here, right now? We have no way of knowing their capabilities after all. We have to figure out what we can whilst it's fresh and new, go over every detail. Something may pop out at us and then we can form some sort of strategy... Tell me, your father, what *precisely* did he do?'

Miles sat up straight and shook off his own fatigue. He rubbed his sore eyes a little, then his arm. 'He worked for the army all his adult life. Joined straight from uni. Medical Corps. High ranking officer. His doctorate was in genealogy and he was considered the top guy in his field in his day. He headed up several thinktanks and committees, had entire teams working under him, managed research projects etc.'

'Okay. That sounds like pretty important stuff. He's hardly storming trenches, so we may be onto something there. I can see how, in some warped parallel universe, possibly in this one too, that kind of role could lead to something worth killing for. If he was heading work into vital projects for the military, he would be privy to all kinds of secret stuff, wouldn't he? Obviously, it would depend on the nature of the projects, but that would most definitely place him at risk, don't you think?'

'Maybe. I never thought of it like that. But who would know? They don't advertise it. In fact, they sign so many acts and take it so seriously, that I've never heard of an issue. Plus, we're just guessing and we could be way wide of the mark. It might have nothing to do with his work at all. Could be something he did *off the books* so to speak? To me, he was just my dad. Hardly ever spoke about what he did on the base and never, *ever* brought it home with him,' answered Miles, honestly.

Jenny huffed a little as the promising lead appeared to be going nowhere all of a sudden. Miles was hard work, like trying to extract the truth from a politician. She could see that she'd have to graft, if she was going to obtain anything useful from him.

'Oh no. You're not getting off that lightly. You're gonna have to try a little harder for me. We're being shot at here, if you hadn't noticed. Think! Try! Wrack your brains and dredge up what memories you can. Go right back to the very beginning. What was he doing back then?'

'Alright, take it easy. I'll try.'

Miles was quiet for a minute or two, much to her frustration. There were things in his past he could see clearly, as well as vast chasms of darkness where an abundance of pictures and memories were missing for some reason. The exhaustion he was feeling wasn't helping any and he soon became exasperated with getting nowhere.

'Nope. I'm sorry, really I am. I want to help but I don't think I can tell you all that much. The little I know, he was an assistant in the lab in his early years, general dogsbody fetching and carrying, making tea and sweeping up… Lots of top-secret stuff he would never have divulged came later on. Official Secrets Act an' all that. It was his stark response if ever work or the lab was mentioned. I remember him saying it was the greatest umbrella ever invented that act, because it shielded him from all sorts of crap. Years and years of whispers and *shut ups*, that's all I can recall… He almost died once though. Big accident in the lab. It was before I was born. I remember my mum talking about it once or twice. Brought her to tears and then she'd stop. She thought he was a goner. He was badly injured and I think she'd started planning the funeral. Though he eventually made a full recovery and ran a few marathons afterwards, so it couldn't have been that bad, and it's probably not relevant.'

'Noted. Anything else?'

'This is damned hard you know. I feel like I'm trussed up and the lights are shining in my eyes. Is it hot in here, or is it me? Let me think… It's not much, only… I once heard him speaking with one of his staff. Someone named Andy who visited our house. That was unusual. He had plenty under his command but nobody ever got close. They certainly didn't appear at our door. Anytime he had to meet with them, it was always away from us. Golf clubs, sports bars, ranges…

Anyway, this one time, they mentioned something they were working on. I think they called it, *Project Ajax*. Can't remember much else. The name stuck for some reason. More may come back to me at some point, I don't know. You have to understand that I was busy doing my own living and took very little notice of anyone else. My father and his job were just about as boring as you could get, to a young lad growing up.'

Jenny stretched her aching limbs as best she could. 'Yeah, you had the latest games to try out, you party animal you. Maybe hacking into MI5 or the FBI or something? You're hardly a goldmine of information. Still, it's something I suppose. More than we had a few moments ago. If that's everything about your father, we'll move on. Who was the woman who warned Jase?'

'Now that one I *can* answer. My mother. Has to be.'

'I'm so glad you said that. I was beginning to think you frequented a different planet and that I'd *never* understand your family. My thinking too. That's why she had the video. Your father was a very intelligent man, way cleverer than us. He left a suicide note, of sorts. Only, he hid it for some reason. That's if it *was* a suicide.'

Miles swallowed a large lump which had just formed in his throat. His eyes moved to meet hers invitingly, even though he was dreading her next reply. 'Come again? That's one *hell* of a leap, isn't it?'

'No. I don't think so. I know this is painful for you to even contemplate, but think about it? Remove all feeling, all bias, try to be impartial. We've just learned that he was doing all this secret science stuff. In charge of it all. Most definitely in the know. The details of which are a mystery. Though, maybe not to others? *Possibly* extremely significant or dangerous, we don't know. What if it *was?* What if it was *both?* Then, he goes and dies, supposedly by his own hand. No depression or gradual decline noted in his behaviour, according to you. By all accounts it was a real shock to everyone. Now, wind forward a few months and you and your brother are both violently attacked, by what looks like multiple pairs of international professionals of some kind. Your mother vanishes into thin air. She's gone dark, as several of the novels I read like to put it. Assuming she's still alive. And, again, I apologise. She's not seen by anyone other than Jase, it appears. If I'm correct, your entire family has been, or is being, hunted to extinction! Sounds like one heck of a conspiracy to me? And again, if I'm right, I'm thinking that it all began with your father... He didn't *kill* himself, Miles. Someone took him out.'

Miles felt a burning rage swelling in his breast. His palms grew sweaty all of a sudden and he felt even more sickly as his beating heart raced to keep up with his pulsating mind.

'I'm too close to this to see things for what they are. I've been blind, haven't I? Too caught up in grief to think straight? If that's so, if he *was* murdered, there *must* be something we can do about it? How could they *possibly* get away with something like that?'

'Do? Without any proof? We'd be laughed out of town. Never mind putting our heads on the block the moment we speak up. They have ways and means to make it look how they want, believe me,' Jenny replied.

'*They?*'

'Oh, come on? You're not stupid. At the level he was operating, there are *hundreds* of suspects. If not his own people, we're talking spy agencies, organised crime, CIA, MI6, Mossad, Triads.... Take your pick. It all depends on the research or project, but I should think there would be no shortage of enemies, if it were serious enough, and word got out. Don't forget that he was military. Their business is finding better ways to kill. You need to establish exactly what happened to him. And why?'

Miles' head was buzzing and looked like it was going to explode as he moved it gently from side to side in utter confusion.

'And just how do I do that?'

Jenny shrugged her shoulders. 'What am I, Brains of Britain? I'm just thinking aloud, that's all. We may *never* know these things. It would probably be too hard now to establish what happened. So, let's start with something smaller. What about this so-called message he left for you? The holiday. Sandringham Gardens. Does that mean anything?'

'No. Not especially. I was about twelve or thirteen when we went there. It was a day trip, not a holiday.'

'Aha! So, the highly-educated scientist *deliberately* misrepresented the facts. Classic technique for fooling captors that. I once read about a Vietnam vet blinking in morse code on a hostage video, sending messages home. Similar thing. The lie, or error, or omission, is known only to you both, so it emphasises the importance of what is actually being said.'

'You're quite good at this. But there was nothing of note on that day. It was drizzly, as usual. We were stuck in traffic on the way home. I recall being very bored and rather wet. Not top of my favourite memories so I'm a little confused as to why he thought it so special. We *did* take a photograph. It was snapped by a passerby for us. One of the few good ones of the three of us together. It was framed and took pride of place on our wall for years afterwards.'

'Well, that's interesting. What was in this photo?'

'Nothing much. Other than *us* obviously. We were dressed normally. Holding nothing. Stood in front of a statue, next to some…'

'Statue? What statue?'

'That *can't* be important, can it? Err, let me think... Eros, maybe? No! It's just come back to me. I can picture it now. It was a statue of Father Time.'

'There you go. That *has* to be it. What significance does that hold for you?'

'*Father* could refer to my dad. *Time*... His watch!'

'The one on your wrist?' asked Jenny, all animated now. 'What about it?'

Dad only left me two objects when he died. Well, three, with a little money in a bank account that secured my deposit on the flat. This watch, and his beloved car. His pride and joy. We shipped it over from the States. Everything else went to my mother as far as I know.'

'Maybe not. How do you suppose Jase was able to buy a garage and set himself up in business? I'm betting he had a helping hand. Now we're finally getting somewhere. Is there anything special about the watch? When someone gave it to you? A remark or story about it? Anything?'

'No. It's just a watch. See for yourself.'

He unfastened it and passed it over. Jenny examined it carefully. It was lovely but in itself unremarkable and she could see nothing untoward. She sighed with disappointment as she gave it back.

'Maybe there's something inside?' ventured Miles.

'Worth a shout. Only one way to find out,' Jenny replied, perking up a little. 'I've a nail file and some small scissors in my bag.' She fished the bag off the rear seat and found the file, handed it over to him. Miles removed the metal casing from the rear of the watch. He examined inside but could see nothing unusual. Then, he turned over the metal in his hand, shined some light over it.

'Here, there's some engraving on the inside. It's rather faint. I can only just make it out. A series of letters and numbers. It seems to be a code of some sort. Here, grab a pen and write this down...

C, Z, Y, Dash. C, F, C, Dash. 5, 3, Dash. A, F… That's it.'

'Got it. Means zilch to me. Anything jump out at you?'

Miles nodded, his mood improving rapidly despite his fatigue. 'Not certain about the rest, but this message was most definitely left by my father for me.'

Jenny's lips curved upwards in relief. 'Hallelujah! Explanation, please?'

'It was his pet name for me. Nobody else knew it. Apart from my mum. I was always getting into scrapes as a small child, falling over, scuffing knees and elbows, tumbling out of trees… Added to that my initials; Miles Andrew Dalton. *Mad?* He thought it was hilarious and took to calling me, *Crazy*. And there you have it; CZY.'

Jenny placed a warm hand on his. 'Sounds like one hell of a papa. So, don't stop there. What's CFC?'

'Not too sure on that, but I know it's familiar somehow. I've seen it somewhere before.'

'CFC gasses maybe?' Jenny offered. 'He *was* a scientist?'

'No, don't believe so. Give me a moment.'

The car fell silent for several minutes and Jenny was just about to explode, her patience running thin as her eyelids fought to remain open, when Miles suddenly spluttered out, '*Paint!*'

'What about it?' she asked, exasperated beyond belief by his one-word announcement, as if that was supposed to unlock everything for her.

'*CFC*. It's the code they use for Signal Red in the industry. The car he left me is a classic. A Jaguar XJS built in 1990. One of only three thousand or so made that year. V12 engine and… Not important. Anyway, I have it in private storage. The colour is *Signal Red*. It's on the log book. It was scratched in transit and I was going to touch it up along with some marks my father would have known about, so I bought a little pot of the stuff online. CFC!'

Jenny laughed and shook away her dreariness. 'A family of geeks. You're on a roll. More!'

'Well, fifty-three is easy, now I know it's the car. The Jag has a 5.3 litre engine. Gas guzzler. He's telling me something is hidden inside the car.'

'And? One more clue,' she urged.

'That has to be exactly where it's concealed. So, it's a part or area of an old Jaguar.'

'AF? We could do with Jase here, the mechanic?' Jenny mused.

An instant response this time.

'No need. He's not made it difficult at all really. Not once we cracked the first part. AF refers to the Air Filter. Has to. Plain as the rather pretty nose on your face.'

Jenny was ecstatic, thrilled in fact, and she threw her arms around him to hug him before she knew what she was doing.

Seconds later, normality returned and rather embarrassed, she pulled herself away sharply. 'Sorry, I…'

'No, it's okay, really,' Miles insisted.

'No. No it's not. I don't feel that way about you…. Let's forget it happened. That's enough excitement for one day. We both need some shuteye. Make yourself comfortable. I hope you don't snore. The first of the residents will be leaving for work in a few hours so we'll have to get moving. Try to access that car of yours. Hope to God that nobody else has figured it out and gotten there first.'

Chapter 11

For Sam Lennox, the nightmare was always the same. An intensely horrific recollection of past events. Distorted over time perhaps, but no less vivid or upsetting for it. Always, she was looking through her own eyes and smelling, hearing, tasting what she did back then, as if she was somehow returned in the flesh. To *that* street. That ill-fated mission. To some little-known corner of Afghanistan nobody had even heard of. In daylight hours, when fully lucid, she had no trouble reciting her incident report of that enemy contact word for word, from start to finish perfectly, recalling every single bullet she'd fired. At night though, in the dark when her mind was free of constraints, the entire ambush took on a life of its own. She knew what was coming each and every time and yet, as she witnessed it happening again, it felt like an entirely new horror. Fresh and unnerving. And whilst immersed fully in the action, the thrill and the mayhem of it all, Sam second-guessed every single decision she had made, each minute movement or deed, so that they played out in slow motion intensifying her overwhelming feelings of guilt and remorse. Because the thought that she had made mistakes out there, where in counted most, let somebody down, was *the* most frightening and troubling aspect of the whole war...

It began with the ride in. The convoy of assorted vehicles. The heavily-armoured Mastiff she'd been assigned to. Luck of the draw, for she could hear the bullets striking the thick exterior and the other vehicles being hit, set ablaze. Multiple explosions, automatic fire being returned, screams and roars... Then the officer yelling at his comrade next to him, 'Don't stop! Get round them!' and the driver answering in a thick Scouse accent, 'Can't sir! We're blocked in!'

Almost immediately afterwards came a roar of, 'Contact! Contact ahead! RPG!'

The command to exit was followed by a mad dash under fire into the nearest damaged building and a tremendous thunder. The air being sucked somehow from her lungs, a brief intense heat, and sand, smoke and dust falling all around the survivors...

All down the line soldiers were trying to find what cover they could. The smells hit her then. Those awful reeks which could now trigger her in an instant and return her to hell. She'd come to hate *them* more than anything. Cordite. Smoke and dust. Burning bodies, garbage and rubber... And damp concrete mixed with mouldy earth? That one always felt weird to admit. But it was true.

To this day, she feared descending into old cellars...

Exhausted and deep in slumber, Sam tossed and turned on the chairs she'd made her bed in the office next to the locker room at the police station. She'd stripped down to her bra and pants so that her clothes would remain fresh for the next day but she was sweating profusely still, as she gave a stifled cry of, 'Left! On your left!!!'

The corporal she was screaming at on the other side of the street in that faraway land reacted too slowly though, as four insurgents carrying AK's blasted away at him, scythed him down before she could react. Sam was up and charging at them before she knew it, her mind completely gone and rage having seized her. She fired from the hip, unloading the entire magazine of her rifle into all four, aided by her concealed position and their bunching, as well as the close proximity. They dropped to the ground in contorted shapes never to rise again.

The loud click of her gun as it emptied almost made her sit upright in fear, for she knew only too well what was coming next. Immediately though, her body dropped and sank back into the safety of the chairs, as if they could protect her somehow this time. Hide her almost...

It still hit her again like a freight train, however. The bullet with her name on it. It *never* missed. Her arm was almost severed. Blood everywhere she looked. She could not deal with it then, had to react swiftly to the threat, or die.

All around her was carnage. Bodies, wounded, the dead and dying. The *whoosh* of RPG 7 rockets, incoming fire of all types, radio chatter and commands, the *zip* of rounds passing by, the *ping* of metal striking metal, flesh, bone and stone, and swearing. A whole lot of swearing. The feeling of complete isolation and helplessness and always, the rotten stench of death...

Somehow, with immense difficulty, she'd managed to get a CAT, a tourniquet, onto her injured arm to stem the bleeding. The humorous bone appeared to be almost completely shattered so that it looked as though the only thing holding her limb on now, was her triceps muscle. A violent wave of pain and nausea swept through her at the sight. She was terrified of losing her arm far more than her life ending right there and then. Strange that. She found though, that she could still just about wiggle her fingers and pulled herself together.

'Come on! Move! Move, damn you!' she yelled.

On went a field dressing, followed by a sharp jab in the thigh of morphine. She reloaded her weapon with maximum effort and re-entered the fight one-handed, helping to see off another wave of determined attackers. Then she used her good arm to drag some wounded and bodies away from the burning wrecks and into relative cover, despite her severe wound, extreme fatigue, agony and the loss of so much blood. All the time she was under serious fire. A close personal friend and colleague, Billy Mac, was hit in the throat as he worked away on the GPMG. She wrapped her one good hand around his wound but knew it was hopeless and watched him bleed out in revulsion, prayed for deliverance...

Back on the makeshift bed, her heart was racing and she thrashed and tossed. She only awoke when a final blast detonated so loudly in her mind, that she almost fell off the sodden chairs. Her breathing was rapid and ragged then and her eyes opened wide and fast in fear and alarm...

She calmed eventually, as she always did. Once she realised where she was. Took a moment and rubbed her left arm, the scar tissue of her wound and the point of incision for the metal pins which still ached so, even to this day. *Another* episode to add to the rest. No cause for concern. The price she had to pay for survival. The reason she was single, despite plenty of offers, for she couldn't allow herself to let anyone in. Let anyone *know*. Sam was just grateful that nobody had witnessed her shame. She'd hardly slept at all. Not *proper* rest. No use trying now. She clutched the gym bag she'd retrieved from the boot of her car, slipped out of the office and stepped into the locker room. Turned on the lights, arranged her toiletries and enjoyed a long, hot shower.

Good as new.

At ten the following morning, Owen James took yet another call on his mobile.

'Spliffer's whorehouse? No Ganja, no flange-a, so tell me you're loaded?'

There was an audible huff of disapproval on the other end of the line and Owen began to think he'd ballsed up again.

'I'm not sure who you think you're impressing with your childish wit. I should have thought that the time for such immaturity had long since passed, Mr. James? Only those basking in the glory of success, ought be so merry, don't you agree?' the eloquent male stated.

'Maybe. Though, there's a lot to be said for humour. Got us through two World Wars, didn't it? Just tryin' to lighten the mood. Brighten the day, you know? Tough crowd though, I get it. Let's talk shop then. What do you have for me?'

'Hmmn... An update... That's a little back to front, is it not? In *my* view, the service provider should be the one providing the *service*. Where are you now?'

'Don't you know? I'm watching her flat, as ordered.'

'Yes, of course. We know everything. I was merely being polite. You should try it sometime. In that case, I have to inform you that you're too late. We've established that they have already been to the residence and fled.'

'Excellent,' stated the top-end merc, sarcastically. 'It would have been nice to have been informed.'

The disgruntled voice once again sighed like it was the most tedious conversation he'd ever had, as if he really didn't want to be there, conversing with the hired help.

'Be that as it may, *James*, listen closely. The systems we've been able to access picked up a vehicle entering and leaving that street in the early hours, some fifty minutes or so before you arrived. Pictures are grainy but there's a ninety-per-cent probability that it's a match to our target. A red BMW. We've tracked it partially and we believe it's heading towards Islington. They have a head start on you again, so we suggest you move towards that location too. The very moment they stop appearing on cameras, we'll notify you of their whereabouts.'

'Received and understood. Show me as mobile.'

'And Mr. James?'

'Yes?'

'I wish to clarify something while I have you, so that we understand one another completely. This constitutes your final chance. You have one more shot at completing your mission. If you fail to honour the contract in *full*, measures will be taken to address that situation. The clients here, including myself, are a little tense as you may have gathered. There is a lot at stake. Frankly, we pay top dollar and expected better results. We need to expedite this termination. I cannot emphasise that enough.'

'You do go on. Good job this is a secure line. There is no misunderstanding. You have been quite clear and your words have been heard.'

'I do hope so. But to overstate the point, if I may? *If* he is still breathing after this, it will be open season on them both. All files will be made public knowledge within our tiny fraternity, and the bounty will be paid to *anyone* who succeeds where you have failed. I need not tell you the damage that would do to your glowing reputation.'

Owen James beat his hands on the steering wheel and bit his lip.

'Open season, eh? There'd be hundreds of shooters, of all calibre. I'm grateful for your... restraint. Goodbye!'

Around an hour later, DCI Farley and DS Lennox were driving an unmarked Audi A6 heading for the address of Jennifer Pearce's parents. They wanted to learn more about her relationship with the deceased, and possibly his twin, Miles Dalton. Both had slept in the station overnight and Edward Farley certainly looked like he had. His hair was all over the place and he hadn't shaved. Lennox, however, looked and felt fully refreshed. All necessary paperwork had been completed and authorised and they had been handed service weapons which were on lease for the duration of the investigation only. A virtually unheard-of event for Cambridge Police and indicative maybe of the increasingly high-profile nature of this case. Farley had called in a close colleague and friend to command the Incident Room. DCI James Darling he'd known for twelve years. He was a good cop and an honest man. Farley had briefed him and explained that although the situation could be considered as wholly unorthodox, he felt that he needed to be on the ground for this one, close to the action and therefore any breaking leads. He was offering to share not only command, but also any of the glory that might come his way afterwards. Darling had accepted at once, knowing that a series of events or capture of this magnitude did not come along every day and could quite easily make his career. Farley's mobile chimed and he pressed the button to place it on speaker, so that they could both hear what was being said.

'Alex? It's James Darling. Just took a call. They've been sighted. They've switched cars now. They're in a BMW, details and pics being sent through to your phone as I speak. They visited Miss Pearce's flat for some reason. Possibly to retrieve an item. Didn't stay long. Appears as though they were in a hurry. She left carrying a bag. Around ten minutes from arrival they are seen heading out of there at speed.'

'Good. What time was this?' Farley asked.

He nodded in acknowledgement as Sam Lennox showed him the car photos and details, which had also pinged up on *her* mobile.

'About zero three thirty. We lose them then. But in the early hours after daybreak, they are seen heading towards the north of London. Too early to say precisely where.'

'Do we know why?' asked Lennox.

'Negative. We know of no family connection in that area. However, you have a fine team here and they've unearthed a gem I feel. A strong possibility at any rate. Miles has a car. A *classic* car. Worth a penny or two. It's being stored in a lock-up garage. DVLA and insurance records show it is in Islington. That'll be costly.'

'Excellent,' said Lennox.

'Yes, pass on my thanks, James… Just a minute! Not so fast,' raged the DCI. 'Why am I only hearing this now?

They were spotted in the middle of the night. We have operators claiming overtime for this kind of thing, cameras manned full time, even allowing for trawling and playback etc. that's a hell of a lag?!'

A slight hesitation in replying spoke volumes. James Darling was clearly not relishing having to explain, possibly angry at being rebuked when he had only just assumed command.

'It was nothing to do with me, I assure you,' he answered, coldly.

'I know that. I apologise for my tone. Lack of sleep. Don't give me that chain of command stuff though. We've worked with each other too long. Who's rubber-stamping the information flow? Who's blocking the channels and delaying communication?'

No response once more. Lennox looked over at her new boss. He had quickly earned her trust and respect. For the first time in a long while, she was working for a guy she would quite happily follow into battle. Not that it would come to that. His face was bright red now and he shook his head at her, instructing Sam silently to say nothing. Protecting her from any subsequent fallout.

'James?' Farley prodded.

'Yes?'

'You needn't answer. I can guess. Only, do what you can for me?'

'I will. You and I both know though, that my hands are tied.'

'Understood. As soon as you can, I want roadblocks in place around that garage. Nothing gets in or out of that area without being searched.'

'Right. That I *can* do. Happy hunting.'

Miles and Jenny arrived at the lock-up without incident. They pulled down the alleyway onto an open area with similar units on either side. Jenny turned the car around for a quick getaway and maintained a constant vigil on the alley, whilst Miles unlocked the door and dashed inside. He turned on the light and made straight for a huge toolbox, took out several screwdrivers and spanners and hauled the tarpaulin sheet off the vehicle. He unlocked the door and pulled the bonnet release catch, lifted the hood, rested it on its catch and got to work. Miles had messed around with cars all his life. It was one of the things he did with his dad when he was alive and he had often worked on this very vehicle. The complete air filter was removed within minutes and tools in hand, he closed and locked the garage and jumped into the Beamer.

'Got it. Let's get out of here.'

'I've been thinking. What if we were wrong and it's somewhere else?' said a concerned Jenny.

'I'd rather go now and take my chances. Can't stay in one place too long. Especially if they can trace it to me. Besides, we're *not* wrong, I can feel it in my bones.'

Jenny gave a tiny smile, reassured slightly. 'Alrighty then. Hey! I've just thought of the perfect place to lie low. Somewhere they'll never find us. It's not too far. Sit back and relax, enjoy the ride.'

Miles scoffed at that remark. 'Hmmph! Enjoy the ride? As if.'

Jenny put the BMW into gear and pulled out of the alley onto the side road. She took the next left and turned straight into the path of a fast-moving missile!

The BMW was blind-sided so fast and furiously, that it had to be a deliberate action. Both occupants were badly shaken but recovered quickly. Jenny instinctively stood on the accelerator and was relieved to hear and feel the big, mangled mess of a motor shudder and roar into life.

The Land Rover Discovery which had intentionally rammed into them was badly damaged but still moving, chasing them now at high speed. The driver appeared to be deranged. He was leaning out of the car as he drove, firing off rounds from a short and stubby machine pistol. Several bullets pinged off the road surface and soon the rear windscreen disintegrated, making Jenny scream out loud.

'Aaargh! That's the same headcase from last night!' she shrieked, as she weaved and raced away as best she could. 'Oooh, I really do not like this joker!'

'Just concentrate on the road,' Miles stated, turning and loosing off two rounds in reply through the now non-existent back window.

Owen James had spotted the BMW at the very last moment, as they pulled out of the alleyway. He launched an immediate assault, as was his way. Royal Marine doctrine still burned fiercely within. He'd tried and failed to stop the car outright, which seriously angered him further. He was banking on his superior fitness and training to give him an edge. However, Jenny's superb driving skills and prompt reaction had scuppered his plans. She'd seen his car and anticipated being hit, accelerated at the very last second, throwing his timing off a fraction and altering the point of impact. All was not lost, however. He was right on their tail and believed for certain that he had them outgunned. All he had to do now was end them and collect his earnings. He raised the pistol and closed to within inches of their bumper, ignoring the twin bullets which smacked into the passenger headrest. His finger tightened on the trigger. There was *zero* possibility of him missing from so close. Not a gunman of his calibre.

An almighty crash sounded abruptly and he lurched aggressively to his left. The weapon fell from his hand and flew out of the open window, clattered onto the street outside. It was all he could do to maintain control of the car and he watched in frustration and dismay as the heavily dented BMW pulled away from him.

In his wing mirror, gaining fast again, was a black Volvo S60 with two military-style males inside. The side of their vehicle showed all the signs of the impact he had felt. The wing mirror was off and it was a complete mess. The men were pointing guns in his direction and he had to throw the car around violently to evade their eyeline. He sighed in vexation.

'Just what I need! These clowns, I take it, are the B Team. Wonderful timing, you shower of...!' he roared, cursing his misfortune.

Owen James had now entered a deadly game of life or death. With complete unknowns. He drew another gun from his shoulder holster as he battled with the steering wheel and tried to keep tabs on his new enemy. He decided to deploy a manoeuvre which certainly wasn't for the feint-hearted. The Discovery was a wreck, a write-off. He'd seen to that by ramming the Beamer. He doubted he could outpace the S60 these goons were driving so it was time to face the music. He shot out the front windscreen of his own car and used the firearm to remove any remaining glass in his immediate vicinity. His face and body were peppered by flying debris and several cuts and scratches ensued. Luckily, none of these entered his eyes. Then, he yanked the handbrake up hard and fast, spinning the wheel so that the motor turned almost completely out of control. Before it flipped, he found himself with a split second to fire out of the space where his windscreen had been at the startled pursuers, who were now mere feet away. He let the entire magazine empty and both occupants were killed instantly, riddled with bullets.

James' battered and now burning Discovery rolled and rolled, finally coming to a complete stop in the garden of a nearby house. He climbed out as best he could, aching and bleeding from scores of minor wounds. He moved swiftly to the Volvo, which had crashed into a wall almost demolishing it completely. The Two occupants were still in their seats. Neither was moving but Owen James put a bullet in each of their heads just to make certain. It didn't do to leave enemies standing in his line of work. He took out the papers in the pocket of one of the corpses and found a Russian passport.

'Figures,' he muttered to himself.

The cool Brit then made his way back to his own car and removed a few items from the holdall in the trunk, including a pistol and mags. The bag was too conspicuous on foot and too heavy to carry. Though it saddened him greatly, he tossed a thermite grenade into the wreck and torched the lot. Then he made his way down a nearby side street and disappeared from sight. Within seconds, his phone was ringing.

Chapter 12

By the time the police were in position to mount any roadblocks calls were already coming in about yet more gunfire and fatalities in North London, near the garage rented by Miles Dalton. Details were sketchy at first but extremely concerning as the police response had once again been inadequate and far too late. Questions were being asked as to why the great city was beginning to resemble a war zone. The top brass, including the Chief Constable, Home Secretary, Prime Minister and most of the Cabinet were agitated and incensed, looking for scapegoats, as they often do. DCI Edward Farley was high on their list. He was furious too. The delay in providing him with accurate, speedy intelligence on Miles and Jenny's movements was unusual and they had very nearly paid with their lives. Not to mention the fact that it made him look like a fool. Farley could only guess at the kind of politics in play at higher levels and the number of unknown individuals involved in that error, so it was impossible to pinpoint at present who exactly was to blame. He had theories and questions of his own now, however, which required answers. Who was in command of this incident? Not *him*, judging by the evidence on show. He may have been the figurehead or point man shoved in front of the media, the designated fall guy if things went south, but the *real* power lay elsewhere, no doubt with the secret handshake, third nipple brigade. He was too much of an old dinosaur for that. Not that he'd ever been considered a potential applicant for membership for he wasn't the type. He'd built a solid reputation for efficient and honest policing over his career of which he was justly proud. Nothing and nobody was going to destroy his life's work. The others could play their games as much as they liked, just so long as they did not hinder him or his investigation. A line in the sand which *somebody* was now in severe danger of crossing.

As witness statements came in bit by bit and were relayed to him over the phone, it became abundantly clear to the experienced detective that at least two different sets of attackers had made determined efforts to murder both Miles and Jenny at the garage. It was presumed Miles had been the priority target, but that Jenny had now become a secondary mark due to their close association. Two of the hostile factions had then become embroiled in their own separate firefight. They were in no way working together, as part of a team, more like competition. Why *was* that?

Because there were more than two parties who were calling the shots here. This was confirmation that Miles had not just made it to the head of one kill list, he'd topped several.

That was some going by anyone's standards and DCI Farley was scratching his head as to what he could have *possibly* done to earn such popularity.

He had just informed DS Lennox to step on the gas as they headed for the crash site and lock-up in Islington, when yet another call came through.

'Ed? It's James Darling again. I'm in a private office and nobody is listening. Are you alone?'

Farley placed a finger to his lips as he pressed the button for the speaker, instructing Sam silently to pull over onto a verge and remain quiet, but listen in.

'Yes, James. I'm all alone. We're parked up and Sam's fetching coffees. What's up?'

'Good. I've been, *contacted*. Need I say more? The kind of discussion you never want to have.'

'Oh, I see. Thought they would. Didn't take them long. Don't tell me, the chief constable?'

'The one and only. Listen, the long and short of it is, you're ordered to back off after today. You're finished on this case. Tomorrow morning, you're to brief those who will be taking over, hand everything to a joint taskforce they're forming. It's going to consist of Met personnel, anti-terror squad and MI5... I'm sorry, Ed, they are taking your case and I'm not certain what you'll be doing afterwards.'

'Cleaning the toilets I should think. It was never *my* case though, James. We're all servants of the crown here. I half expected it to be fair. It's grown too large in such a short space of time and it's politically sensitive that's for sure. Still leaves today, however. They'll take some time to set up and organise. I have another pair of corpses to identify and...'

'No. No, you don't,' interrupted his old friend. 'That's the second part of this message. It came straight from the spooks. They're pulling the gaffer's strings as usual. One of them, I can't tell who, has his hand so far up her back that he's twisting her tonsils. They're moving fast. By the time you arrive on scene, I imagine the stiffs will have already been whisked away. They want no witnesses they can't control. MI5 are taking them to their own facility. Who knew they even *had* one? Thanks for bringing me on board pal, 'cos I'm learning so much... I'm told they will share their findings in due course, though *I'm* thinking we will be drip-fed baloney like they always do. We're all just going to be fetching and carrying for the special ones now. Glorified waiters for faceless suits.'

Farley seethed inside but was determined to maintain his cool. His upper lip was trembling a little. 'Not to worry, James. I'm sorry you came all that way for nothing. Though, I might as well make use of the day. Maintain standards right to the end. What about the motor in the garage?'

'They've taken ownership of that too. Once they begin and the covers are off, they sure don't mess about, do they?'

'No. Unfortunately. Not leaving many crumbs for us to follow. Which, I guess, is by design.'

Farley shook his head at Lennox warning her not to speak, even though he could clearly see that remaining silent all that time was absolutely killing her.

'Well, that's all I have for now. I'm sorry to be the bearer of bad news, Ed. If I hear anything else, you'll be the first to hear,' James Darling stated. 'Enjoy the rest of your day. May as well kick back and relax until the morning, my friend. We've effectively been demoted.'

'Nah, not my style. Catch ya soon for a pint and a curry away from all this. See ya.'

Farley turned off the phone and waited for the damn to burst. Which didn't take long at all.

'You're... You're not *taking* that, are you?!' Sam fumed. 'They've shafted you big style! What the actual...?! They can't do this!' she screamed, absolutely livid, in need of punching something.

'They *can*, and they *have*. Privilege of rank. They're paid to make the big decisions, and they've just made one. I think it's an epic mistake but I'm just one guy at a relatively low level. It's as simple as that.'

'But...!'

'Enough! Put your eyes back in their sockets, unclench those fists and keep quiet. You'll blow a gasket, the way you're going. It's the way of the world, Sam. Has been for a thousand years or so. You have a decent brain on you and will hopefully go far in this service, but you must learn quickly to pick your battles or you'll be dead in the water. We've been given the command to leave it for others now. *From tomorrow morning.* I heard that loud and clear. Nonetheless, this thing's moving fast and furious. I'm out from behind my desk right this minute and wading through the mud alongside you. Of all people, you should know that the fog of war can be intense. They really haven't a clue *what* we're up to. And that plays massively in our favour. We have the rest of the day, plus tonight. So, let's make it count. Let's catch these two fugitives and maybe solve a few unanswered questions. Plus, take out or find the lone shooter. That's twice he's come close to killing them and he's murdered the latest duo to have a dabble too. From the descriptions given, it sounds as if he's the same driver and sniper who chased them in Cambridge. We need to identify him ASAP.'

'Received and understood, gaffer. I could reach out to a contact I have in MI5?' Sam ventured.

'Yes. Good. Do it. I don't like going cap in hand to those guys, it goes against all of my beliefs, but I'm betting they know a *hell* of a lot more than they are letting on. If you think you can trust them, we need a little inside information. And we need it fast. Somebody is running interference here, to use an American saying, I'm certain of it.'

'I knew you wouldn't lay down like a tame puppy waiting for a tummy tickle. On it.'

'Oh, I'm tame alright. When I need to be. Set up a meet for today. While you're doing that, I'll study the map, try to figure out likely destinations for our desperate pair of runaways, given their direction of travel. They'll need to ditch the car at some point, if it was damaged as badly as we've been told. They'll know it will be reported and traced. Not too many options open to them that we haven't covered. Snap to it!'

Sam stepped out of the vehicle whilst she made a call to the mobile of an old friend who was now working for MI5, based in London. Ten minutes later, the door opened and she climbed back inside.

'Well?' asked an impatient Farley.

'Sorted. We're on. There's a pub I know not far from their headquarters. I'm to message him when I get there and he'll make an excuse to step out for no more than fifteen minutes. That should be long enough. He'll meet me around the back by the tradesman's entrance, out of sight. Just so long as I come alone and not wired, obviously.'

'Ha! They're a suspicious lot. And are you happy to do that?'

'Sure. I've known him for years. We served together and go way back... I'll be fine, boss, I promise,' pleaded Sam, sensing his unease.

'That's the stuff. I have a duty of care to you though. If you feel at any point that it's too dangerous, just say so. I'll pull you out in no time. I'm desperate I know, but your safety is my primary concern. You call me at the first sign of trouble and I'll come running with all guns a-blazing.'

'Ha! You sound like Eliot Ness.'

'Do I? Always fancied myself as a movie star.'

Farley instructed Lennox to check out a couple of the roads whilst they were in the area, having been informed by Grippa that Miles and Jenny's BMW had been spotted on ANPR cameras heading in a north-westerly direction, avoiding the motorway. On a long and straight stretch of the Henley to Oxford Road, Lennox spotted them ahead in the distance, hardly able to believe their good fortune.

'There they are sir!' she cried out excitedly.

DCI Farley was astonished but looked up from reading his messages on his phone as calm as you like. 'Then put your foot down, sergeant, and let's do this.'

'Certainly. Though, shouldn't we wait for back up?'

'And risk losing them? Not on your life. Besides, you heard what happened with the intel. If we call it in, we'll be ordered to stand down. Is that what you want? The cavalry will take an absolute age to get here and we'll miss our chance. All I want to do is talk to them at this point. Anyhow, I don't seriously believe that these two are dangerous to anyone, apart from acting in self-defence. They won't harm us, just so long as we make our credentials known and are careful. I think *they* are the ones being hunted. That might make them jittery, but I'd like to bring them in safely. Let's try and learn why they're considered such an enormous threat to half the known world that they've thrown London and Cambridge into turmoil, shall we?'

Before long, Lennox had closed the gap. She was just passing a slip road when a white Toyota Land Cruiser driving very fast and erratically joined the carriageway ahead of them, between their unmarked car and the BMW.

'Damn!' Lennox exclaimed. 'Where the *hell* did they come from?!'

Farley drew his pistol and put a round in the chamber. 'Don't know, don't care. They've made their intentions clear. They look like they mean business.'

The Land Cruiser had three males inside, which wasn't immediately apparent until Sam Lennox somehow managed to draw up level and they instantly attempted to ram her off the road. Only her expert driving skills saved them but by that time, she had identified a white man in the passenger seat with a gun in his hand, a rear seated male of mixed race and a heavily-built white driver, also male. The guy in the back was armed too and soon both gunmen were attempting to fire out of open side windows on either side of the vehicle, with serious hardware, probably MP5's or Mk18's.

Lennox slid the car rapidly over to the Toyota's driver's side, using every inch of the road. The BMW was a little way ahead and now going flat out. They were approaching heavier traffic and she was growing increasingly anxious.

Bang! Bang!

Farley fired off two rounds, hit the Toyota twice, the second bullet tearing into the rear driver's side tyre which exploded and shredded so fast, that the vehicle careered across the road and Lennox had to stamp on the brakes to avoid a heavy collision. The police car turned through one hundred and eighty degrees in the ensuing skid and came to an abrupt halt. Both officers undid their seatbelts quickly in record time and exited on opposite sides of the car, weapons at the ready, opening doors to provide extra cover. A succession of incoming rounds hit the motor and the road as they tried hard to locate their new adversaries, holing the doors with ease, but thankfully missing their targets.

The three unknowns had reacted swiftly to the loss of their own vehicle and now determined to take the police car in order to continue the pursuit, or escape. Farley and Lennox began taking a serious pounding as a result and the strangers launched a clearly well-practised, co-ordinated assault.

Bang! Bang! Bang! Bang!

Lennox all of a sudden morphed into a different beast. She'd snapped completely, as a bullet very nearly smashed into her head. It was like a time warp. She was all of a sudden thrust back to Afghan, could feel the intense heat and dust around her, her mind so alive and focussed now, that she almost felt as though she was actually on fire.

Pain and grief were forgotten in that moment as her immense training instinctively took command. She and her new boss were dead anyway, if they sat it out like this. And Sam Lennox wasn't about to go out like that. The former warrior moved to the offensive in extraordinary fashion. Her first two shots missed. But they came close enough to gain the target's attention and the second two hit the guy she had forced out into the open squarely in his chest, exactly as planned. The driver was hit in his left leg as he ran forwards soon after. He fell down in a crumpled mess and she put another round into his head, which switched off his lights for good. Not content with that, Sam moved straight away to eliminate the sole remaining threat.

On the other side of the car, the extremely competent mixed-race guy was providing covering fire for his comrades. Now that Lennox had revealed her position, his head popped up an extra inch in order to take a shot. The former soldier however, was too quick for him. She rolled, adjusted her aim and fired her pistol the very moment she felt it was on target, relying on feel and instinct.

One shot, one kill. *Outstanding* marksmanship. The bullet tore out his trachea and he bled to death in seconds.

Seeing this, Farley broke cover to check she was okay, astonished to have witnessed such fantastical deeds by a police officer on British roads. As he walked over towards her, the first of the attackers, who was somehow still breathing, still able to hold his weapon, fired straight at the passing DCI from almost point-blank range.

The double tap was inaccurate and rushed. The first bullet missed by two inches. The second though, passed straight through Farley's right eye and into his brain, taking off a small portion of his head on the way out. He was dead before his body hit the ground.

'Nooo!!!'

Sam Lennox wailed in rage, consumed by grief and bloodlust. She lost it. *Totally* lost it. Ignored all of her military training and broke cover, reloaded her gun as the wounded shooter tried to escape over the central reservation. Walked behind the professional killer slowly and deliberately until, when she was ready and he had nearly bled out, was just about to drop, she emptied an entirely fresh magazine into his back and head. Pulverised him. It was overkill of the grandest kind. He was probably dead already, given his wounds and having expended the last of his energy, but Sam made doubly sure. Hang the consequences.

When the smoke eventually cleared and she'd regained control of herself a little, Lennox knew she was extremely lucky to be alive. Had she have missed *any* of her initial shots, had one or more of the men survived their first encounter a little while longer, or she'd stepped out in the open like Farley, then she would have been a sitting duck for trained men of this quality.

Luckily for her though, she didn't miss. She *never* missed.

She turned and made straight for the body of her fallen colleague, sat down in the road and cradled his bloody and lifeless form in her arms. Rocked back and forth for what seemed like an age, tears streaming down her face and the smell of burning rubber in her nostrils, making her convulse and turning her stomach.

Her hands were shaking violently again now.

Chapter 13

The cigarette between her fingers was two-thirds ash by now. It just hung there, unmoving, like *her*. Samantha Lennox was utterly distraught, beyond consoling, consumed with a vile, familiar blend of outrage, grief and exhaustion. Just like that fateful day back in Afghanistan. She'd sustained some whiplash injuries and the paramedics attending to her were seriously concerned about shock. Also, the short and long term affects of the psychological trauma she had just experienced. Withstanding such a violent attack as the one she had described, seeing her partner and manager killed in front of her in such a fashion, would have been debilitating for most people, rendering them unable to function at all. And yet the turmoil within Sam Lennox was far worse, invisible, beyond their sight or reach. Disguised too. Way past their understanding. At least they hadn't read her file, or whatever emergency powers these medics possessed, would have been enacted swiftly and she would have been driving nothing more dangerous than a desk for the remainder of her career. As it was, they were content to check her over and let her rest a while, whilst they took care of the deceased and handed over to colleagues.

The police had arrived on scene speedily but had still walked into sheer bedlam, like somebody had released a pack of hungry lions into a schoolyard. The excessive force employed in the murder of one of the assailants was clear to see, but *nobody* was speaking of it. Blood, bodies, debris and gore lay everywhere they looked. It littered the entire carriageway, which had been closed for a mile or so in both directions. A situation which was now causing severe havoc on all roads in the area. Teams of every size and description were combing through mountains of evidence on their hands and knees in no time, conscious of the ticking clock and watching world. The severely mutilated corpse was loaded onto a van as soon as it arrived, breaking protocol. It was draped in a white sheet, despite being zipped inside a bodybag. An excess that amused Sam a touch. Her sense of humour at times was something even *she* did not get. She was sat on the steps of the ambulance in the same spot she had refused to vacate since the time of her first examination, the medics original decision to *let her be*, only now coming home to roost. All subsequent attempts to render first aid had been sternly rebuffed as she replayed events over and over inside her mind, obsessively visualising each and every scene, every kill a thousand times, trying to recall fully what had happened and questioning *everything*. Every minute detail.

Specifically, if she could have done more to save her superior's life.

DCI Farley had died a hero. Not that it would have meant much to him. He'd have liked to have been remembered as a good cop though, and *that* at least was a given now. The manner of his passing would only cement his stellar reputation amongst the rank and file. He'd broken cover in a misguided attempt to back up his partner, when in reality she had needed no such assistance. It was a cruel twist of fate that had he have been a coward and remained hidden, he would in all likelihood have survived the encounter. The thought plagued Sam and she found it nigh on impossible to concentrate on anything else. The shakes had remained and she badly desired a shot or three of the good stuff, to raid that drinks cabinet in her flat and crawl up into a tiny little ball, disappear from sight into a black hole somewhere. However, the desperate need to create something tangible out of all this mess, something wholly positive, was gnawing away at her very soul like rats chomping through rotten flesh. It wasn't about to let go. She simply *had* to finish what Edward Farley had begun. Crown his legacy. She owed him that much. Even if it ended her own career. Her life in fact.

The latest of the paramedics to try to convince her to seek medical help at the hospital finally conceded defeat and she was left alone again to brood. Not long afterwards, the police helicopter soared overhead and landed in a nearby field. A smartly-dressed man led two others in her direction. One was the Chief Constable, Elizabeth Barker, in full dress uniform with a host of medals on show. Sam knew this encounter would prove important and she studied their approach. The first man she did not recognise. He was tall. Very tall. Early forties, with a wide muscular frame. Extra large neck. Rugby second row in his youth, maybe. Dressed in a brown suit and matching tie. Expensive shoes. Looked as though he could handle himself in a bar fight and had had a few back in his day. Won most of 'em without breaking sweat. The third guy following behind him like an obedient hound was her old friend and contact at MI5 she had spoken to earlier. What was he doing here? Had he ratted her out? He appeared mightily embarrassed to be there, to be seen in such lofty company. Good looking as always, fit and lean with light-coloured hair and green eyes, he smiled warmly at her as he approached. She thought it a false greeting though and he said nothing, deferring to rank.

'DS Lennox, is it?' said the brown suit.

This was new. This chap she did not know quite obviously carried *serious* weight within the upper echelons, to beat the chief constable to the punch. And to not fear her wrath for doing so. Sam looked him up and down with a renewed sense of suspicion, though she was weary and also remained silent.

'You've been through quite an ordeal I hear? Care to take me through it, blow by blow?' he continued.

Sam lowered her eyes to the ground as if she was too far gone for that.

'Not really.'

The chief constable, a stern-looking lady at the best of times, looked distraught, mortally wounded. She coughed loudly to make her displeasure known.

'Not good enough, Lennox! We've left a high-level function to be here. Just *try*, why don't you? You've refused medical attention I hear. So, there's nothing else the staff can do for you. Life goes on. And *we* need information now. These murders we've been having are bad enough, but the death of one of my finest officers cannot go unanswered. Will *not* go unpunished. Your part in it we will get to in the fullness of time. There will be an investigation of course. In the meantime, this gentleman is Mitch Lovell, Deputy Head of MI5. *He* is now in command of the joint taskforce which will manage this case. I know where your allegiances lie. Nevertheless, you will tell him *everything* he wants to know. If you can't do that, I'll…'

'Yes, thank you, Elizabeth. Very gracious of you but I'll take it from here. I think Sam just needs a little time to process everything that has happened,' Lovell intervened.

That brought Sam Lennox back to her senses. This goon was at the top for a reason. She hadn't figured out yet if he was one of the good guys, though early impressions told her he was no fool. She lifted her eyes and gazed straight past the distinguished pair to their much lower subordinate.

'Hello, Jack. Long time no see.'

'That's right, you and Jack here are old buddies, aren't you?' stated Lovell.

'We went round the block a few times. Though, never behind the bike sheds. Served in Afghan together. Saw a few things out there,' Sam confirmed. She smiled at the younger man. 'Cat got your tongue? These friends of yours won't mind. How's it hangin' then? I *heard* you were pushing a pen? That true? Waste of talent if you ask me.'

Jack replied to her in a soft Scottish accent. 'I was about to say the same. Thought you'd hung up the six-shooter for good? Took up knitting or such? Then I hear about some mad woman tearing up the highways and conducting her very own private war. I'm thinking to myself, that canny be Sam? Didn't take long to come to my senses. I s'pose some days, the world's just out to get ya, no matter what you do. Or some big, bad tango is anyhoo.'

Sam broke into a slight smile for the first time since the cars were sighted, upon hearing the military jargon. She almost immediately burst into tears but managed to catch herself and wiped her brow to hide the pain.

'I... Sorry, sir. I was being rude and discourteous before. It is unforgiveable of me. It's just... DCI Farley. He was a fine man and he deserved better. I've took his death rather harder than I thought I would. It's still raw. So... We were checking out a hunch of his. I was driving. Came across Miles Dalton and Jennifer Pearce travelling on this road in their reported ride, a BMW. Window was gone at the rear. Almost caught up with it, only the Toyota there tried to ram us off the road. It was a deliberate act and we began taking fire. The DCI returned it as best he could and whether it was luck or extreme skill, he managed to take out one of their tyres. All hell broke loose after that. I narrowly avoided a crash but we turned the car and were blind. We scrambled to get clear but by the time we were out, they had decamped and were shooting at us with superior firepower. I think they were ex-military, as there was a pattern to...'

'They *were*,' confirmed Jack. 'German regulars.'

'That explains it then. They were solid tacticians. Good drills. Well trained and motivated,' said Sam. 'We got lucky. Which raises a whole new load of questions.'

'Hmmn... Lucky, is it? They were not well trained *enough*, apparently? For you were able to best them?' said the chief constable in a snooty tone.

'Yes, ma'am, I've had a little training of my own.'

'I think what Chief Barker meant to say, is that you showed excellent ability and remarkable courage under fire, sergeant. We were very fortunate you were at hand. Three more lethal weapons are off the streets, thanks to your actions. Ordinarily, of course, you would be immediately taken off duty, pending enquiry. The postmortem would be troubling, given your *enthusiasm* for your work, shall we say? But these are trying times. There are no families here and no press. Plus, they killed one of our own. That's a gamechanger for me. The Prime Minister has granted me temporary emergency powers. I pretty much have a blank cheque book. And a Get Out of Jail Free Card. What to do with you? I can make all this disappear... Tell me, what are your plans right now, Sam? Do you want to sit at home kicking your heels? Think you need some time off? Because it's perfectly understandable if you do. You've been to hell and back, so nobody here will begrudge you that.'

Lennox bolted upright as if addressing an army officer and stared him straight in the eye. 'I most certainly do *not!* To sit on my backside at home whilst you lot try to stop or catch these thugs? *Hell no!* That would be the absolute worst thing you could do to me. I've just lost my boss. Never knew him long, but he was shaping up just fine as far as I was concerned. I liked him, and I need to see justice served here. Please, don't you bench me?' she begged. 'Give me a role in this and I won't let you down, I promise?!'

'No can do. You're too close. Take the days offered to you, Sergeant. Relax a little and get your head around things. It's standard procedure after an event such as this anyway, as stated,' began the chief constable.

'Err... Yes, yes it is. *Normally*. Never liked it though. We lose our best assets to protocol. Those in touch with events and up to speed. *Not* today,' answered Mitch Lovell, overruling the chief constable, much to her shock, disgust and fury.

'But you can't...!' she protested.

'I'm in command here, Liz! Or didn't you get that memo? I can forward it again if not? The DS here has proven her worth. How many others do you have in your ranks of this calibre? I believe she's far too valuable to be sidelined. If she's happy to work, I say we let her work. I need all the experience I can get and I'd like her seconded to my team from this point onwards... It's a done deal in fact. She can partner up with young Jack here.'

'Sir?' questioned Jack Walters.

'I've already had it sanctioned at the highest level, lad, so save it. Anti-Terror Command can do without you for a little while. The desk can drive itself. Don't want you getting splinters in that young ass of yours. Take Sam over to her house and do it now.'

'It's... It's only a flat, sir,' said Sam. 'Police pay as it is.'

'I stand corrected. Okay then, flat. Let her freshen up and collect some things if she needs to, maybe get a change of clothes. Then, the pair of you, go out and hit those streets hard, pump any sources you have and find me those two fugitives. Bring them in alive. If you do happen to cross paths with any other teams or gunmen, lethal force is authorised right here, if you believe lives are at stake. Now, disappear!'

'Yes, sir!' answered Sam, almost saluting him in her joy but thinking better of it.

She grabbed Jack by the arm before Lovell could change his mind or be dissuaded, sprinted for the parked cars. A young detective had just arrived and was exiting his, so she demanded the keys leaving him gobsmacked in her wake. Once inside the commandeered ride, the two former soldiers began the process of getting to know each other again. After a great deal of catching up on the journey to her place, Sam was beginning to feel a little better. The conversation inevitably then turned back towards work.

'So, tell me what you know,' Sam stated. 'We were going to meet up anyway, you and I. And you know you can't say no to me.'

'True dat. Up until this incident today, you mean? Relatively little. It's a mess. Everyone is panicking, but nobody appears entirely sure that they know *why*. There are guesses and theories of course. The most prominent among them is that this Miles of yours is in possession of a real spanner, something that has the whole world doing cartwheels. A piece of research, a weapon, design, chemical or something which will totally alter the balance of world power and mess up the works, crash stock markets, plunge us into an arms race, or a new Cold War... It's mad, I know, but the trouble he has caused is so huge, conventional wisdom has it that it *must* be on that scale. Then again, the targeted hits are well heavy and they don't support that notion. The Americans are in constant contact over this. They're flapping like the fox is in the henhouse. His dad, *James* Dalton, is like the world's worst traitor to them. If any of their agents play darts, I bet his face is pinned to a board in every club on every base in the free world. They are badmouthing him all over the place. All the players we have unearthed so far, or found, dead or alive, have diplomatic immunity. That's *really* pissing the PM off, I can tell you. Your German mercs will be the same, you can put money on it. *And* the Brit.'

'Sorry? What did you say? The Brit? That's an American term?'

'Yes. I thought you knew. Their people at Langley identified your shooter from the Cambridge incident. And Islington too, at the garage, no doubt. *Owen James*. Captain, Royal Marines. Or *was*. Good soldier by all accounts. Decorated for gallantry. His records were devilishly hard to obtain, as if somebody was protecting him. Though the yanks opened doors we found firmly shut. He's a merc for hire now. Top of the tree and well regarded in the darkest dives on the net.'

Sam pulled up at some traffic lights that had just turned red. She twisted his chin in her direction so that he was looking directly into her eyes. 'Are you telling me that our side is now playing dirty, Jack? *Are* you? Have we sent someone after him? Be straight with me, I beg you? *Is* there a kill order out on Miles Dalton?!'

'No. Not in this country, not that I know of. Though, I wouldn't put it past them. And we appear to be just about the only nation who haven't.'

'Then, you and I have plenty of work to do. We need to get our heads in gear and get back in the game. I'll start. The BMW is all bashed up and it's too conspicuous now. They'll change it as soon as they are able. They were heading towards Oxford, the gaffer said. He was switched on. A real diamond in the rough. I'm not inclined to dismiss him nor his ideas easily. We need eyes and ears around that locality. Looking for a dumped car, a local theft, or carjacking etc. Anything out of the ordinary. Checks on public transport…'

'Right. I'll make a few calls whilst you freshen up. Check in with the cameras and with our team at HQ. We'll find them, don't worry… And Sam?'

'Yeah? What is it?'

'Nothing. Just that, it's damned good to see you again.'

Chapter 14

Jenny fished around in her bag for some time and eventually retrieved the small key she was searching for. It was usually kept in her purse but everything had been thrown into one holdall in her haste back at the flat and it had fallen to the bottom. She always carried it around just in case it might be needed at short notice, or on a whim. The tiny door to the narrowboat was opened and she ushered Miles inside, turned the lock, switched on a couple of lamps, drew all the curtains for privacy and rummaged around in the cupboards for something to eat. Two microwaved tins of beans were unceremoniously dumped onto rounds of buttered toast in no time. It was hardly gourmet food and in no way showcased her excellent culinary skills, but it was fast and stodgy and would fill their empty stomachs.

Whilst Jenny was preparing the meal and making herself totally at home, evidently fully conversant with where everything was, Miles took a good look around their new surroundings. 'So, tell me again how all this works?' he asked, barely able to believe the somewhat unusual arrangement she had earlier described to him.

Knelt at the open fridge, Jenny looked up at him with a, *what, again?* face, having put away the butter. 'I've already explained. It's not *that* unusual, so I don't know why you're struggling with it. Amanda's an old friend of mine from our university days. She's what you might term, a *free spirit*. Would have been more at home in the sixties, rather than part of today's judgemental society. Not sure you two would hit it off. Rules and regulations mean nothing to Mand, nor possessions. What's hers is mine, always has been. We shared everything at uni from clothes, cars and food, to men and… Ooops! A little too much information, me thinks. Anyway, I always leave her some cash behind if she doesn't show, to soften the blow a little, pay my way. Not that she'll mind. She'll never change and that's why I love her so much. She goes where she likes, when she likes. *Does* pretty much the same. She's had a thousand and one jobs. Right now, she's a freelance artist. Sells her stuff to magazines and the like, sometimes for big money. I've had a key to this place from the time she bought it. It's been my hidden sanctuary over the years, my retreat, the one place I can come to and totally relax, away from everything. Whenever I need a break, I…'

Never mind all that,' she continued. 'I'm going over old ground. I thought she'd be here. Probably at her new boyfriend's place. Zack, his name is. Not met him yet, but he sounds like a real knob. Make yourself comfy. Nobody knows about it, so we should be fine for tonight. Can't imagine how they could trace us here and as long as the car remains undetected until after dark, we'll be just fine. We'll have to move on in the morning mind, because I don't want to bring any trouble to her doorstep. Mand has a top-notch laptop in her cupboard over there, courtesy of her dad. He's mega rich. A barrister of some sort. The password will be the same as it always has been since her teenage years when she discovered Bob. Dillongroupiegal69.'

'Groovy,' Miles quipped. 'As soon as we've eaten, we'll check out what's inside this bad boy,' he said, holding up the air filter. 'I'm feeling a little weird about things now. That crash behind us looked bad. I know they were probably after us, but I hope nobody innocent was involved, or hurt.'

Jenny had driven the wrecked BMW into a nearby wood where it was camouflaged, covered with branches and leaves as best they could. From a distance, they could hardly tell it was there when they'd finished. The dense trees were off the beaten track and isolated. The thick canopy overhead rendered discovery from the air highly unlikely. They knew it would be found eventually but were banking on being far away from that location by the time it happened. Surely, one night's uninterrupted rest was not too much to ask for?

The meal was devoured in no time and Miles set about breaking apart the Jag's air filter. Hidden inside was a small SD card. They sat down, each with a mug of steaming hot coffee. Jenny fired up the laptop, punched in the password, inserted the card and worked the pad expertly with her fingers.

'We're in. Two files only,' she stated without delay, licking her lips in anticipation. 'The first is a video file. The other one is a large data file. It's taking up most of the storage capacity on the entire card. Which do you want to open first?'

Miles chose the video without a moment's hesitation. He was almost white and looked awful, as if he might hurl beans all over the place. He sat back expectantly however as the screen came to life. His dad was soon staring back at him, raised from the dead by modern technology. He looked a little older than he remembered with stubble, unkempt, as if he hadn't slept for days. That wasn't right somehow. His father rarely wore whiskers. He was a military man through and through. Even on his days off he'd be up with the morning sun, shaving and showering, waking everybody else in the house with the noises he made. A real creature of habit, discipline personified. So much so, that Miles used to envy all of his friends when they spoke of the Sunday morning lie in's they'd enjoyed. His curiosity was instantly piqued as a result.

On the screen, James Dalton was sat alone in his car filming himself on his mobile, which was presumably propped up with something on his dashboard. Emotions stirred wildly within Miles as he stared straight into the eyes of his beloved dad, whom he would never see alive again. Jenny couldn't help but notice. She placed her drink down and took his free hand in hers, just as Major Dalton began to speak.

'Miles, my son, if you're watching this video something has gone drastically wrong.'

All I can do is apologise to you, though I'm certain it will never suffice. I had hoped you would never need to view it, that we'd spend many more wonderful years in each other's company. Given the situation that has developed, this outcome was always a distinct possibility.'

The video is my insurance policy. Let me explain. For years I have served the crown, as you know. Immensely proud to do so. Done their bidding without question. Gave my life for what I believed was a noble endeavour. I was rewarded handsomely of course; in that it enabled me to raise you in relative comfort. We had a good life. Just lately though, I have begun to have some serious doubts. About the things we've done. What I have done. I'm not the man I wanted to be, Miles... Oh, where do I begin?'

...At the very beginning, I suppose. Yes. I've shielded you deliberately but you have to know something of what I do. Genetics, in a nutshell. Research and Development. And a whole lot more besides. I won't bore you with the technical stuff. You never were that way inclined, unless it was computers. At the very outset, I was a fresh-faced, eager recruit trying too hard to impress. Much too willing to bend the rules back then, and I began taking way too many risks. Liberties which placed myself and all the staff in harm's way. I got away with it for a while but eventually it came back to bite me in the ass.'

'Bite him in the...? The accident in the lab!' declared Miles, hanging on his father's every word. 'Has to be.'

They both continued staring intently at the screen, thoroughly engrossed now.

'Something went awry. The mighty veils of secrecy were erected and it was all hushed up, as we do from time to time, to prevent hysteria amongst the public. Everything was my own fault though. I ended up being exposed to a cocktail of dangerous toxins and it cost the entire team I was working alongside their jobs. Almost took my life too.'

You weren't born as yet, and you very nearly never happened. If it were not for the quick thinking of Doctor Steven Lawson, the medic attached to the base, I don't think I would... Well, remember that name, that's all. I'll come back to him later.'

My behind was chewed up good and proper and my fingers well and truly scorched, but we advanced light years in terms of our understanding and results. I shared the findings only with a select few in the military and before long, I had received mountains of fresh funding. I was assigned my own laboratory and a whole new team of experts. University graduates, scientists, professors... I was in my own little Utopia and as happy as I could ever be. This was all I had ever dreamed of.'

Then, after the tempest came the lull. For years I tried to replicate what had happened, but to no avail. Something was missing. And I could never quite manage to pinpoint what. It was a stupid accident you see that cast light down upon a darkened pathway. We tried everything, and I mean everything, threw the kitchen sink and more at the problem, came mighty close to solving it, but always that one anomaly evaded discovery. Some unknown variable was toying with us. We failed to identify it, though I was not prepared to contemplate defeat. Frustration and fury got the better of me, Miles, I'm ashamed to say. My relationship with your mother crumbled to dust as a result of my obsession. To my eternal shame, I began an affair. She was young and attractive and I was a willing fool. A lieutenant called Stephanie. We, of course, told nobody.'

I'm sorry son, that you have to hear of this in such a fashion. That you have to learn of it at all. I know what you must think of me and I don't blame you. There is more though. I have to inform you now that Stephanie was not only my lover, but she was also your real mother.'

'Holy...!' began Jenny, before stopping herself as she immediately thought of Miles.

He paused the video. The look of abject horror and disgust on his face could have soured milk. He was shellshocked, mortified. Silence reigned for several minutes as he took it all in. Every extremity appeared to be shaking. He wanted to run, just run. To stick in his air pods and pound that treadmill as if there was no tomorrow. At the same time though, he felt awful, sickly and weak, his insides like mush, the improvements of recent hours all reversed in a single second. He wished in that moment that the Koreans or someone would drop the bomb right on top of this little barge, obliterate everything.

Eventually, in a crestfallen tone he stated, 'That's just tops. Given what I've been through, I genuinely believed that I had hit rock bottom. Now, I know I hadn't. How could things *possibly* be worse than this? That's my *hero* talking. My da. I've looked up to him all my life, despite his faults. He was the only person I was always desperate to impress. In some ways, I idolised him... *Him!* An adulterous, crackpot scientist! A lying, cheating toerag!'

Jenny couldn't think what else to do so she took the cup from his hand and placed it down, put her arms around him and squeezed him gently.

She pulled away a little while later and whispered, 'I'm sorry. Truly, I am. I can't imagine what you're feeling right now, to have learned all of this on the back of recent events. Nevertheless, we have to continue you know. It's the only way any of it will ever make sense. The only source of information we have. I know it must hurt like blazes, but you have push on.'

Miles said nothing in reply, just wiped away a tear, reached forwards and tapped play.

'Before you fly into a justified rage and go off on your mother for not telling you, know that she was innocent of any wrongdoing and sworn to secrecy. You see, by that time we were working on something which had the potential to be huge. Massive. Up there with Oppenheimer, I kid you not... Project AJAX, we called it. Genetic programming and enhancement...'

Things had moved on at an alarming rate. My own blood was being used now for testing. For further understanding. To learn what is needed to produce the finest warriors ever to walk this earth. For that is what it was all about. We tested umpteen batches of senior NCOs from the Special Air Service and similar regiments. Only those who had served with distinction for ten years or more and excelled in combat were selected. We isolated enzymes, genes, whatever it was that made them extraordinary, the best of the best. In around eighty-five per cent of cases, the exact same blend of contributors was present in their samples. And yet, we were still missing that last piece of the jigsaw; whatever it was that activated them all together, brought them to the surface at exactly the right moment and accelerated or triggered the subject's response, on demand. I was still fascinated by the endless possibilities. But in the midst of all my fervour, Stephanie fell pregnant and several months later she went into labour at the base. She was rushed to the local hospital but died just minutes after giving birth to you.'

Miles gasped aloud. The question of whether he'd plumbed the depths had been answered. He was still sinking as fast as a stone in the abyss.

'...And your brother too. That's right, Miles. You heard me correct. You have, well had, a twin.'

More explanation needed I reckon...'

Words will never be enough but here goes... I lost it completely. I panicked. Maybe it was the grief, or everything else happening to my mind and body at that time, but I hadn't even confessed about the affair to my darling wife at that point, whom I realised I still loved dearly. I have no excuse. Couldn't stomach the thought of losing her. We're all human, Miles. None of us are perfect. We make mistakes. And I sure made plenty of those... I figured maybe your mother might accept one child, if I came clean and told her everything. But not two. Plus, crazy thing I know, but I couldn't bear to look at him; your brother. He was the last out and the one who in my mind had killed her.'

James Dalton looked thoroughly ashamed of himself on screen but determined to tell it all, in every damning detail.

'I've had to live with that decision and it almost killed me. I made a terrible, awful choice I have regretted all this time. It has haunted me daily. And keeping it from you has been the hardest thing of all.'

I must finish what I have to say... We eventually patched things up, Sarah and I. She was an angel to forgive me. I'm not certain I could have been so magnanimous, if the roles were reversed. Your twin brother, Alex, was given a new name and placed up for adoption. Jason Murphy. I contacted him and tried to explain, to make things right between us, to...'

I could never really succeed.'

I have to be quick now. I'm sure there is someone following me... The work continued but the real breakthrough never came. Not until a few months ago. I was on my own in the lab and working far too late, testing all sorts of concoctions from various animal samples. The tiredness I suppose played a part, but I dropped some vials, needles, test tubes all over the floor. They were mixed up and some had smashed, blending who knows what, covering the needles... One of which punctured my flesh when I rather hurriedly and carelessly in my anger went to pick them up. Of course, I hardly felt it at the time and it did not register, so I never noted what was involved.'

The following day though, I awoke with the world's worst fever and called in sick, leaving my assistants to clean up the mess, and therefore the evidence. For four days I did not move out of my bed. I genuinely thought I was dying. On the fifth, I had made a miraculous recovery. I returned to work and some days afterwards, my sample showed remarkable results for the very first time. Exactly what I had been searching for. I kept this to myself, having learned my lesson.'

Because, what I was witnessing, what I was seeing, was beyond frightening!'

That accident all those years ago altered my DNA somehow. However, here is the real kick in the goolies this latest episode taught me; there exists in nature, in the animal species we are trying our hardest to destroy alongside our planet, the means to produce a supreme catalyst, Miles. A natural chemical or combination that takes my altered DNA not only further than you could ever imagine, but right into another stratosphere!'

There is nobody like me. I am unique. The product of a mishap. But, if they manage to harness this power I have attained, they'll be able to build entire armies which will sweep aside any force put before them. I'm not a good man, I know that. Though, I don't believe I can live with it on my conscience anymore.'

So, I'm going to destroy it all!'

Just in case they learn of it by some means and ever threaten my family, I'll need some leverage. This is it. The insurance I spoke of. Keep this file safe but never let it see the light of day! Not unless you have absolutely no other choice. Seek out your brother and try to repair... I have to disappear now! There's a car coming. If I manage to escape, I'll see to it that you get this file. A second one too, which has details of all my research. It's encrypted though. You need a password to unlock it. Can't say it on here, in case this falls into the wrong hands. The stakes are too high. Remember Stephen Lawson? Look to him.'

I love you, son. You are by far my greatest achievement. Sorry I failed you. I'll love you always.'

The video stopped playing abruptly and a blank screen popped up. Miles' jaw dropped open and very nearly hit the floor. He really didn't know where to begin.

Jenny though, was more than a little vexed. '*Encrypted?!*' she fumed. 'Who does he think he is, Jason Bourne?!'

She leaned forwards intending to play the next file but her stunned companion stopped her by placing his hand on hers.

'No. Leave it be, please? Not tonight. Not now.'

She huffed in disappointment but relented. 'If you say so,' she replied, her head shaking from side to side gently.

'I do.'

'Then, I'm going to take a quick shower.' She picked up her bag and disappeared into the tiny bathroom. 'There's a bottle of wine in the fridge,' she called out to him, before closing the partition.

Miles needed no second invitation. He poured out two glasses, downed his in one and then refilled it. He tapped play on the video again, froze the screen on a still of his father and stared at him for a good while. He was seeing him through different eyes now. With mixed emotions, uncertain how he should feel about the man he'd once loved and respected like no other. Thinking of his poor mother.

Chapter 15

Miles soon had a change of heart. A soothing glass or two of the good stuff, as well as the awkward silence of his new female companion, who just didn't appear to know what to do or say around him now, made him suddenly reach for the laptop again like a man on a mission. He opened it up furiously and waited for it to load before double-clicking on the second of the files and declaring, 'We've come *this* far together, may as well keep going. I'm not sure I can take many more surprises like that but let's open Pandora's Box again and see what else jumps out.'

Jenny was thrilled and couldn't hide her excitement. She scooched up close and took his arm in hers as if they were watching a blockbuster movie. All she needed was the popcorn.

Major James Dalton reappeared on screen. Only, this time, he was resplendent in military uniform and clean-shaven, speaking even more eloquently, professionally. He also appeared a good few years younger, though whether that was due to the lack of five o'clock shadow on show, Miles couldn't quite decide.

'Hello and welcome. To whomever is watching this video, I'm James Dalton, lead scientist at this facility. I've been ordered to deliver a presentation. First off, if you do not possess the correct security clearance to hear what I am about to say, please make this known to staff immediately and exit the room without delay. The onus is on you to declare it. Failure to do so will result in prosecution in all cases. You have been warned...'

After a slight pause to allow people to leave, Major Dalton continued.

'I'm assuming all is well... So, this is, An Introduction to Project AJAX. Hopefully, few of you will have heard that name. For those who have, we'd like a little chat with you afterwards as to how and why. From the outset, I should say that the intention as I speak is to shelve this project indefinitely, in favour of others which demand more urgent resources and funding. This, is therefore a recap of what has happened to date, so that any who come after will have a rudimentary understanding of the progress made. Also, an explanation of the work undertaken and results achieved over the past thirty years or so, as well as an appraisal as to where we are right now when measured against current targets. It's important to remember that AJAX can and will be reinstated once certain conditions have been met. That's the promise we have and these are explained in full.'

So, what is Project AJAX? And why was it created?'

In reply, I'd like to pose further queries to you all which are at the very core of what we are striving to achieve. What is it that makes people who and what they are? Fundamentally. How is it, for instance, that some of us can kill without batting an eyelid, whilst others baulk at the idea of swatting a tiny fly? Why do certain soldiers excel in a battlefield environment, whilst their comrades run, or turn into gibbering wrecks? Is it nature? Or nurture?'

In the 1980's the Ministry of Defence commissioned a top-secret programme to answer these mysteries and more. Their overriding remit was to discover why seemingly ordinary men and women rise to the very top of the pile, become the finest of the elite. Science has proven now that although citizens can be taught certain skills and evolve into effective warriors, the ability to go above and beyond, to flourish, to excel, has always been there inside each of us from the very beginning, to a certain degree. Which means, the tools we require to see the job done, no matter how extreme or difficult, are already in our locker. We merely require the key or combination to unlock it. And that, is purely down to genetics.'

The United Kingdom has punched well above its weight for centuries in military terms. This small island off the coast of Europe developed the largest empire the world has ever known. However, all that is in the past. New threats have emerged and our potential foes right now, are likely to seriously outnumber the resources we can deploy against them, should war be waged. The empire has come and gone, ladies and gentlemen. We live in different times and we can no longer rely on our once loyal dominions for support. Nor our supposed allies.'

Imagine, if you will, a hypothetical scenario. A time of peril akin to 1940 when we are under siege, the wolf clawing at our door. Only now, our beloved nation has the ability to field an entire army of soldiers with every single recruit of similar calibre to the very best of the SAS. Elite in every way. Handed all the ammunition and equipment required to wreak havoc. Faster, technically gifted, able to react to any situation with extreme competence and devastating force... Expert warriors, every one a Spartan, let loose amongst inferior foes, who would be most certainly annihilated. Numerical advantage would count for little. It would be akin to employing an assault rifle at the Battle of Waterloo, or Rorke's Drift. Anarchy. The Dogs of War truly unleashed.'

This is exactly what AJAX was attempting to create.'

CRISPR gene editing. It stands for, Clustered Regularly Interspaced Short Palindromic Repeats. A real mouthful. Hence, why it was shortened. It was officially patented in 2013. I'm afraid that date is a bold-faced lie, however. 2013 is when it first became public knowledge. In reality, we were experimenting with that technology twenty years earlier. And by, we, I mean the British... You see, the army knew that top soldiers aren't made, but born. Extensive studies of the SF community revealed concentrations of the same blend of enzymes, genes, proteins etc. existing in all successful veterans. Bar none. Many of these were present in others too, but lying in a dormant state. They were there alright, but they were in need of awakening. We tried therefore to replicate the make-up of, and impregnate, countless volunteers. Living hosts. We met with minimal success. A missing component could not be identified or sourced. An unknown, unidentified catalyst existed which sparks the change in the host. The growth and assimilation that allows the increased powers to develop or surge on demand.'

AJAX was searching for that elusive chemical agent.'

In the following segments of this talk, I will walk you through every step of our research, from inception and a promising beginning, through early trials and tribulations, to modern technological feats and our current impasse, where we are teetering on the brink of a breakthrough that would eclipse all before it. It's a fascinating journey and it's not yet complete. Not over by any stretch of the imagination. So, sit back and relax. Break out the sweeties and light 'em up. It's quite a story and lengthy to tell.'

For we are close, people. Very close.'

The screen darkened again. Almost immediately, a three-letter caption appeared, over a set of asterisks.
Please Enter Password
****

Miles looked to Jenny, who was equally as dismayed as him. He tried to think of anything he could, entered innumerable guesses ranging from old names for pets, cars, bikes, addresses and bands, to football teams and heroes etc. *Nothing* worked. Eventually he was out of options.

'It's no use. We're locked out for good. All we have is the intro,' he stated, his frustration clear to see. 'That's not enough. We need to know everything.'

'Yes, but at least we have a good idea of why your father was murdered. I mean, I told you, I'm not buying suicide at all. Things like this don't stay secret for long, Miles. There's always a leak, even in the military. No, scratch that; *especially* in the military! Us and the Americans would *never* have let him fall into enemy hands given what he knows, so I'm afraid we would head any list of possible assassins. And the Russians, Chinese, Koreans and all? They would do anything to stop this madness, if it had any chance at all of success. Especially, if they learned he had destroyed years of his own work. That makes him unstable. A loose cannon on deck. An inside man who might be disposed to sell out to the highest bidder. They couldn't risk failure in trying to apprehend him too, or publicity neither. Knowledge of any such attempt would be enough to spark World War Three.'

Miles was quiet again as he deliberated. Finally, he said, 'I suppose you're right. I have to get into this file though. There is more to tell. The answer must lie with this Stephen Lawson geezer my dad mentioned. I've never even heard of him before but he must be important. If he's still alive, we need to track him down.'

Jenny raised her eyebrows, confused. 'How? Where do we begin, detective? It's not as though we can access his bank records, or the DVLA. We don't even know where he lives.'

'I have an idea,' replied Miles, smiling once again.

Jenny was glad to see it. A few minutes earlier, she had feared he might do something silly. He'd had a whole load of troubles thrust upon him in such a short space of time, enough to break the strongest of us.

Sam Lennox and Jack Walters were mobile again. Sam had taken a little longer than expected at her flat, relishing the opportunity to refresh and change. She'd experienced another brief episode in the shower, where the events of the day had mingled together with another vivid memory from Afghanistan. The finding of the mutilated corpses of one of her interpreters and his family. It flew into her head and turned her stomach, almost as much as the recollection of the vicious reprisal she and her squad had inflicted upon those responsible a week later. The flashbacks triggered her so badly, that for several minutes she burst into floods of tears, her body and mind perilously close to shutting down completely. In the end however, the warm water worked its magic and she'd shook it off like it was nothing.

    She quickly dried herself and with the towel wrapped tightly around her, water still dripping everywhere, she'd raced to the whisky bottle in the cabinet and downed a few full swigs like water. It soothed her anxiety a little and calmed her somewhat but the resulting pang of conscience and guilt struck like a juggernaut and was almost too much to bear. She immediately raced to the bathroom again and brushed her teeth so long and hard, that her gums turned to red. Several gulps of mouthwash stung as she gargled, before she moved rapidly over to the closet and picked out a nice trouser suit. Then, she dried her hair with the blower, fixed her makeup, slipped on some matching shoes and stepped up to the full-length mirror. She looked for all the world like a highflyer ready to do business. No sign of her troubled mind. How easy it was to mask the pain inside. To put on the show that deceived them all.

    Sam bounded out of her flat and into the passenger seat of Jack's navy-blue, unmarked Mazda 6. He put the car into gear immediately and raced away at high speed through several side roads until they reached a dual carriageway, where he opened her up and set the cruise control. He'd remained silent so far which Lennox was immensely grateful for, as it gave her time to collect her thoughts, lose the tremor in her voice. Though, Jack clearly thought he needed to apologise.

'Sorry about the cold shoulder. No time to waste. We've had a spot of good fortune while you've been tarting yourself up. Nice threads by the way. You still scrub up well. I'm guessing you'd still rather be back in camo's though, eh? Yeah, sure you would. Another time though. Another world. We all have to move on, so let's bring you up to speed. Your lot did well. They put out an alert on the call I made. It pinged straight back, believe it or not, faster than an echo. Slight exaggeration, perhaps, but you get the idea. A female officer sat in a layby manning a speedtrap was really on the ball. South of Oxford. She clocked a dented BMW doing *exactly* ten percent over the speed limit. It matches the ride taken by our perps.'

'*Not* perps, Jack. Persons of interest,' corrected Sam, being careful to breathe well away from him and towards the window she'd cracked open a little. 'We're not convinced they are involved in the killings. In fact, they may even be innocent of anything but acting in self-defence. Time will tell but at present, we're keeping an open mind.'

'Powtarto, powtayto,' he answered, cynically. 'I've heard it all before, Sam. Whatever they are, no action was taken at the time by the locals. She had a side view mainly, our traffic officer, so she never noticed the rear window and other damage, or called it in. But *then*, our shout came through almost immediately afterwards and she was bright enough to radio through to a colleague who was waiting to intercept wrongdoers further down the road. Only, the BMW vanished into thin air. It never passed the guy at all.'

'They turned off someplace,' Sam responded, enthusiastically.

'Yep. We checked, there's only one turning they could have taken, according to local plods. A small lane leading to a dirt track. Runs up to a little clump of trees they laughingly term a wood. Not big enough to swing a cat in, if you believe the report.'

'Perfect place to ditch a car though? God bless the woodentops. Gotta love 'em. I kinda enjoyed pounding the beat, it was a little boring at times but I met some damned fine sorts. Tell them we'll be with them shortly. Dish out some instructions too. They're to set a perimeter, watch and wait. They are *not* to approach them unless absolutely necessary. Detain only if compromised.'

Jack shook his head in disappointment at her. 'Not my first shindig you know. If we're going to function correctly you and I, try to remember who you're dealing with? Already done all that,' he stated.

'Point taken. I'm not myself at present and sometimes I forget. I'm getting there though and I'm really glad you're on board, watching my back.'

'Oh, I'm always given the tough jobs, me. I'll always be up for watching that little tooshie of yours,' he quipped.

'Oi! Cut it out, you dickhead.'

Sam was happy to find that the military banter she so enjoyed came back naturally to her now that she was once again in the company of another ex-squaddie. It was an environment she craved and felt comfortable in. Like slipping on a second skin. *Missed* like crazy. Civilian life, even within a disciplined force, had taken her by surprise. There was a lot of adjustments to make and hardly any of that was by choice. The autonomy was scary at first. Still *was*, if she was being honest with herself. She longed for the regimen and structure of the army once again that had vanished upon her discharge. The comradeship and support that was never-ending there. The purpose behind every single day, even if it was just maintaining fitness and standards. Nowadays, time off was an absolute curse. Empty hours of meaningless drivel. Nobody was pushing her on to succeed. Together with her particular set of issues, which made it almost impossible to find anyone to love, it was a lonely, tough existence. She was trying hard in her own way but at present, the demons were winning. The job was about all she had to keep them at bay.

My God! she thought, horrified by a sudden revelation. *I'm turning into Edward Farley!*

Not long afterwards they were approaching the wood on foot, weapons drawn and at the ready just in case. They cleared the search area tree by tree, for old habits in soldiers of their calibre die hard. The wood was empty though and so was the car.

'Damn!' snapped Lennox, slapping her palm against her forehead in exasperation. 'I'd cuss a lot louder and shock you with some newly learned expletives, but we've only just met again and I'm worried your ears may have grown a little delicate sitting behind that desk. We were so close!'

'Be my guest. Don't you worry about me. But stay the course, Sam. It's a marathon, not a sprint. All's not lost yet,' her new partner replied. He put away his gun and joined her. 'Let's do this the old way. Let's run it through.'

Lennox moved close to listen to his words.

'The terrain works in our favour. Wet, muddy ground in places. Hard not to leave a trail. And yet, no tyre marks leaving the scene. They are on foot. We're in the middle of nowhere, almost. Not too many come this way I should think. From the looks of it, they only have three options open to them. *One*, to double back to the road. Which is unlikely, increases the risk of being seen in the open. *Two*, to follow that path over there up to the village I can just make out on the horizon. Possible. Or *three*, to go straight over the fields down towards that canal.'

Jack was pointing to the valley below and a long stretch of water with around four or five moored narrowboats, each some way apart from the next. It was a picturesque scene which would have looked great painted on the front of a postcard or box of chocolates.

'I'm with you,' said Sam. 'Well, the road we can rule out, I think. Busy. No sightings reported, crawling with cops. They're not gonna like those odds. They must have arrived here with some kind of a plan. These are not stupid people, not by any measure. Quite clever actually. You don't dump your car in the middle of nowhere unless you have transport or a place to go. Don't cut yourself off like that.'

'Agreed. Now we're getting somewhere. Then, that leaves the village or the canal. You take the field. I'll go for the path and do some searching.'

Sam rushed over to the edge of the wood and ventured out onto the mud and grass. She began examining the ground for clues. It didn't take her long to find a size ten or so footprint clearly stamped into the soil.

'Over here!' she rasped. 'That *has* to be Miles. Yes, there's a few more. There are two distinct tracks and they are leading away from the trees. They're heading for the canal. Let's go!'

Chapter 16

Owen James didn't know whether to laugh, or shoot himself in the head. He was raging inside and his hands were trembling. But, the more he thought about things, the more is anger subsided and he actually began to see the funny side of what had occurred. Twice now he had been foiled in his attempts to kill this, Miles Dalton. The supreme assassin had been outwitted somehow by a rank amateur. *Or*, fate, possibly others, had conspired against him on the guy's behalf. The dorky-looking waster had managed to avoid termination by a blend of his own decent cognizance, and the rash and foolhardy actions of Owen's competitors. Neither *should* have been allowed to happen. The former Marine Officer turned professional hitman was far too good for that. Or at least, he was *supposed* to be. He'd taken out marks all over the world, in situations far more complex and dangerous than this. And yet, he'd let this scrawny private citizen escape without so much as a scratch. Perhaps, his old comrade had been correct and he should contemplate settling down? Was he beginning to lose his edge? Age catches up with everyone, eventually. And in a profession where speed, agility and quickness of mind were very much kings of the battlefield, it was only natural that contract killings were perceived as the domain of the young.

Of course, *Owen* held a different view. He valued experience above all, was convinced it gave him an advantage of his own. He gazed in the rearview mirror as he drove and dismissed the notion out of hand. Age was not a factor here. He was as fit as he'd ever been. His record to date was the stuff of legend, his kill count second to none. He was up there with the very best money could buy. There was no way he could have foreseen events as they played out, being spotted so early back in the park. It was either just sheer bad luck, or there was something he wasn't being told about this Dalton fella. *Something* he didn't know.

The impromptu ambush which had stopped his car supported that belief. The crazy fools who had rammed him, those bloody *commies*, had clearly been blinded by greed, knew he would have completed the kill if they had not acted so swiftly. Hung them out to dry, with nothing but pathetic accounts of his all-round superiority and brilliance to take home to their clients or handlers. They'd blindsided him from out of nowhere in panic at the thought. Without warning. How was he supposed to have prevented that?!

You can't stop what you can't see. Bad luck, that's all.

On the upside, Owen was enjoying the new set of wheels he'd acquired. Following the contact and collision by the garages, he'd retrieved his weapon and phone and a small first-aid kit he'd noticed in the boot of the car. Angry and frustrated but still very much in the hunt, he'd performed a little minor triage on himself, glueing and covering the many cuts he could see which were oozing blood. The multitude of minor scratches to his face where tiny fragments of glass or debris had impacted would have to heal themselves. He looked a complete mess but almost every wound he was certain was superficial, would not affect his performance in any way. Aches and pains came with the territory sometimes anyway, were simply a matter of mind control. He'd had worse. Far worse. Consequently, not long afterwards, he found himself walking through a fairly affluent neighbourhood in search of an exfil option. With a smile larger than any he'd worn in a very long time, he'd then stepped out into the road and stopped an oncoming vehicle at gunpoint. Not just *any* car mind. Oh, no. Owen had suffered an unexpected, virtually unheard of, setback. He felt like indulging himself now. After passing on a few *lesser* motors, he targeted a shiny, new Porsche 911. The updated version, with all the gizmos. It was being driven by a man mountain happily cruising the streets as if he owned them. The whole scene was like something from *Beverly Hills Cop*. The original. Which he'd once watched on DVD with his parents back in his youth. Only, Eddie Murphy never had this guy's immense physique.

He'd promptly relieved the giant freak of his pride and joy at gunpoint and seeing the state Owen was in at the time, with blood stains everywhere on his torn clothing and cuts and bruises galore, Mr. Universe lost whatever bottle he may have possessed in a flash. He made no protest at all and almost left a little puddle on the driver's seat as he climbed gingerly out.

Owen took off in no particular direction and soon found a quiet backstreet in which to park up, free from the gaze of any unwanted surveillance. He made a rapid call to his former SBS colleague, who was now his handler and mentor.

'Christ, Owen!' the guy hollered down the line, without affording him the chance to speak. Which was *not* the response he had expected. 'What the...! What have you been playing at?! This is madness! A cockup of the first order! I send you off on a nice little jolly, a fun run that even my granny could manage without messing up, and *you* turn it into the mother of all cake and arse parties! You! The whole thing is a shambles. It's blown up in my face good and proper. It's a breech explosion, that's what this is. Nearly took my nose off. My phone has been ringing constantly. In case you hadn't noticed, publicity of any kind is seriously unwanted here, so you've made me a tad anxious. Especially *bad* publicity!'

Owen casually checked himself over in the mirror, removed a tiny piece of glass from his front teeth as his friend ranted. 'You through whining? Good. I've done the analysis myself and things don't add up. I was compromised by bad intel. Provided with false facts. Or I was set up. I'll take the hits coming my way gladly, *if* I'm at fault, you know that. But the *real* blame on this one lies elsewhere... Lay it out for me. How bad is it your end?' he asked.

'Mate, you're off their Christmas card list, that's for sure. And I don't think I'll be having many nights out either. I may be the only friend you have left. You'll be lucky to get security for a kid's birthday party after this one. You'll be the bouncer for the trampoline, unless you make things right, never invited out again. The money guys are hopping mad and they're not messing about. They've doubled the bounty on his head already, offered it up to the masses. The plebs are loose in Rome. Civilisation as we know it, may be a thing of the past. Honestly, there's no controlling the outcome from here. You're more or less cut adrift. They'll feed you stuff, maybe, but *only* because they want the job completed. You're an asset only as long as you're an asset. After that...? I suggest you watch your six.'

'Good to know. Thanks for not sugarcoating it. Appreciate it.'

A slight pause, followed by, 'Owen?'

'Still here.'

'You want a sitrep from an old warhorse?'

'Always.'

'Then cop this... As I see it, you only have two viable alternatives. You can walk away now, give up the ghost and retire to some little island somewhere with the fortune you have already made, leave this clown alone and hope that for some reason they forget all about you...'

'Hmmn... Doubtful. Not *me*, is it? You and I are *players*, pal. Not cheerleaders or clerks. Though you managed to find a way out of sorts, old age is not for the likes of us. It's a pipe dream that's all, to those of us still active. We chase it in our thoughts perhaps, but inside, we have no real expectations of getting there. Are more than happy to forego it.'

'Yeah,' the voice agreed, 'at least you know it. The choice we made. The bargain with fate. Some misguided fools dream big and long, and the fall is all the more bitter for it. They drag others along with them; family and loved ones. Not you though. Then, that only leaves option two. You have to kill every living soul connected to this mission. Pray that if you *do*, it will clean the slate so thoroughly, that all parties will be satisfied with your contribution.'

'Now, *that* sounds more like my kind of plan. I'll take door number two, Bob.'

'Bob?'

'My old platoon commander, Bob Betts. Tough as nails, but looked like a gameshow host. I'll need resupply? And up to date intel?' Owen stated, knowing instinctively that his old friend would come through for him despite the downturn in his fortunes. 'It has to be you. Not certain I can trust anyone else.'

'No problem, seeing as you asked so nicely. For old times' sake. I'm tapped in to their systems as we speak… Bingo! I'm sending you an address. It's local, according to the tracker we've placed on your phone. Just turn up there and say nothing other than you're supposed to collect a bag. Message just despatched. They're expecting you. Payment has already been made so you should encounter no problems or delay. If there *is* an issue of any kind, shoot your way out. Fire first, ask later.'

'Have that. Really lovin' your work. I owe you for this. You know I'm good for it. Either in death or victory, you'll be looked after,' James stated.

He meant it too.

'Ah, get out of here, ya soppy git. You're beginning to worry me. I think you're turning soft. And too right you'll pay,' quipped just about the only real friend Owen James had left. 'You can *begin* by leaving my daughter alone, okay?

She's bright enough to have a future, too young and pretty to be a widow. I *mean* it! Let her down gently but move on.'

Now, to business; your young couple… Do we think they are lovers yet? May be something to factor in, if you need to get creative? Love does funny things to young 'uns and you may need some leverage. They have been sighted and backup has been requested. That means the law is breaching, not hanging around. They are believed to be on one of four narrowboats, on a canal in Oxford. Get a skate on and you may just beat the boys in blue to the prize. They're overly cautious as a rule. They will plan, plan and then plan some more, if they're true to form. Lot of confusion in a thing like that. And you will arrive on scene with enough firepower to start a small war.'

'Nice. Only one thing concerns me then. What about the clients?'

'Just you leave them to me. Though, if this all goes south again as it may, the whole lot was entirely your idea. I was against it from the very beginning. I'm claiming that you held a blade to my daughter's throat.'

'Ha! Sounds reasonable. Not something *I'd* ever do, to a mate. But reasonable.'

DS Samantha Lennox had another serious problem. Four barges had so far been flagged up as possible locations for her fugitives, who were thought to be armed. So far, she had only two small fire teams in attendance. Just two firearms-trained officers had turned up, along with seven or so local coppers who were all unarmed. Cambridge and surrounding forces had units already deployed to other incidents. The Met were too far away. She would have liked to have hit all the targets simultaneously but the requirements of the force and police protocols, dictated use of two-person teams. Effective backup was essential to protect lives and she wasn't about to risk any of her colleague's safety. Certainly, not with the death of Edward Farley so fresh in her mind. Delaying further was not an option either. The light was fading fast and she didn't want to risk allowing Miles and Jenny to escape in the darkness. Who knew when she might be afforded another chance to apprehend them?

She therefore conducted a rapid risk assessment and decided to do away with planning and caution. The size of the potential win outweighed the jeopardy. She would launch immediate raids on the barges in turn, the two armed police on one team and her and Jack forming the other, with unarmed stoppers comprised of the locals at either end of the canal. A visual deterrent, if nothing else. The resident bobbies were instructed in no uncertain terms to remain out of sight, though their fresh-faced eagerness was there for all to see and Sam had operated with rookies before, so she had limited confidence that they would obey her commands. She only hoped that her snap decision would prove the correct one in the fullness of time, that they would detain the young runaways without any further loss of life. However, they had proven elusive to date and had already shown the lengths they were prepared to go to in order to avoid capture.

Together with Jack Walters, Sam moved into a position near to barge number one, concealed behind a large tree trunk. There, she waited for the two firearms guys storming barge number two to do likewise. The signal eventually came and she immediately gave the order to advance. Having retrieved some gear from the local police cars, Sam and Jack moved forwards in a close formation which afforded maximum cover in all directions. They reached the small door to the barge in no time and Jack grasped the crowbar hanging from his belt. He took the door clean off its hinges with one powerful pull and they entered the vessel at speed, screaming orders to surrender to any possible occupants and clearing the boat in seconds.

Nothing there. The whole barge was empty. Sam was just cursing her misfortune and making ready to storm the next barge, when her radio suddenly crackled into life.

'Sarge! You'd better get over here.'

It was the officer in charge of the second team and they both raced to his location. Inside Amanda's narrowboat, the two firearms guys looked completely relaxed when Sam and Jack came running through the open door. They were stood next to the sink, holding up two unwashed plates covered in bean sauce residue. A couple of glasses lay discarded on the side and a pair of coffee cups were in the bowl, some with telltale lipstick marks. The lamps were on and the cushions were ruffled.

'We've just missed them!' roared Sam. 'Outside, now! Area search. Get on comms. I want all nooks and crannies, all bushes, hedgerows, sheds and barns turned over. Dog support. Someone call in dog support!'

She turned to Jack, her eyes alive and burning with fierce determination. 'Come on! You're with me. They *can't* have gotten far. We're more use out there than in here.'

Jack followed her outside without complaint, even though he technically outranked her and should have been the one giving the orders. When they reached the canal towpath, Sam bellowed loudly to the locals, '…And *somebody* make certain those other barges are empty!'

A short while earlier, Miles and Jenny were still processing all they had learned. Jenny had showered and dried her hair, put on a casual, light-pink tracksuit that she clearly kept on the barge for lounging in. She explained they were her *snugglies*. The pair began giggling a little and Miles cast a surprised glance in her direction. She had struck him as the prim and proper type, always immaculately turned out, not the kind of girl who owned such attire. Jenny was just about to fire another question at him in response to his ridiculous reaction when Miles raised his finger to his lips. He had a really weird sensation all of a sudden which was impossible to ignore, like somebody was watching him from afar, but poking his chest from the inside at the same time. He'd never felt that way before and he had no idea what it meant, but it was a powerful feeling that overwhelmed him and he knew for certain that *something* was wrong.

He darted to the small window and peered through a gap in the curtains, glanced around in all directions, unsure what he was looking for. Then, he caught a momentary glimpse of a police officer's head and shoulders, near the corner of a nearby cottage.

'Game's up! We've been made. Not sure how, but put something on your feet quickly, grab a coat and follow me,' he whispered forcefully, sliding on his trainers and picking up the laptop, then shoving it into a case he had retrieved from the cupboard.

As they slipped silently past the canal door and into the water, their bodies now hidden by the barge and the waterline, Miles tried desperately to keep the laptop dry by balancing it on his head. Fortunately, it was shallow enough to stand, but the slime and sludge on the bottom made it hard going. They kept moving however, using the towpath ledge as cover, slowly made their way noiselessly past the other barges. They could hear the police officers talking openly as they waded through the water but eventually there was clear distance between them and the barge.

'Eww... I feel really riffy now. My snugglies are ruined. And I had a shower too,' said Jenny, in a voice held intentionally low. 'What now though? Surely, it would be better to hand ourselves in? We have some evidence now. We've done all we can do and are bound to be caught? Somebody's got to listen? They can't all be bad?'

Miles shook his head. 'I'd love to. Believe me, I've had enough of running too. We still have no way of knowing who we can trust, however. It's you who has been saying that all along. Nothing's changed… Come on. There are some buildings over there that look abandoned. We can make it inside and reassess our options. If you still think that's our only choice, I'll listen.'

They scurried onto the site of an old farm, long since left to decay. The house had no roof, windows and doors and was sprouting a variety of wild vegetation from all aspects. There was an old barn made predominantly of corrugated iron to one side. It was absent numerous panels but somehow still standing, defying time. Here, they stopped for a rest. Jenny was shivering now in her drenched clothes so Miles threw his arms around her and held her tight.

'I've said it before I know, but a thousand apologies for dragging you into this mess. I'm beginning to see things your way. I think we've run our race. We're through. We have no transport, our faces are probably all over the news like Bonnie and Clyde, and these detectives seem to be the relentless type. I…'

Jenny gave a few exhausted nods of her head. 'Well, if we're going to do this, I'd much rather surrender to the law, than a hit squad.'

They sat down on an old bundle of hay, huddled close for warmth and waited for the end to come.

Owen James pulled up quietly onto a patch of muddy ground between a small clump of trees which lined the edge of the field. He could see the farm in the distance. The sun was setting and it would soon be twilight. Perfect. Adequate visibility and a semblance of added cover. In a flash, he had moved to the rear of the Porsche and opened the boot. A HK 417 rifle was wrapped in a grey woollen blanket. He had three twenty-round magazines and two boxes of 175 grain Sierra Matchking ammunition. He looked down at the rifle.

Nah, this will be a quick in and out, he mused. *No time for all that.*

He grabbed the black leather holdall and unzipped it. Inside, was a G36K rifle and four thirty-round magazines that the previous owners had kindly loaded. He took a roll of electrical tape and quickly fastened two magazines together, one pointing up, the other down. This would speed up his reload if he needed more rounds. A third he shoved into the back left pocket of his jeans, the bullets facing down. He shrugged on a brown leather shoulder holster and slipped in a CZ 75 pistol, after first checking the magazine and chambering a round. A spare mag went into the holster on the right-hand side. He donned a zip-up hoodie to hide all this from any onlookers then mooched again through the bag, found a Cobray machine pistol, the kind drug dealers and gangsters favour. He moved it aside and took out two RDG-5 hand grenades. With one in each pocket of his hooded top, he closed the boot, being careful not to let it slam, made his way silently into the trees.

Chapter 17

Sam Lennox and Jack Walters split up to search the old farm. Jack took the house whilst Sam made for the abandoned barn and surrounding undergrowth. She proceeded carefully, her weapon drawn and tucked in close to her torso as she cleared the corners, then extended her arms ahead of her forming a solid shooting stance when in the open, her former military training and keen senses warning her immediately of another presence in the vicinity. She had no way of knowing for certain if it was Miles and Jenny at this point or a hostile force hunting them down with orders to eliminate the pair on sight. She made good use of the terrain and whatever cover she could find just in case. She thought of calling Jack over but it was little more than a feeling inside and she did not wish to give away her own position with any noise that might make. Besides, Sam had been out of action for a good while so what if she was just being a little jumpy?

Around twenty yards or so from the dilapidated old barn she halted for a closer inspection. It was surrounded by ditches and greenery which afforded superb natural hides for any potential enemy. The soldier in her grew a little more anxious. The *feeling* had now blossomed into a strong potential threat, though she still pushed on alone to the edge of the structure.

'Armed police! I know you're in there! Come out now with your hands raised high!' she called out into the mounting gloom. 'It's over, Miles. You hear me? You have no chance of escape. I have several teams combing the countryside and even more on their way. You're surrounded. The dogs will be here soon and all forces will converge on this location. Do yourself a favour and end this!'

At first there was no response from inside. All was quiet and Sam even began to doubt herself. Then, she heard a faint noise emanating from within and she lifted her arms ready to open fire.

'I'm not stepping out in the open,' answered Miles. 'But you can come in if you want? I won't shoot.'

Lennox entered the dilapidated old structure slowly, hesitantly, weapon poised in case it was a trick. She gazed around at the many dark shadows which were interspersed with brighter spots here and there where panels were missing from the sides, and a little light shone through. Several dirty old bales of hay with plants growing all around littered the soil, some piled two or three high still. Out from the gloom, from behind the wreck of an old thrashing machine, stepped a very nervous Miles Dalton. He cut a wet, bedraggled and sorry figure. He was shivering slightly and inching forwards with his hands up as high as he could manage, as if expecting to be cut down by a hail of bullets at any moment. When she did not shoot, he turned around and reached out a hand, walked Jenny out slowly by her fingertips to face the music. A laptop case was hanging from his shoulder and Miles reached behind him slowly, watched like a hawk by the supremely alert DS.

'Take it steady now. No sudden moves. *Lose* it,' Sam ordered, her command resolute and unyielding.

Miles very carefully threw his weapon on the ground ahead of him, out of reach. 'I suppose this makes you our...'

He meant to say more than he had. The sun was in its last throes now however and as it peaked out from behind some clouds, a flutter of his heart sent an urgent distress call straight to his brain. He yanked Jenny's arm and dragged her swiftly behind the old thrasher, just as a couple of bullets whistled by their heads and tore holes into the rear of the structure, crying out loudly, 'Shooter!' as he did.

Lennox turned like a cat, her eyes instantly wide in fear. 'Grenade!!!' she yelled, and dived onto the ground with phenomenal speed as a third and fourth round only just missed her on the way down.

Miles instinctively made a dash for Jenny who had moved slightly, looking for a better vantage point. He pushed her back behind the old farm machine, shielding her with his body. The grenade exploded with a loud crack, followed immediately by the tell-tale, dull ringing in their ears and the sound of dirt and debris raining down over the detonation area.

Miles and Jenny were fine. They'd been several metres away and shielded by hard cover. Sam was in a worse state, however, the concussive force of the grenade having knocked the wind from her. The barn was spinning but by some miracle she had no shrapnel wounds and nothing was broken or leaking.

Her army training had saved her. She had dived and remained low, her feet pointed towards the blast. 'What the hell...?!' she hissed, now up and alert and scanning for the threat. 'How did you...?'

'I caught a glint of light reflected off something,' Miles lied.

He tried to move closer to Sam but the side of the barn suddenly burst inwards in a shower of splinters, raked with automatic fire from James' G36.

The weapon soon ran dry and he quickly swapped the magazines around, inserting a fresh thirty rounds and yanking on the charging handle, sending the bolt forward. Cautiously, he cleared the threshold of the barn.

Big mistake.

Miles had retrieved the pistol he had previously discarded and he emptied the entire mag, firing towards the blackened shape that stood in the entrance to the ruin. James was struck four times, in his thigh, stomach, shoulder and left arm. He was in a bad way, but he wasn't out of the fight just yet. As he stumbled to his knees, he lost his grip on the G36 and it fell into the mud. He fumbled for the pistol under his hoodie, but he was too late as the incomparable Lennox sent two rounds his way before Miles or Jenny knew what was happening, lightning quick. The first hit him in the chest. The second struck him a fraction of a second later, made a real mess of his left shoulder. A mighty yelp of shock and hurt sliced through the evening air and echoed through the countryside, shattered the peace of the night, and Sam Lennox was on Owen James before he had the chance to do anything else, despite his wounds.

James knew the game was up, probably for good. He was dripping claret everywhere. He fell back to the ground on his right side, his breathing heavy and laboured. Some opponents you just don't test. Don't mess with, regardless of your own prowess. And with Sam Lennox, it was *all* in the eyes. Which now told him all he needed to know.

'Remain perfectly still! I am going to search you now. You so much as flinch, and you die right here!' she warned ominously, her Glock trained on his head at all times.

Sam placed the pistol he had reached for inside her belt, at the small of her back, kicked the G36 away by the butt and pulled his phone and knife from his jacket. She patted him down. Content, she retreated a pace or two and took a good look around outside for any more hostiles. Nothing doing. Moments later, she was glad to hear the sound of running feet.

'My partner will be here soon to cuff you. I'd like to take you in alive but any smart moves on your part, and you know what happens.'

Owen grimaced a little and did as he was told. He really had no other choice. He looked up, thereby allowing the others to gaze upon his face fully for the first time. His numerous wounds were serious but perhaps not terminal, if they could stem the blood loss in time. Though his face was all cut up, clothes shredded in places, holes everywhere.

'That's...! That's the maniac who has been shooting at us!' cried Jenny.

'Thought as much,' replied Sam, as Jack Walters finally arrived and surveyed the scene, his mouth wide open in astonishment and his own weapon pointing straight at the deadly contract killer.

'So, you're the Brit everyone's been referring to. The one whose been paid to kill this pair. We've been looking forward to capturing *you*. Talk, and we'll apply some first aid. What's your name? Who are you working for?' Sam demanded.

Owen James had thought to hide behind supposed diplomatic clearance if by some miracle he was ever taken alive. It would halt any interrogation straight off and buy him some much-needed time, until the Met discovered he was actually lying his ass off. By that time though, his well-connected friends in extremely high places would have hopefully whisked him away to some none-extradition haven. Truth was, he hadn't *planned* to be taken at all. Was a kill or bust kind of guy. That shot of Sam's to the shoulder though... It was a thing of genius. Swift in the extreme, with the other one already damaged, it had incapacitated him and after that, he'd had no time to deploy more firepower. My God, she was fast. So good in fact, that his extremely large ego now had the better of him and he had other ideas. Besides, given the actions of his clients to date, even if the wounds did not kill him, he was still a dead man, so why not enjoy what little time he had left on earth?

'You've real flair. It's not often I'm bested like that. Which branch did you serve in?' he asked, smiling sweetly at Sam through gritted teeth.

Lennox immediately shook her head, hardly able to believe his nerve. 'Nope, that's *not* how this is going down. Answer the questions.'

He gazed around at the farm and surrounding countryside, then straight back into her eyes. 'Have it your way, Sam... *James*. My name is James, okay? Owen James. Royal Marines, in a former life. Officer and most certainly a gentleman. These days I work for hard cash and thrills. I was tasked to...'

Bang! Bang!

A couple of well-aimed slugs fired from close range in rapid succession ripped into the flesh and bone of Owen James' head. It exploded at the rear and he dropped backwards onto the ground in no time, never to rise again. The action was so swift and unexpected that Miles and Jenny hardly had time to flinch before Sam Lennox reacted speedily again, out of pure instinct, on auto-pilot, raising her weapon and firing before she had even blinked.

Her own partner caught the full force of her venom this time and he was hurled backwards, somehow still managing to stay on his feet. For it was Jack Walters who had gunned down Owen James in cold blood, an unarmed prisoner he *should* have been taking into custody. The through and through high on the right side of his chest was not a fatal shot. The follow-up round which entered close to his heart, most definitely *was*.

Holed twice in quick succession, Jack collapsed in a bloody heap and his gun flew from his grasp. He began coughing and spitting blood, which trickled down his chin and cheeks, violently gasping for air in very short, rapid breaths, all too aware that he was about to journey to hell.

Sam rushed over to him and holstered her Glock, knelt down at his side, shaking her head as Miles and Jenny looked on in bewilderment and fear.

'You numbnuts! Now why'd you go and do a stupid thing like that for?' she asked. Her heart was breaking inside. 'Damn you! You gave me no choice, Jack. Why, you imbecile, *why?!*' she yelled, tears forming in her eyes but point-blank refusing to fall.

'I... My wife... Kids... Don't tell them I...?'

Jack Walters stopped breathing and at that very moment, the phone in his pocket began to chime. Sam located it quickly and placed it on speaker, the treachery of her closest colleague throwing all of her previous loyalties into question. She gazed up at Miles as she pressed the button to answer the call, warning him to remain silent.

'Mr. Walters? What in heaven's name is happening? Where are you? Are they dead?'

'Oh my God! What *have* I just done?!'

Lennox was beside herself, now that she'd had time to think things through. Intense feelings of shock, remorse and rage had consumed her and her head was whirring like a washing machine on spin cycle. The caller had hung up swiftly when no reply was given, adding to her fury.

'Apart from anything else, and most important of all surely, you saved our lives?' answered Miles, as he walked Jenny over to her slowly. 'As grateful as we are though, that still leaves us with a problem or two. They *won't* stop here. They'll get at us wherever we are, even in your police cells. You can't protect us. Nobody can. You've just witnessed how strong they are. They have people *everywhere*. You take us in, and you're probably signing our death warrants.'

Sam looked at them both with fiery resolve and sheer grit. '*You* do not know me. I can give it a damn good try! Wait here. Do *not* move a single muscle, the pair of you. You must trust me now. You have to trust somebody sometime, so why not me? This has to end, or you will be running for the rest of your life.'

Lennox took a calculated gamble, left them all alone and intercepted the armed officers responding to the gunfire, just as they entered the old farm grounds slightly ahead of the local coppers. She waited for them all to arrive and then held up her badge.

'Listen in quickly. We have a major incident here. A homicide that will be of interest to several law enforcement agencies. The eyes of the world will soon be upon us. As the ranking officer here, I'm assuming command. We have two fatalities; an as yet unidentified shooter who attempted to kill the two civilians over there, *and* an MI5 officer killed during the execution of his duties. Exact circumstances to be determined. The priority now is the safety of these witnesses... You!' she called, to a young officer at the rear. 'Fetch the car keys out of the detective's pocket. Bring his motor back here in double-quick time and report to me. Go!'

The police officer scurried away and Sam turned to address the senior of the two firearms officers. 'Thanks for the backup. We'd split up to search, me and my partner, and I'd taken the house. It was nearly over by the time I arrived on scene. He did it all. You have command here from this point. Set a perimeter and await the cavalry. They shouldn't be long. Don't let anyone touch or move anything. Preserve the evidence. That's all for now. Nobody goes in or out until SOCO and senior detectives have arrived and given the go ahead. I'll save you some time. They are both deceased, checked and verified by myself, time of death five minutes ago. That's your confirmation. Start a log.'

'Right, sarge. Only, this is highly irregular, isn't it? Won't they expect you to stay and give a statement?'

'Yes, they will. But I *won't* have any more deaths on my conscience. I'll be contactable and they can chew my ass over it some other time. I need to get these two safely stashed away somewhere and then I'll conduct a full handover, okay?

Once I've arranged and briefed a protection detail to relieve me.'

'Understood.'

'Good man. Call it in. I'll take full responsibility for my actions. I'm not risking any more firepower showing up here, for we're in no shape to fend them off. It's dark now and if they *do* show, they'll probably have night sights, which will seriously outclass us. Round up his weapons. He'll have a motor too. Find it, search it quickly and bring any gear he has to my car. I'll take everything with me, for security. No point making a present of them to those we may face.'

Jack Walters' Mazda turned up and once the holdall had been stashed in the car, Lennox spirited Miles and Jenny away without further comment.

She drove in almost complete silence to her cousin's house, knocked her up out of bed. Explained she was in real trouble and needed help, that she had parked her friend's vehicle about a mile away in a busy car park and needed a replacement. *Hers*. That she could tell nobody until she heard from her. The cousin was a little put out to say the least, but something in Sam's tone sounded desperate and she eventually relented. Handed over the keys to her old Audi A4 and stressed that she now owed her one, of the mightiest variety.

Not long afterwards, they arrived at a bungalow in St Albans which was owned by Sam's favourite uncle. Again, she begged for help and the former paratrooper offered to do whatever she asked with no questions and no strings attached. There, she garaged the car and settled Miles and Jenny in the lounge, closed the door and poured them all a glass of scotch. Downed hers in one gulp, thereby steadying her now trembling hands. Then she pulled out a packet of Malbrough and her lighter, lit another one up.

'This has gone far enough. It's time to confess all,' she said, blowing smoke out of the side of her mouth. 'Are you going to tell me everything you know now, or am I turning you over to the authorities?' Lennox asked Miles, who was still clutching the laptop. 'I can't blame you for being scared, but I must have earned *some* points with you? I've obliterated whatever career I may have had. I've made my identity and my involvement known, so I'm probably at the summit of their kill list too. Whoever they are. And I've shot dead a guy who in my eyes, was both a genuine hero and a trusted friend.'

Jenny suddenly piped up with, 'Go on, Miles. It's what we'd agreed. Can't see as though we have much of a choice? And she's right; she's certainly earned it.'

'Okay,' said Miles, relief etched all over his face. 'I could talk but it's probably easier if I show you, then try to fill in the gaps.'

He took out the laptop, plugged it in and powered it up. Tapped on Jason's video file and message to Jenny. Watched her intently as she absorbed what she was seeing, paused it where necessary and answered her questions as best he could. Then, he immediately played the introduction section to the Project AJAX research file. When the password prompt appeared on the screen, he turned off the device.

Sam was speechless at first, before she finally regained her senses.

'Now that's a body blow. This entire thing is... Well, it's beyond the scale of anything I've ever heard of... *AJAX?* Mythical warrior of ancient Greece. Apt title for a plan to genetically manufacture entire legions of them. International conspiracies. Agents, assassins and mercenaries running amok on British soil. Murder, and who knows how many other crimes? Corruption in the Met Police and MI5, maybe elsewhere. To what extent we can only guess at. And a top-level scientist destroying his life's work and blowing the whistle on practises probably outlawed by... Killed by... Who? And why?'

'Unknown. And because he couldn't live with himself. Feared for the future,' answered Miles.

Several seconds of stunned silence followed before Lennox felt she needed to add something. 'I'm stumped. My concerns are multiple. Let's begin with the two things that smack me straight in the chops. The voice on the phone. The one seemingly controlling Owen James and probably Jack Walters too. Maybe, the whole lot of them. The one who ordered James' death no doubt, before he could spill the beans.'

'He deserved to die. Probably thought he knew too much. They couldn't risk him squealing like a pig,' offered Jenny.

'Colourful language, for a civvy. Though, you're right. And I have the feeling he was about to. I knew... I think I know that caller's voice. It's familiar to me somehow, but I can't quite place it.'

'And the second thing?' asked Miles.

'Obviously, where to now? This Stephen Lawson guy, you think he is the key?'

'We're not certain of anything but Miles' father stressed his involvement, as you heard. Miles had an idea about that,' Jenny retorted, remembering his statement.

'Err, yeah. I've been thinking it over. If you listen closely, my dad said, *Look to him*. That's a weird thing to say, don't you think? Not like him. It implies that there's something to actually *look* at. A photo maybe?'

'Did your father do social media at all?' Sam enquired.

Miles scoffed a little. 'Pah! Are you joking? He never had time. Work was his entire life. And in retirement, he was decorating, golfing, or tinkering with his car.'

'Pity. Then we'll have to contact Mr. Lawson. You two sit tight here whilst I make a few calls. Better still, get your heads down. You must be shattered. Jenny, you have the couch. Miles, a choice of chair or floor.'

Blankets and pillows were thrown in and the pair slept soundly. They were awoken bright and early by Sam, her uncle keeping out of the way as asked. She had already showered, eaten and dressed. She entered carrying an electronic tablet, drew back the curtains for a little light, another lit cigarette dangling precariously from her lips.

'Help yourself to breakfast but first, I contacted a colleague of mine last night, was informed of Stephen Lawson's home address and contact number. I chanced my arm and gave it a try. Didn't expect him to answer given the hour, but he did. I said I was dealing with a possible homicide involving your father. He was anxious to help in any way he could. They were work colleagues, nothing more. Not especially close. Though Lawson recalled that they *did* row for an army club together at one time. Said he had a photo of them at a meet where he won first place. The prize was the Samuel Curran Cup, named after a Scottish scientist who worked on the Manhattan Project with Oppenheimer. That's why he framed it and kept it. And guess what?'

'What?' asked an enthralled Jenny. 'Oh, come on! Don't leave us in suspenders?!'

Sam's lips curved into a smile. 'He fished it out of the frame, took a clear photo of it on his phone and e-mailed it to my uncle's address.'

She turned the tablet around to display the picture.

'He's next to my... He's holding the trophy!' exclaimed Miles. He raced over to the laptop and pressed the power button. 'Come on! Hurry up!' he yelled at the screen.

He opened the research file, clicked in the password prompt box and typed away. Pressed enter. Nothing.

'Bit of an anti-climax. What did you type?' asked Jenny.

'Sam Curran,' replied Miles.

'Capitals and spaces?'

'Yep.'

'Try, Sam Curran Cup.'

He did. No joy. The disappointment ladened the air like mustard gas.

'What about trophy instead of cup?' suggested Sam.

Miles entered in *Sam Curran Trophy*.

The screen burst into life. A new title page in army green appeared, with big bold words dominating the centre.

PROJECT AJAX

****

TOP SECRET.

Chapter 18

It happened again. Worse than before. More intense and vivid. Maybe it was the stress of this current investigation, of everything that had occurred, the death of a close colleague, the betrayal of a supposed friend…? *Whatever* had triggered her, the recurrences this time were especially penetrating, powerful and real. So much so, that after a good while in bed tossing and turning, crying and screaming out, Sam's uncle heard her distress loud and clear, came bursting into her room like a Scots Grey charging down Napoleon's finest. It was the early hours of the morning and he shook her violently to wake her, even though he probably should have known better. Not a great thing to do. Not to a warrior who believes they are in the midst of a firefight, even if the whole episode was safely contained within the confines of her mind. For Sam did not know that and she reacted as soldiers do, almost killing him as her hands clamped so rapidly and forcefully around his neck, that she very nearly crushed his windpipe. At the very last second strangled cries somehow managed to convey his desperation and she awoke from her stupor, immediately realised what was happening and where she was.

Horrified, mortified in fact, she released her favourite uncle and her face was a picture of horror. For the next few minutes, she professed her deep sorrow and guilt over and over again, begging for forgiveness. Her hair was all over the place, her clothes wet through, the bed an absolute wreck, as her impassioned pleas turned eventually into floods and floods of tears.

Funny thing was, Uncle Wayne had put up no fight at all, almost let her end his life, hardly flinched as the air was choked from him. Just let it happen. Went as limp as a doll and began to sink in her arms, calling out her name unceasingly. Then coughed and spluttered as she took her time to fully come around. When she'd *finally* calmed, Sam simply gazed into his eyes and began to sob once more, like a babe. He'd hugged her then as if she were his own sweet little girl afraid of the dark, told her time and again to, 'Let it all out.'

In many ways, she *was* afraid of the blackness. Of the night. Of the terrors it wrought. Had been for some while now. But alone together in that room, the two veterans found a little peace in each other's company. Understood one another at long last.

'I'm so sorry, Sam. I never knew it was so bad for you. I should have seen it,' the ex-paratrooper stated sympathetically, after an absolute age of silence. 'Lord knows, I've known enough of my mates who've gone through something similar. Many who never made it through safely to the other side.'

She stared blankly back at him, uncertain what to say but feeling like a great weight had been lifted off her chest all of a sudden. This giant secret she had born stoically for years had finally been aired and at last, somebody else was in the know. On her side. Not just anybody too, but a former squaddie she loved, someone who might just understand all she had endured. Sam reached for her cigarettes on the nightstand. Her hands were shaking so badly, she couldn't work the lighter properly. It just flickered and spluttered pathetically, showed no sign of igniting the way it should.

'Damn!' she cursed, somewhat perversely not wanting to swear in front of her uncle, despite all he knew, had seen and heard.

'Here,' he said, 'let me,' and he took the lighter from her hand. Cooly, he clicked the mechanism and easily sparked a strong flame.

'Thanks,' she murmured, as she put a cigarette into her mouth and dipped to light it. She pulled deeply, holding the smoke and the sweet nicotine in her lungs for more than a moment, before slowly exhaling. Bliss.

A strange sense of achievement then. Why hadn't she confided in him before? She knew why. The terror that never left her.

'You can't say...! You can't breathe a word of this! Please, uncle, I'm begging you?! They'll take my badge. I'll be chained to a desk if I'm lucky, sent back to therapy for...'

'Hey, hey! Take it easy. This is *me* you're talking to. We'll get through this, I promise. *Together...* You're going to have to open up though. If not to me, then I'll find the nearest veteran group or charity? You can't keep bottling it all up, Sam. It'll eat at your insides like a cancer. It's like a fizzy bottle of pop; you keep shaking it the way you've been doing, and it's gonna explode on you one day! I mean it. It'll take you out easier than an RPG blast.'

'It's not that easy, uncle.'

'I know that, kid. Course it's not. Name me one thing worth having in life that *is* easy? But this thing is your biggest fight yet. I'd be going through work if I were you. Seeking the professional help they are obliged to provide, though I understand completely why you might feel that isn't an option. You can't go on like this, that's for sure. I know what I'm talking about. That was *bad*, what little I heard. I've had similar nightmares, but nothing on that scale. I bet you're drinking too?'

When she remained silent on him, he took that as a resounding yes.

'You got the shakes yet?'

'It's nothing. I can handle it.'

'Oh, Sam. You've got to *want* to get better first off. Lying about it won't help at all. Nobody can drag you to meetings, or make you talk. Listen to me. You have a problem. The only way you are going to fix it, is to start by admitting that. Promise me you'll deal with this? I'm here whenever you want to begin and first thing tomorrow, I'm looking for those chat groups an' all. I'll say it's for me. Nobody need know a thing. What do you say?'

Sam's shoulders sagged somewhat and she nodded her head extremely slowly. She stubbed out the remnants of her cigarette and went for another.

'And you can pack those things in too!' her uncle declared, though it was said with a smile this time.

Sam laughed a little. 'Yeah, they'll be the death of me.'

'That's my girl. It's just another objective to take, that's all. A big one maybe, but you've just laced up your boots.'

'Thank... thank you. I'll do whatever it takes, I promise. I have to see this case through first, but I swear, once it's done, I'll be coming back to see you.'

Her uncle smiled and stood up. 'That's all I wanted to hear. I'll leave you in peace now, let you get back to sleep, not that there's much of the night left. Our sort never pass up a chance of downtime though.'

'Or scran.'

'Ha, ha... Too right. See you in the morning.'

He turned to walk away but her voice calling out stopped him before he reached the door.

'Uncle Wayne?'

'Yep?'

'I love you.'

After breakfast, once Jenny had changed into some clothes from the local charity shop that Sam had purchased, they spent a few hours going through the long video presentation on Project AJAX that they had unlocked. Even then, they had to skim past a lot of sections for the majority of the content was way over their heads. The *recap* was both long and intense, no doubt thoroughly entertaining to anyone clever enough, or with a vested interest in the subject matter, but to the average Joe in the street the multitude of explanations, references, theories and technical jargon made the whole thing tedious in the extreme. Not for Miles, however, who was enjoying simply being able to watch his deceased father again, a spark shining brightly in his eyes as his dad clearly derived great pleasure in sharing his passion with an unknown audience.

The introduction they had already viewed was followed by numerous sections with grand titles including Human Genetic Variation, Defining the Norm, Public Response, Enhancement and Training, Responsible Scientific Research, Evidence Gathering and Recording, Somatic (Nonheritable) Genome Editing, Fairness, Unfair Social Advantage, Nonheritable Somatic Editing for Enhancement of the Individual, Heritable Genome Editing and Enhancement, Eugenics, Germline Enhancement, Findings - Testing and Analysis, Budget Requirements, The Future, Stakeholder Engagement, Education and Dialogue and Conclusions and Recommendations. Each of these headings was a separate lecture in itself. Though, by forwarding past droves of intelligence explanations, they learned how James Dalton had gradually become completely and thoroughly obsessed by his work. To a degree which nearly cost him both his marriage and his life, in one way or another. He grew blind to the ethics governing his endeavours, every bit as much as the scientists who worked for Adolf Hitler conducting medical experiments on human beings, or developing gas chambers... *His* was an all-encompassing voyage of discovery with virtually no limits and minimal oversight. There were *zero* indications from the film that he had given any thought or consideration to the potential consequences of his actions, should he actually succeed in achieving his ultimate goal. The ramifications of a new world order were beyond him it seemed, or more likely ignored. As were the lengths others might go to in order to stop such a thing from becoming reality, as well as the clear target he was painting not just upon his own back, but on the backs of all those around him.

At numerous points during the lectures Sam and Jenny posed their own questions and Miles stopped the recording each time, tried to answer as best he could, admitting ignorance on more than one occasion. It was towards the end of the lengthy monologue when Major Dalton alluded to the fact that he had been testing his theories out on himself. They paid closer attention then, began to show signs of real concern. Testing his *blood* was one thing, but his body?

'He never states it clearly, but it is implied and I don't think we can discount it. Not enough to incriminate himself though. And he doesn't state when it began,' Jenny commented.

'Yes, but he must surely have known it was *way* beyond acceptable? No way his superiors would allow that, surely? It's potentially extremely dangerous. Life-threatening even,' added Sam.

'I say we video the lot on a phone, post it all over social media. Let the cat out of the bag. If all this becomes open source, then maybe, just maybe, whoever they are will leave us alone?' ventured Jenny.

Miles remained quiet, horrified by what he was hearing, his mind all fuzzy.

'Miles!' she cried, determined to hear his thoughts on the matter.

'What? Can't you just let me be? I never knew anything about it, if that's what you're asking. Whatever he was going through at the time, whatever heartache and sorrow he put my mother through, they both appear to have shielded me completely. I'm as stunned as you two by all of this.'

'*Shielded?* Good way of putting it. As all good parents do,' Sam remarked.

'Yeah? Not from my standpoint. Not now at least. I wish he'd have let me in, confided in me a bit more. He's gone, my brother too. If it all links back to *this*, maybe I could have helped, talked some sense into him?'

Jenny placed a reassuring hand on his shoulder again. 'Stop that. You were a child, Miles, a boy. And I think he was past all that anyhow.'

Miles gave a deep sigh and tapped the screen again. The video continued along the same vein but in the last but one section, Jenny spotted something, asked Miles to freeze the frame.

'What? What is it? What am I looking at?' he asked, completely blank.

She took the tablet out of his hands and held it close to her face.

'Can you screenshot that page and zoom in?'

'What you thinking?' Sam asked.

'It's... I'm just wondering why our major has *two* test tubes, and if we can see the labels on them clearly enough to make out the writing. He's repeating everything he does, have you noticed? *Exactly* the same each time, no variation at all.'

Sam drew in a sudden gasp of air. 'You're right!' she exclaimed.

Jenny replied in a soft voice which nevertheless showed that she was obviously pleased with herself. 'I'm a researcher myself. It's what I do. And if you ask me... Okay, I think this whole thing has been deceit and deception from the get-go. What if somebody else was in that lab at the time of the accident all those years ago? What if they too were affected in the same way? It's only an observation, but it could mean there is, or was, a secondary source of the altered blood.'

'Now there's a thought. It would mean a secondary target too. And this video would be kryptonite. The kind of thing countries go to war over,' Lennox added. 'And that's exactly why we can't put it all on the internet as suggested.'

Miles continued the video. No more revelations surfaced but James Dalton was seen repeating experiments and using items marked Sample A and Sample B over and over. The inevitable conclusion was that he had been concealing the truth yet again.

After dinner, Miles helped Sam's uncle with the dishes, whilst Sam and Jenny were left alone to get to know each other a little better.

'It's Wayne, isn't it?' Miles ventured to begin the conversation.

'That's right. And you're Miles. Don't know more than that and I don't want to. I've been warned to keep it that way, for all our sakes.'

'Fair enough. Smalltalk it is then. How close are you to Sam?'

Wayne Dalton answered as he washed the dishes with a cloth and handed them to Miles to dry. 'As close as any uncle I suppose. Career soldier, so I had none of my own. Children, I mean. I'm probably the reason she joined up. I loved it you see, couldn't help but talk of it. Though, she was always a clever one, Sam. Never just infantry. Took after her father, not me. Thank God.'

'Your brother?'

'Yeah. Our parents died early. We're two halves of the same person. Only, he's as decent as decent can be, whereas I'm a rough sort. He involved me in her upbringing as much as he could. Didn't have to. I used to sleep over when on leave and tag along on days out. Broke my heart when she was deployed and caught one, came back all knocked about. Thought we'd lost her. Don't know how I'd have handled that. I served in hot zones all around the world, took lives and fire. Lots of fire. Saw comrades fall. In all that time, I never once received so much as a scratch. Just lucky I guess. And there *she* is, goes and gets herself ambushed by a small army, in some little hole nobody's even heard of. Not that it was her fault. She did us proud. She was hit bad and still kept fighting. Saved her mates.'

'I didn't know that. She's a real hero,' Miles agreed.

'You don't know the half of it. And look how they treated her afterwards. Forced her to leave the job she loved. Made to start from scratch again and given a hard time by others not fit to lace her boots. I had hoped she had done with fighting. I'm wrong though, aren't I?'

Miles said nothing. He didn't have to. And besides, Sam had warned her uncle not to ask.

'Ooops! As you were! I've been told to stand down on this one, and I will. But you listen to me!' the former para stated, realising his mistake, his tone now stern and deadly serious. 'She is *not* as strong as she thinks she is. It will catch up with her again at some point. When it does, she'll need your help. So, you *be* there for her. Promise me!'

Miles took a tiny step backwards as the old soldier leaned in a little too close.

'I... I hardly know her.'

'That's no excuse. I know nothing of what you face but I can tell my niece is scared, and that don't happen easily. If she's letting it show, it's for good reason. And likely to be immediate. You just make certain that you watch her back! Or you'll have *me* to deal with!'

'Okay, I promise. If I *can*, I will.'

Sam Lennox had had enough of idle chatter. It wasn't her forte and to be honest, she was bored of it. She was more at home in the officer's mess, than on a girly night out, so this forced and false discussion thing, was her idea of purgatory. She therefore decided to cut straight to the chase.

'You and Miles then?' she asked, taking Jenny completely by surprise.

The young beauty blushed a little, before replying, 'There is no, *me and Miles.*'

'Really?'

'Really. Whatever ideas are in your head, whatever Miles may have told you, you're wide of the mark.'

'Alright, if you say so,' said Sam, eyebrows raised. 'I'm not entirely convinced, however. I have eyes. He'd *like* there to be.'

Jenny dipped her chin a little. 'Maybe. I mean, yes, probably. I've seen the way he looks at me and I suppose I've led him on a little. We've become quite close in such a short space of time but that's only natural, I think, given what's happened. It's been one hell of a ride. But we're just friends in my eyes, thrust together by extraordinary circumstance, nothing more.'

'Then why are you still here?'

'Why, you're just as blunt as they come, aren't you? Good question though. Can't say that I have a decent answer. I can see how it looks. When you break it down, it maybe makes sense? These murderers are heavy duty. High-tech killers. They have my photo, car details and who knows what else. I have to consider that they know precisely where I live and that they want me dead too, in case I've been told anything of importance and speak to the likes of you.'

Sam nodded in agreement. 'There is that. You sure that's all?'

'You don't back off. You're like one of those little terriers tearing away at the postman's trousers. A proper copper. Alright then, let's put all our cards on the table. What *exactly* do you mean?'

'You protest too much. I think you're hiding something. And he's not bad looking?'

'Back to Miles, are we? I thought I'd dealt with that. *Not* my type. Too g*eeky.*'

'You could do a lot worse. His heart's in the right place... So, remind me, what is it you do again?' Sam enquired, pushing her for answers merely because she could, killing time.

'I told you. I work for Johnson's Pharmaceutical. I'm in research. I enjoy it, and the pay is great.'

'Yes, so you did. That's a nice little earner. Probably how you can afford that flat of yours. And that's based where?'

'Head office. London. Look, why the tenth degree? Shouldn't you be shining a light into my eyes or something?'

'*Would*, if I had one. I see. Have much to do with the millionaire who owns the company? Sir Nicholas?'

'No. Of course I don't. He's way above my pay grade... I wonder what those two are talking about? They're taking ages just to do a few plates. Much longer, and you'll have me banged up, tried, convicted and swinging on a rope... No more questions, okay? I'm not the enemy here and we have better ways of spending our time together. We need to plan our next move. Unless, that is, you're intending to hide us here for the foreseeable? Is that your master plan? Feeling a little lonely and needed some company, did we?'

It was quite an abrupt change of subject and the hostility in her voice was clear, but Sam let it pass.

'No, you're right. Give them a shout. I have some decisions to make. And so do you.'

Chapter 19

Uncle Wayne very obligingly agreed to take his black labrador for a long walk, leaving his niece and her guests sitting around the kitchen table in complete privacy. Sam waited until she heard the latch on the gate as it closed, before opening the discussion. Even then, her voice was held low.

'I love him to bits but if he hears *any* of this, I won't be able to hold him back. And he takes some stopping, believe me, when his blood's up. One man army. Still thinks he's twenty years old. He's rather protective of me and would walk through fire if I asked him to. Miles has only lasted this long in his house because he thinks you two are an item. I may have given him that impression. Forgive any funny looks he's thrown your way... Now, it's time to get to work. We have to talk this through and devise some kind of a plan, or strategy. It's been a lot to take in but I think I have my head around it now. Time to decide our futures,' Sam began, noting the determined eyes staring back at her. '...However short or long they may turn out to be,' she added, which notched up the tension in a heartbeat.

'For every action, there's a reaction,' Lennox continued. 'My absence will be setting off alarms just about everywhere by now. Police H.Q. will be doing their nuts. I've a few enemies at the station who will be stirring things up too, feeding disinformation to discredit me, make me look bad. I should have reported in an absolute age ago to let them know we are safe and provide details of what happened, our current location, arrange protection details and the like. The police have a real problem now that I'm no longer contactable. One of their own is missing, possibly gone rogue. They'll respond in kind. Swarm known haunts or local landmarks, check all associates and family, last known sightings... They are bound to turn up here eventually. And they'll soon find my car. They can't assume anything, so time is short.'

I can phone them right this instant, if that's what you'd like? Explain what happened with the shootings at the farm and agree to surrender myself, take you both in straight away, give my statement in full. Hand you over to a protection squad who hopefully will not have been compromised. I can maybe even salvage something of my career, if I'm smart enough. Get to keep my job. As you may probably have figured out, I don't have much else going for me right now, so... You never know... Well? That's option one I'm bringing to the table, what do you think?'

Miles looked across at Jenny, trying to gauge her reaction, then straight back at Sam. 'I'm sorry, but no. Not for me. I can see how that might be the favoured choice for *you*, but we have no way of knowing if we will be safe taking that route, if we do as you say and turn ourselves over to the law. The police are infiltrated. And shifts change, people rotate, take days off... A watch detail like that will be large and it only takes one rotten apple to create mayhem. Can't see that we will last too long. We won't see it coming either, because it will arrive from within, when our guards are down. I may be wrong but worst-case scenario, it will be like a brief stay on death row. Feel like it too, awaiting execution. Plus, MI5 were compromised also. We have just learned that to our cost, very nearly our doom. I don't think he could have come much closer; your pal, Jack. If, between you, both your organisations as big as they are couldn't protect us, what chance do you have now with local police? Word has spread since then. We're national news. Everyone will have heard of us. And nobody can say to what extent both forces are breached. Nor how long we will have to remain in hiding. The longer that is the case, the more potential assassins are bound to learn of our whereabouts. Money buys courage, and the motivation for foul deeds. They appear to have an endless supply of that. This pursuit of theirs could last forever.'

'Miles is right,' voiced Jenny, scratching her chin as she deliberated. 'Though a nice cosy little house in which to sit things out sounds appealing, we have no real timeline here. We know next to nothing. Except that the threat is very much *now*, made by those with unlimited resources. It is *real*, and it comes from every direction. Unknown numbers are seeking us intent on murder. Pretty much invisible until they are right on top of us. How can we defend against that? They could be everywhere. I can't see how we will tell friend from foe, or when an end to this nightmare might be in sight. They *have* to have learned by now that Miles is not Jase, and yet they still keep coming! Staying still in one location doesn't sound too appealing. Like making it easy for them. And maybe it's not the time to bring this up, but what about that scratch on his arm?'

Sam's brows furrowed and her chest moved up and down as she sighed deeply. 'More secrets? What scratch?'

'On the train,' Jenny replied. 'Miles felt certain he was caught with something by Jase, possibly injected. He's been off-colour ever since. His arm has been hurting and he saw a needle.'

'The auto-injector! Is this true?' demanded Sam, astonished and a little perturbed to only be hearing of this now.

Miles nodded like a schoolboy who'd just been caught raiding the cupboards. 'Well, yes. Though, I'm starting to feel much better than I was and...'

'Why didn't you mention this before?!' she fumed.

'I... There's a lot happened and we...'

'You brainless clot! You need to be completely honest with me from now on. Well? What *was* it, do you think?'

Miles shrugged a little. 'I have no idea. This was Jase we're talking about, not my father. I was in bits at the time.

I'd never even met the guy and I've been too busy trying to stay alive ever since. I never really thought about it too much until we watched that video. Now, however, I'm a little bit concerned.'

'A bit?!' Sam scoffed. 'I don't blame you. That's the understatement of the year.'

'Why? Do you think it's all related?' asked Miles.

'Duh! I should say so. It's one heck of a coincidence if it isn't. You know, for somebody supposedly quite bright, you can actually sound very...'

'That's *not* helping!' interrupted Jenny, her voice stern and sharp. 'We don't know what it was and though it may have affected him, he appears to be none the worse for it now. We have to keep an open mind and push on. You shouldn't scold him like that. He's not your subordinate and he's doing his best in a horrendous situation. He's lost a lot and doesn't need to hear it. Move on.'

Lennox looked at Jenny with eyes that could kill, though she relented a little after a while, just about managing to see the truth in her words. After a long pause, she continued speaking in a more conciliatory tone.

'I'm going to have to do some more thinking around that extra little revelation. For the moment, it's shelved, to be revisited later. So, option one is a bust then. Not appealing in the slightest. Fairy snuff. Two's up next; It's a little extreme but... You and Miles disappear completely. Off the radar and off grid. We can set you up with a witness protection gig. You'll have new identities and passports, jobs, plastic surgery if you choose, the works. But *only* after you testify and turn King's evidence. That way you could go wherever you like. Abroad perhaps?'

It was Jenny who answered this time, almost instantaneously, in a forthright manner. 'Never! I already have a life that I love very much, thank you. I have family and friends who care about me. A beautiful flat and a semi-decent social life. I'm *not* willing to throw all that away.'

Sam turned her head towards Miles.

'As *she* said. No. She shouldn't have to. Not because of me,' he declared. 'Besides, those same police officers and agents we were so frightened of before, would no doubt be involved in setting up this change, arranging for those papers you mentioned and entering it all onto computer systems etc. MI5 would most certainly be able to find out where we went, surely? It's what they do. And then what? Stuck in a foreign land with no help to turn to and nowhere to run? We'd be no safer than if we stayed right here and took our chances.'

A shake of her head showed Sam's frustration. They were getting nowhere fast. 'I appreciate you have problems galore at the moment, but you have to meet me half way here? I'm trying my best to come up with something you can work with. You're not easy difficulties to solve, either of you.'

'We know. And this *difficulty* right here, is extremely grateful to you for even trying,' snapped Miles. 'So, what's option three then?' he asked.

'Three's a beast. That's the one I like least of all. The nuclear option. I can't believe I'm even proposing this. I'm a police officer after all. A damned good one at that. Until you two came along I... Never mind. We come clean. Completely. Lock, stock and barrel. Though, I don't take you in, as they will expect. Demand even. No, we arrange a neutral venue. Test the waters so to speak. You show up there and only when satisfied, you hand them the file. Tell them everything you know from a position of safety.'

'What?!' exclaimed an alarmed Jenny. 'Impossible! Then, what was all this for? Why did we even resist? He'd be shot on sight and you know it. His father's research would be used to further the interests of whoever paid the most money and laid their hands on it. Copied to any foreign power willing to cough up the dough. Terrorist states. No, that's just not gonna fly. It endangers everybody and it's suicide.'

Sam threw her hands up in the air and struggled to control her fiery temper. 'I agree, it would be a *massive* gamble, but what do you want from me? I said I had options. I never said that any of those choices were *good* ones. You're on the canvas in the last round with a broken jaw, it would take a miracle to win this fight.'

Miles coughed to clear his throat. 'There *is* an option four. One we haven't considered.'

The two ladies looked at him expectantly, inviting further enlightenment.

'What if…? Hear me out on this before you fly off the handle… What if, we *did* arrange that meet? Only, when we showed up, we were the world's clumsiest rabbits and it leaked all over the internet before we arrived?'

'Then, every man and his dog would show up and it would descend into our very own version of Armageddon in short order,' answered Sam. 'I'm not liking it so far. It would be a bloodbath, bullets flying in all directions.'

Miles nodded his head gently in agreement. 'That's what I thought. Nevertheless, I think it's worth further exploration. I could go on my own. You two would then be free. Jenny could return back to her life, as she desires, for everything would be out in the open. You needn't do any more than you have and I'm sure we could explain that away. It's a win-win… The only casualty would be me… Look, let's get real for a moment. I don't think I'm meant to survive this thing anyway. My game is over no matter what I do. At least *this* way, Player 1 and Player 2 walk away into the sunset? Can't see any other alternative. And I could take a few guns along with me, try to take out a few of the bad guys while I'm there, before they can…'

Jenny suddenly grabbed hold of his wrists and pulled him to her. '*Kill* you?! Are you completely insane?! You're not that guy, Miles! Why would you even suggest such a thing? After all we've been through. You'd be throwing your life away and for what?!'

'For you,' he murmured, quietly.

That short reply hit her right where it hurt. Her heart burst all of a sudden and it felt like the wind had been plucked from her sails by some supernatural force. She couldn't help herself and she wept openly, tears as big as raindrops tumbling from her cheeks.

'You're mad, it's true,' she blurted out between her tears. 'A full hamper short of a picnic. I've never heard such rubbish! You're serious, aren't you? Miles, you're a grown man able to make your own decisions but I'm not the one to sacrifice yourself for. I can't give you what you want. I just don't feel that way…'

'I know. I'm still going though,' Miles interrupted, defiantly.

He looked a little hurt but they both turned immediately towards Sam, for different reasons.

'Oh no. *Impossible*. Get over yourselves. I'm sworn to protect but there *is* a limit…' was her immediate reaction.

As she thought on it some more however, she began to come around to the crazy idea.

'…If you do this thing, I don't know if I'll be able to keep you alive, but if I alert the right people at the right time, we'll have some serious firepower there also, which *may* just even the odds.'

'You're both mental!' cried Jenny, exasperated. 'You have absolutely no idea who will be coming and in what force.'

She turned to face Sam and stated, 'You'll be using him as bait!'

'She's not using me. You can't use a willing volunteer, Jen,' Miles corrected her.

'Oh, for Christ's sake! This is the worst plan ever. Dreamt up in seconds by a computer gamer with no grip on reality. Only, this isn't a *game*, Miles! You bleed and you die. You'll be thrown to the slaughter. You only have one life, don't throw it away? What's the aim? What's the end game, eh?'

'Simple,' he answered, 'to flush out all of the main players at once. To bring them out from the shadows. All of whom want to be the first to find me, and kill me, so they will all show I'm certain of it. The stakes are too high *not* to. Losing is not an option for these people. This seemingly foolhardy action on my part will bring everything to the fore. And if by some miracle I do survive, *I* will then control the narrative. Only we three know the truth. If that comes to pass, I will be sure to be very economical with it. What the world doesn't know, won't hurt it. The file can be destroyed once we're certain we no longer need it. No harm, no foul. If I die, then you can do the honours for me. *Or*, we leave it with Sam's uncle, with instructions to smash it if he doesn't hear from her by a certain time. She's stated he's a guy to be trusted. Either way, this promises to be such a gigantic event, that nothing will be able to remain hidden. Questions will be asked from all quarters and any subsequent action will be taken in that knowledge, within the glare of world scrutiny.'

Silence once more. Broken eventually by a now rather beaten and subdued Jenny.

'I still don't like it.'

'You don't *have* to like it,' replied Sam, harshly. 'Not *your* family, is it? So, it's not your decision to make.'

'Let me finish!' Jenny responded, lifting up her head. 'I don't like it, but I want to help in any way I can. I'd never forgive myself otherwise. What can I do?'

Lennox grinned a little, surprised by the fighting spirit in this slight city-dweller, whom she thought would run a mile from the thought of combat.

'I'll need a good spotter.'

'A spotter?'

'Affirmative. Miles is going in alone to face an unidentified threat. He needs our eyes and ears. I intend to be on overwatch for him. Sniper cover from above. All good operators work in teams of two. I can range the area beforehand. We'll be static, on ground of our choosing, and Owen James very kindly provided us with an excellent weapon. Give me a few rounds to zero it in to my eye relief and I should be good to go. Anyone steps within a hundred yards of our guy with hostile intent and I'll make Swiss cheese of 'em. You've just volunteered to be my mate. You call out the shots when you see anyone approach, warn me of danger.'

'Sounds... Sounds simple enough. And what if they have their own sniper?' asked Jenny, shaking a little inside, scarcely able to believe what was being proposed.

'Then, things will be a little tricky. It's only fair to warn you that a static position comes with quite a few risks, but I don't intend to give them long enough to set that up. However, if they *do*, you call it, I'll drop it.'

Chapter 20

DS Sam Lennox had a busy afternoon. First, she drove over to visit a technical wizard Miles had recommended. A fellow Nerd in fact, in so much as she was an active member of his not-so-secret society. A woman he had played online games with almost every night for the past five years or so, until his recent misfortunes. He quite bizarrely classed her as his closest friend. This, despite the fact that they had never *actually* met face to face, and *her* take on that was unknown. It was an embarrassing admission which spoke volumes of his previous lack of social interaction, though Miles was beginning to feel he had turned a corner in that particular department, with his surprisingly easy, developing relationships with Jenny and the fiery ex-soldier turned police officer, whom he was beginning to rely on more and more. The pretty researcher had rebuffed his advances, sure. However, she was so far out of his league that this had met his expectations. It was enough for Miles, that he had plucked up the courage to say something. Half a decade of practising that very moment hadn't been wasted at least. As for the tough DS, Lennox was a complicated and fearsome creature he would normally have avoided like the plague, for fear of being devoured alive. The kind of superwoman he happily observed from afar on his morning commute, usually froze to the spot in fear lest she should cast a glance in his direction. That he had remained in the same vicinity as Sam for a period of time without completely falling to pieces, was triumph enough. Yes, Miles was a different creature now, flying high after an entire lifetime of lows, as far as the ladies were concerned at least. Baby steps they *may* be, but at least he was inching forwards. It had taken a few killings and some near-death experiences to finally bring him out of his shell, but nobody is perfect.

The tower block was large and falling apart. Like a set on a seventies T.V. show, it looked as though it should have been demolished years ago. Litter, discarded toys, needles and used condoms were strewn about the place like decorations, hidden amongst the pervading filth. Sam had seen a lot on her travels and during her time on the beat but the state of this dump shocked her even so. Eyes were everywhere, hidden in a multitude of shades, corners and recesses. She was about as handy as they come in a ruck, she knew that. Nevertheless, countless shivers running down her spine as she trudged past several spaced-out, emaciated youths on the stairwells, made her pat her service weapon for comfort.

She knocked on the battered door of a dingy fifth-floor flat. Heard a stifled whine and a moan in response, then the heavy sound of shuffling feet like a mini-stampede of wildebeests. A pair of beady eyes appeared in the letterbox, which opened with a squeak, and a deep female voice shouted through the opening to ask who she was in an unmistakeable North London accent. Sam showed her warrant card and could hear the occupant gasp in horror. Four chains rattled as they were released, each one distinct from the next. Finally, the door swung inwards and standing before Lennox was a total vision.

The extremely large lady occupant filled the entire hallway. She was dressed in a dirty and stained, grey tracksuit, smoking a cigarette, looking for all the world like she was about to explode. It was abundantly clear that she resented the uninvited interruption to her day and was in a hurry to return to whatever important activity she had been undertaking.

'What *you* want, piggy? That badge gets you a glance at my hall, that's all. Say your piece and then leave, will ya? Can't be seen squawking with the likes of you. Got a rep to maintain.'

Sam's initial inclination was to shove the fag where the sun don't shine.

But she'd promised Miles she'd be nice to his friend, on her best behaviour, so she reined in her rising anger.

'We have a mutual friend in Miles Dalton,' she offered, by way of introduction.

The female occupant licked her bottom lip a little as she contemplated what that meant for her. Or *to* her. Sam could see her eyes working overtime, twitching and moving along with her brain no doubt. Which evidently operated quite speedily.

She leant her head out of the door to check who was watching. 'Step inside one pace, quickly, no further,' she hissed.

Sam followed her instructions. As soon as she had cleared the door, it was slammed shut behind her, almost catching her arm.

'Steady on!' Lennox warned. 'You almost had my skin there.'

'What is this? Why are you here and what has happened to Miles?'

'If I can just come through, I'll explain?' Sam ventured.

'No can do, missus. You're five-oh. The enemy. This is as far as you get.'

Sam huffed. She didn't have time for this. 'Look, Miles is in real trouble and he needs your help. Plus, there's two hundred and fifty pounds in it for you, no questions asked, if you aid me right away.'

The woman's eyes seemed to glint a little at that and the licking of the lips returned. 'Did you say, *no questions asked?* You promise?'

Sam was losing her patience. 'Love, I don't care if you're keeping the Crown Jewels in there, I just need you to listen to what I have to say and act on it.'

The cash was snatched from Sam's hand and she was led through into the bedroom, where there was only one single bed and a desk laden with state-of-the-art computers and accessories. Many of the parts were still in their boxes and had clearly arrived via mail order. The remainder of the place was a pigsty, no evidence of wealth or pride at all, but the computer gear was all top-notch stuff and worth a fortune. Though, strewn everywhere was an assortment of empty wrappers from chocolate bars, biscuits and crips, as well as used and crunched up coke cans and bottles. The cheap stuff, not the brand name. And it smelt like she had slept in there for a month or so without washing so that Sam had to turn away numerous times to hide her disgust.

'What do I call you?' asked Lennox, anxious to move things on at pace.

'The Minxster will do,' she replied, staring down at the cash in her hand and almost salivating. 'What do I have to do to earn this? Nothing illegal, I hope? I ain't on the game you know.'

'No, don't worry. Thought hadn't crossed my mind. You're not my type anyway. All you need to do, is send a few e-mails for us. I want to deliver a message or two. Though, you do *not* want the recipients to be able to trace them, trust me. They are very bad dudes. It could be extremely dangerous for you if they ever find out you have assisted us.'

She scoffed a little in derision. 'No problem, lady. It's what I do. I watch the news. The state-sponsored propaganda. The lies to feed their own agenda. How do you think I afford all this stuff? You're not dealing with amateurs you know. I have friends, many friends, the type who will bounce it around so much, anyone trying to trace it will throw their guts up. You look after *your* end and I'll take care of mine. Is that all you want of me? How do you know Miles? What sort of trouble have you got him into? He's not the sort to do this kind of thing on his own. To upset anyone with that capability. *Me*, yes. Him? No chance. It's like the Pope smoking pot.'

'The details are none of your business. Our interests are aligned on this one and I'm just trying to ensure he survives, gets to return to his gaming. Are we doing it, or what?' Sam asked, forcefully.

'We are. But know this; Miles is a good sort. Heart of gold. It's only because of him that we can work together, just this once. I don't *ever* want to see you again after we're through, ya feel me? And if you wrong him, or me, there *will* be consequences!'

'Good to know,' Sam replied, not too impressed but going with the flow. 'Now, take this scrap of paper. I want you to type it word for word. No variation at all. Send it to the e-mail addresses on the reverse side. Just follow the instructions.'

'Consider it done.'

Sam wasted no time in vacating the flat. She drew in some deep breaths of almost fresh air the very moment she stepped outside, then drove back to her uncle's house and grabbed the bag of guns that had been supplied very kindly by Owen James, sat down at the kitchen table next to Jenny and Miles.

'Is it done?' asked Miles, his eyes bright and alert and looking much better.

'It is.'

'Great. She's a total babe, isn't she?' he said, perfectly serious. 'Her parents are rich beyond belief you know. That's why she has her mail sent to a Post Office box. Hides the address and foils kidnap attempts. She's dated pop stars and actors in the past. Not surprising with that Coke bottle body of hers. I've seen her online in some magazine pictures, looking gorgeous at premieres and galas and that.'

Did he say Coke bottle, or Coke can? Sam thought to herself.

'Err... I'm really not much of a judge in these matters, but yes, yes, she's quite something alright. Very slim,' she answered, trying to keep a straight face.

Just how had *The Minxster* pulled that off?

'So, we're on. It's gone then?' asked Jenny.

'Yes. The first three e-mails went to Chief Constable Elizabeth Barker, her secretary, and DCI James Darling.'

'Okay. Why that particular group first?' Miles asked.

'Secretaries are notorious for gossip. Just in case I might be doing this particular person a great disservice and stereotyping though, we know that either the Chief, or James Darling, are dirty. Or both.'

'How do you figure?' questioned Jenny.

'Police instincts. And because our investigation from the very beginning was plagued by problems. Delays in communication, the blocks put in place, the little things I did not see at the time as issues, they all add up. It was anything to slow us down. Only two ranks at that time had the authority and access to pull that off. The man in charge of the Incident Room. Or the lady at the very top.'

'Sounds plausible. Did you keep a copy of the text?' Jenny added.

'No need. It was as we agreed. I don't have a photographic memory like some, but it's not far off. I have it up here,' Sam replied, pointing at her head. 'It read...

This is Miles Dalton. I am alive and well. I have what you seek. All the evidence you will ever need. I will come in and hand myself over to police custody.

But only if Jennifer Pearce is allowed to walk away free and unharmed. If she is ever hurt or threatened in any way, all deals are off and I will go straight to the press. Otherwise, I promise I will remain silent.

I have captured your Detective Sergeant Lennox and am holding her at gunpoint. She is innocent of any wrongdoing. She was trying to help when I overpowered her. She is now locked up with Jenny at a safe location, which I will divulge once I am taken into custody and out of harm's way.

The meet – 11AM tomorrow. I will be alone and unarmed. You will receive an e-mail exactly one hour before this time with all the details.

I place myself under your protection.

With the first of the e-mails despatched and instructions left for the rest, Sam handed out the weapons and gave both parties some rudimentary training in the handling of guns. For Miles it was almost a refresher, having fired a variety on ranges in the USA. He also appeared to pick things up increasingly fast. Before long, he was looking like a seasoned pro.

Sam disappeared with the HK 417 DMR - or Designated Marksman Rifle – plus a box of 175 grain Sierra Matchking ammunition. She drove to an abandoned quarry, set up a small range and had a little fun, careful not to stay too long in case anyone reported the noise. Though, with a suppressor mounted, she wasn't overly concerned.

With the Vortex Strike Eagle 1-8x24 scope zeroed, she arrived back at the house around teatime carrying two gigantic pizzas. As they ate that evening and enjoyed what could possibly be their last night on earth, they discussed what might happen the following morning.

'How do you know for certain that the news will reach the right people, and that they will take the bait?' enquired Miles.

'I suppose I don't, for *certain*,' admitted Sam. 'Just to make sure, the exact same message was *also* sent to the Deputy Head of MI5. I only met Mitch Lovell once and to be honest, I'm not sure what to make of him. We're short on allies though. These guys who have tried to take you out have already tracked your cars, turned up everywhere, whatever you did to evade them. They've monitored police chatter too I believe. They have proficiencies beyond the norm. I'm as confident as I can be that they will show. And as a little extra surprise, I also sent it to an old pal of mine who heads the Trojan firearm teams around here. That's our armed police units. More friendly fire, I hope.'

'Excellent. Another old army buddy?' asked Miles.

'Nah, Navy actually. Good sort though. Met him in police training.'

Jenny reached over to grab another slice of pizza. 'That all sounds good, Sam. I'm surprised I'm able to eat like this. My stomach is a mess but I'm famished. How'd you make out with the weapon?'

'So-so. I'm a bit rusty. Haven't fired one like that for a good while.'

'Oh great!' cracked Miles. 'I'm trusting you two with my life you know. *Rusty?* What does *that* mean?'

'Nothing. Don't worry yourself. I'm sure I'll be fine tomorrow, when it matters,' Sam answered, winking at Jenny, '...I think.'

Miles seemed to lose a little colour from his cheeks. He gulped down the food in his mouth and then responded by saying, 'If... If I don't get the chance tomorrow, if things turn to rat poo, I just want to say that I'm immensely grateful for all you have done. All that you have agreed to do. I'm pretty certain I've never met anyone quite like you before, Sam. I think you're my new avatar actually. You'll make a great heroine for one of my games.'

'Yeah,' Jenny agreed. 'Bit warped, when he puts it like that, and I don't know quite how to take you at times, but we'd certainly be stone-cold dead without you, that's for sure.'

Sam put down her food and took a sip of her drink. 'Enough of the mushy stuff, please? You're both very welcome... I suppose I am built differently to most. My mind works on a level that I've always known might get me killed. I don't see the danger others do. Tend to rush into contact, when I *should* be running or diggin' in. Or I'm not afraid of it at least. *Enjoy* it almost... You want the truth though? I have an opportunity here to take down those who killed DCI Farley. A decent guy trying to make a difference. I'm not passing that up. I *also* get to set my sights on some corrupt coppers and more. Take out several huge threats to national security. Who knows, possibly to prevent an arms race, or World War Three? Basically, I will be upholding the law, protecting the weak, and making the world a better place. *Exactly* as I'm meant to do. What's not to love?'

'Oi! I ain't *that* much of a geek, Jen!' protested Miles.

He broke out into a grin almost immediately and winked at her, before addressing Sam again. 'And you! When you put it like that, maybe *you* should be thanking me?'

The next morning, at a disused industrial estate fourteen miles north of St Albans that Sam had reconnoitred on her way to see The Minxster, Lennox drove them around and around in the A4 pointing out the layout, as well as the range to her hide and several locations she had planted weapons, time and again, just in case. A host of derelict units were arranged around a large square that used to be the car park, now festooned with grass and weeds growing through the concrete and tarmac. This was designated the Killing Ground and she'd divided it up into grids, worked out ranges, arcs of fire etc. Debris of all sorts littered the place, providing reference points. Metal drums had been upended and now contained the remnants of old fires. Burnt-out cars and bikes were abandoned here and there and had become play things for the local youth. The square was overlooked by an old Victorian factory building which was several stories high and safe from demolition courtesy of its Grade 1 Listed status, though long since devoid of life apart from the occasional squatters, or homeless persons seeking shelter at night. Because of this, the place contained numerous items of discarded furniture and bedding. Sam eventually took them up to the top floor, carrying the remaining weapons. From there, she had an excellent view of the approaches and surrounding area, as well as the square itself. This was enhanced for Jenny, who had been handed a small set of binoculars that Sam's uncle had actually once taken to war with him.

The trap was almost set. It was ten o'clock by the time Sam had completed her guided tour and the final e-mails would be going out. Lennox went over the plan one more time. Inside the factory was a pile of blue, wooden pallets. These were carried over towards a window which offered a commanding view. They were set down a good twenty feet back from the opening, to conceal the shooter in the darkness and hide any muzzle flash or smoke. The 417 was set up in such a way that Sam would be able to fire from the prone position, lying on top of a few sheets of cardboard, which they had topped the pallets off with. It was soon time for Miles to make his way to his position. He carried an old Browning High Power pistol at the small of his back. As well as a five-shot .38 Smith & Wesson Airweight revolver shoved into a pair of Uncle Wayne's bright red football socks that he'd borrowed. In his right jacket pocket was a Benchmade Infidel automatic knife.

'You sure about this?' asked Sam. 'There's still time to back out but it has to be now.'

He was scared, she could tell. His hands were shaking a little, though he appeared to be handling his probable demise far better than most would have, in the circumstances.

'Do or die,' he answered. 'Isn't that what you hero types say at times like this? No retreat, no surrender? That sort of thing?'

'In the movies maybe. Not in real life. At least, not the heroes I've had the pleasure of knowing. Though, I don't believe any would agree with the use of that word. Let others talk of heroes if they choose. We squaddies just want to make it home alive, nothing more. To do our jobs. Protect the guy or gal to our left and right.'

Miles held out his hand and she shook it gratefully. 'Good enough for me. Let's just see what happens? Can't go on like this. It's killing my social life.'

Jenny laughed along with him, gave him a big kiss and a hug, said, 'One way or another, it will all be over soon. Thanks for keeping me alive. Just you keep your head down and come back to me, okay? We're friends now, *good* friends, and nothing's gonna change that.'

Chapter 21

Miles left the relative safety of the old factory and drove the A4 into the very centre of the square, reversed it to within twelve feet or so of the open rear units and switched off the engine, so that it was facing the entrance and exit. The only other route in and out of the small complex had been blocked off years ago by the council with the addition of concrete bollards. A gentle wind whistled its way around the empty shells of the abandoned buildings and vehicles. No sound could be heard otherwise and Miles began to feel completely alone, exposed. Mainly because he *was*. It was a hopeless task almost certain to have no happy ending. He was bait, a sacrificial lamb, pure and simple, had volunteered on that basis and accepted whatever might happen. But that didn't stop his beating heart racing like a thoroughbred at Ascot. He was parched, his stomach weak, the palms of his hands clammy as he stared up at the sun in the sky and wondered if he would ever see another.

Jenny was watching the approach road avidly through the binoculars. Her hands were visibly trembling and she looked pale. Sam's trained eyes could not help but notice and she decided that she ought to say something.

'Hey, how you doing? Just try to relax. I know it's hard, but try to concentrate on the job in hand. You're nervous and scared, that's all, because it's a new experience for you. That's only natural. You'll be fine once the action starts, trust me. Do as we discussed, stick to the plan and don't deviate in any way. Call out any suspected enemy as a *Tango*. Try to feed me numbers and descriptions as they arrive, like blonde hair, red top or something, direction and distance… Short and sweet. Nice and clear. No mumbling and no waffle. Don't over-complicate things. If they look like they might be on our side, call them out as *Friendlies*. But identify them for me either way, so I can make the decision for myself using the scope. Remember, above all, I *hate* surprises. I'll have tunnel vision. You're the only one seeing the bigger picture. If you don't spot them, they will be quickly amongst us and we're done for. I'm relying on you, and so is Miles.'

'Oh, thanks. No pressure then? We've been through all this already. I'll do my best. It's just that…'

Through the silence, the faint rumble of approaching vehicles sounded to interrupt their little pep talk. Nerves vanished rapidly, replaced by tension and fear. Moments later, Jenny began her day's work.

'Tango's incoming! Two times Range Rovers, it looks like. On the road some way out. Half a mile maybe?'

'Excellent. Keep it coming just like that. Our guests are a little early. Hope they've brought a bottle. Yes, I see them,' Sam replied calmly, picking the hostiles up on the scope of her HK 417 DMR. She sighted the driver of the lead vehicle, followed him all the way in. 'Let them come. I have these guys. You look for others… *Miles*, the first group are arriving in two vehicles. I have eyes on,' she added coolly into the microphone of her PTT, or Push-To-Talk radio set.

Sam had acquired some cheap walkie talkies and earpieces from a nearby click and collect retailer so they could maintain direct contact. These were very much basic items, in no way military standard, but they would function adequately at such short notice and over the limited range. For everything else, she was grateful once again to Owen James and his choice of equipment. She flicked the scope of the excellent rifle quickly to Miles, saw him touch his earpiece gently and nod his head. Message understood.

The Range Rovers had blackened windows and they sped into the square just as planned. Sam let them enter, not wishing to give away her position too early and reasoning that the opening exchange would be verbal and need to be heard. They came to an abrupt halt around fifteen yards away from Miles. The passenger door opened swiftly and one of the largest hulks Miles had ever seen, earbud prominent in his left ear, exited the vehicle. The stranger looked all around warily as he walked to within six feet and then stopped. He looked Miles up and down slowly, as if he were complete trash.

'The elusive, *Miles Dalton*, I presume?' he enquired, in a loud, authoritative, snobby voice clearly used to command.

Miles answered with a simple, 'Correct.'

'Good. Nice to see you are a man of your word. I am from British Military Intelligence. You are to come with me quickly, if you want to live. We must leave this place right now. There are others en route and it will not be good if they find us together.'

Miles stood firm. 'Nah, I'm not moving until I see some I.D. and have some assurances. I have no way of knowing that you are who you say you are, and I'm not prepared to take that chance.'

The suited and booted man-mountain appeared severely disappointed with his response. 'Very well. We do this here then. You have something of value to us I believe? Do you have it on you?'

'Yes, it's...'

'Gut! Then I don't need you alive!'

The pointman tried to pull out the weapon in his shoulder holster with astounding speed but a 7.62mm round holed the back of his head before his fingers touched metal, smashing into his brain. His body tumbled to the ground and Miles drew the Glock 19 from his belt, raced to take cover behind his parked car. Two more supposed MI5 operators exited the Range Rovers and were cut down by Sam in just the same way, without mercy, a superb demonstration of deadly accurate sniper fire. The remaining occupants hesitated but when single shots began to pepper the vehicles too close for comfort, smashing glass and slicing through the metal exteriors, those still breathing inside decided to take their chances out in the open. Of the eight original occupants, four now joined the fight in the square, some carrying wounds and all firing directly at Miles, the only target they could actually see and identify. One began talking rapidly into a comms set or phone, summoning further assistance.

The blood in Miles' veins was tingling now alright. Adrenalin was coursing through his entire body and he was alive and alert in a way he had *never* been before. Speed of thought and action were brutally enhanced. The weapon in his hand felt like an extension of his own limb, a part of him now as familiar as his thumb or finger. So much so, that he hardly had to think to point the thing, instinctively knowing for certain that his aim would be true and the target would fall. He downed the nearest two unknown aggressors without thought, hardly blinking at an action he probably never thought himself capable of, prior to boarding that train, ducked out from behind the motor and loosed off two rounds for each, hitting them centre mass, putting them out of action for good, like he was slaying cattle in an abattoir.

He watched as the third was nearly cut in two at the neck by Lennox, then dived to the ground, rolled swiftly over and put one in the centre of the fourth guy's forehead. It was a blindingly fast manoeuvre that really belonged in the movies or a game and as he darted back behind cover, Miles surveyed the carnage ahead of him with complete astonishment. Mere seconds had past but dead bodies and gore lay everywhere. Smoke was billowing from one of the gang's vehicles and the entire place was deathly quiet once again.

Miles, however, found to his surprise that he was perfectly calm and hardly out of breath, fully focussed.

The earpiece sounded with a voice he recognised, though it too was evidently the reaction of a person overcome with shock.

'How did you...? Miles, either that gaming is an excellent training tool, or you have just... I don't know what you did. I would never have believed it, if I hadn't witnessed it for myself,' Sam remarked. 'When did you learn to...?'

Jenny interrupted her again, screaming excitedly, 'More! There's more of them!'

Sam turned to focus on the road. 'Call it!' she barked.

'Sorry. Black Transit inbound, almost on us. And there's a dark coloured saloon behind it.'

'Targets acquired... *Miles*, you have more company and not much time. They're close and will be able to see you soon. Might be an idea to play dead.'

Miles immediately sprinted over to where some of the alleged MI5 agents had fallen. He slapped a load of blood on the back of his head and lay down on his stomach, his legs twisted and the Glock in his hand tucked firmly out of sight. As the transit entered the square, Sam put a nice neat hole in the driver's head, who died instantly. The van careered into one of the burnt-out vehicles and smashed into an empty unit. The rear doors flew open almost immediately and around six guys jumped out. Another exited via the passenger door. Sam dropped one at the rear of the group for certain, wounded another, but then Jenny suddenly wrenched her attention away.

'Another four Tangos! One is female. Exiting the car short of the square. They're looking straight at us!'

'Stay calm. They must have been in contact with the first ones to arrive. Keep watching and shouting, but draw your sidearm just in case.'

'Err... Okay,' replied Jenny, taking up the Cobray M11/9 machine pistol she had been handed back at the house. 'One of them is looking in the boot.'

'I see him. Oh no you don't!' said Sam, and fired a well-aimed shot straight through his upper torso which took him completely off his feet. The others went to ground in the nearby rubble and vegetation rapidly, began skirmishing towards her location.

She fired again, caught another in the leg as he ran.

'Yah! I hate it when they know what they're doing. You'll need to do more than spot now, I'm afraid. Take the far window. You should have a good shot from there as they approach. They'll be close and bunch up as they look to breach. That thing fires a lot of rounds in short order. As soon as you spot them, hose them down with all you have and then move back here immediately afterwards. Hopefully, you'll hit something. I'll try to help Miles for as long as I can.'

In the square, their silent comrade was trying to keep perfectly still as the bemused crooks searched everywhere for their prey. Miles heard shots being fired but not impacts, realised that it was Sam otherwise engaged. Reckoned he was alone with at least five enemy in his immediate vicinity, closing in on him fast. He decided to wait it out but didn't give much for his chances, began praying that Sam could free herself and come once again to his aid. He was just beginning to lose hope as the sound of two henchmen nearby made him tighten his grip on his weapon, when Lennox unexpectedly opened up again with the DMR and a couple of their comrades further away were slotted. Miles figured that was about as good as it was going to get by way of assistance and he sprang into action with amazing speed and ferocity. The lead guy was only a foot away from him. The stranger's eyes widened in fear and extreme alarm as the body on the ground ahead came to life, and two bullets ruptured his heart. Another landed squarely between his eyes and almost simultaneously, Miles twisted his entire torso and put three into the next closest; two in the chest and one in the head.

Tripple tapped. Astounding, almost legendary close quarter drills from a man who had never seen combat before.

Next, Miles turned over and flinched a little as the only guy left standing fired his weapon and sliced off a little of his left ear. More rounds zipped off the concrete at his feet, missing by inches, as the frantic assailant who had witnessed the extraordinary downing of his comrades rushed his shots. Miles rose hastily now and scurried away into the darkness of the nearest unit, more incoming trailing his run. Once inside, he turned and dropped to one knee, waiting for the shooter to follow.

Jenny was doing as asked. From the window but far enough back in the shadows, she watched the two military-trained operators work their way steadily and professionally towards the factory, no doubt with orders to eliminate the sniper team. As soon as they were out in the open, once they made to enter the building itself, she jumped forwards and up like a Jack-in-the-box, squeezed the trigger of her machine pistol emptying the entire magazine and sweeping it from left to right and back again, until it all fell silent. The thing kicked like a mule and she had to fight to keep it steady but it was all over in a flash. Thirty rounds don't last long on full auto.

The male of the two was a little slower in finding cover and a lucky shot caught his hip. He fell and dragged himself into the greenery, screaming like a maniac. His female counterpart, however, waited for the gun to empty and then darted into the building at speed.

'I missed her! She's inside! Tango inside the building!' screamed Jenny.

'Right. Over here now! Do what you can with this. Fire at anything that moves. Except Miles, obviously. Keep their heads down. Leave her to me,' Sam ordered, still remarkably, annoyingly, cool.

Back in the square, things were getting dangerous. Only a fool enters a darkened room without altering their silhouette or possessing *serious* firepower. And this guy was no fool. He was though, desperate to complete his mission and on the clock. He needed to ensure that he beat others to the main prize. Consequently, he rounded the entrance crouching low and fired his weapon blindly into the gloom, hoping to put Miles on the back foot, or for a fluky kill. However, his targeted victim was ready and waiting for him like a man possessed, his mind working overtime and skills he never knew he had, racing to the fore. Miles predicted the action and flung himself down to the ground, raising his arms and firing twice, even before a third bullet had left the attacker's gun. Both deadly projectiles sent by the enlivened fugitive struck the luckless would-be killer in the stomach. He fell in a crumpled heap. Miles checked his magazine. Almost empty. He put one in the guy's head and reached for the Sig Sauer P365 taped to his back, winced as the tape tore at his skin. It wasn't enough. He needed something heavier, to make it to one of the stashes Sam had shown him. Pistols were fine when facing isolated targets but he knew he was outgunned here against trained opponents with serious hardware. He gazed out onto the open square to find there was a momentary lull in firing and decided to make good use of it.

Jenny had positioned herself behind the sniper rifle as instructed, though she had absolutely no idea what she was doing, other than firing as Sam had shown her. The gun was zeroed in for Lennox at long range and was therefore pretty much useless anyway. She turned to yell at her partner that she had just spotted two red SUV's racing towards the square, but Sam was nowhere to be seen.

In fact, Lennox was now using all of her considerable experience and skill to stalk an assassin of her own. One who had already proven her ability entering the factory. Sam was taking no chances. The hired gun was most definitely already on the floor below, working her way up. Lennox could hear movement on the stairs, inching relentlessly forwards in a cautious but determined fashion.

The private merc took the steps one at a time, weapon outstretched, ready to spit death. She was packing a Glock 19, with a surefire weapon light she put to good use clearing the dark corners of the stairway and halls. As she reached the top step and her cover was exhausted, she had no choice but to expose herself. Just in the nick of time, she ducked down low as two bullets smacked into the concrete behind her.

'You cow!' the mercenary snarled, and the impressive fighting machine was up fast. *Very* fast. Hammering rounds at Sam's muzzle flash, zipping them at her head and moving aside as Sam was sent scampering for cover.

Lennox altered her position, moved to a nearby pillar, only just making it in time. Tiny missiles of death followed her every move and chunks of masonry and dust exploded into the air. The sounds were deafening. She returned the compliment and it soon became a high-class game of cat and mouse, with Sam unsure if she was Tom, or Jerry. If she had *finally* met her match.

'Why can't you just be a good little bitch and die?!' the mercenary called out, followed by more shots as she raced forward at speed trying to close the distance between her and her prey.

Sam knew what she was up against now. She withdrew a little, into the vast second floor office complex, invited her on. Distance and angle was what she needed. The semi-open plan office had a few old desks and file cabinets dotted around the centre of the room. Doors had been kicked off hinges and the walls were covered with graffiti. She did a quick ammo check. Only three rounds left. She instinctively reached for the spare magazine that should have been on her left hip, only to find nothing there, and she almost swore.

Somewhere ahead, broken glass crunched under military boots. The white light of a weapon was sweeping the room vigilantly. Sam pulled out her zippo lighter. She tossed it the length of the office and it clattered off a filing cabinet. Instantly, metal disintegrated as the cabinet was lit up by a hail of bullets. Sam's weapon was up fast scanning for the shooter and she caught a glimpse of her shadow as she ducked back into cover, followed momentarily by the metallic clank of a spent magazine hitting the ground. A moment later an audible click sounded.

'Oh-oh. You're running low,' Sam called out into the darkness, in desperation trying to make her opponent do something stupid.

'No,' came the staunch reply, 'but it's telling, that you should ask. How many do *you* have left?'

The mercenary, safe behind a pillar and with a fresh magazine now in her weapon, took a moment to remove her jacket, skilfully swapping the pistol from one hand to the next. Hot work. Her physique was beyond impressive, the result of countless hours of hard gym work. Her heavily tattooed arms and shoulders were huge and she had a black sleeveless tee, over a low-profile bullet-proof vest. Skinny jeans showed of her honed glutes and thighs and short blonde hair slicked back on top, shaved at the sides, made her *really* look the part. With a couple of gulps of air, she sprinted to the next support and slid into cover. Her next three rounds sent pieces of masonry flying off the pillar protecting Sam. She was now only one column away.

Sam was empty, literally backed into a corner, with nowhere to run. She scanned around in the gloom, spied the fire exit and made a dash for it, but she was halted in her tracks by a thick chain and padlock barring her escape.

The hired killer goaded her now. 'Why don't you just come out? I'll make it quick. Pinky promise.'

Sam said nothing, her mind racing, trying desperately to come up with a solution.

The merc once again stepped out from behind cover, this time with her weapon outstretched. She fired with each step and advanced relentlessly. Soon, she'd reached the pillar she was sure Sam was taking cover behind and darted out, firing into a blank space. Bemused, she scanned around frantically.

Then, it hit her, literally, as Sam whacked the leg of an old desk across her back.

The force of the blow was enough to send the muscled freak sprawling to the floor, the weapon sent flying from her grip. Sam readied a follow-up blow and moved in, but her opponent somehow recovered in time to deliver a kick of her own, into Sam's knee, that sent her reeling backwards.

The killer was up speedily and now her blood was boiling. She reached into her rear pocket and produced a knuckle duster, which she slipped onto her right fist, a glimmer of a smile on her face.

'Let's dance,' she spat out as she swung for Sam.

Sam knew immediately that if she was clocked with that steal fist, she'd had it. This girl was massive, at least when compared to her, with arms that looked like they could tear the horn off a rhino. The blonde-haired killer threw fast jabs and hooks, her footwork excellent. Clearly, she boxed to a high standard. It was as much as Sam could manage to defend herself with the length of wood she was clinging on to for dear life. Then her chance finally came. Her opponent, in a bid to make an opening, threw a roundhouse kick but Sam anticipated this and swung her improvised club down onto the killer's shin. She heard the wood meet bone and blondie instantly screamed in pain, her tibia most likely fractured. Unperturbed though, she hopped and grimaced as she tested the weight on her damaged leg.

This move had levelled the playing field.

'MI5?' Sam asked, expecting and receiving no reply. 'Is it *me* you're here for? Or him?'

'You? Don't make me laugh. *You* are small fry. You're in the way, is all. Though, the Headshed can't understand your reasons for sticking your neck out so far, over a lost cause. It concerns them. Makes you a loose end in need of tying off.'

'Maybe I'm just a Good Samaritan?'

'Possibly. Then again, *perhaps* you're just a fool! Military?'

'Yep. *Was*. You?'

The lone fighter nodded her head and smirked.

'We probably fought on the same side then?' said Sam.

'It's possible. Though not anymore.'

Further discussion was pointless and they both knew it. Sam raised her fists and beckoned her adversary on. The blonde beast then rushed her, tackling Lennox around the waist and the pair went sailing through an office window, ended in a heap on the floor, each desperately trying to out-manoeuvre the other. The power of this woman was something to behold. Sam has sparred against many of her male colleagues in the army but few had hit with such force. She desperately needed to land a decisive blow, and to do it *now*.

She found one.

Sam grabbed an old and discarded biro from the floor in the tussle and started attacking the blonde in the face and neck. An agonising scream told her that the pen had found its mark, puncturing the left eye of her attacker. This sent the hulk scuttling backwards but Sam was not letting up. She was on the front foot for the first time in this fight and she wasn't relenting. She unleashed a devastating front kick which caught her foe straight under the chin.

Unbelievably, she *still* didn't go down.

An astonished and exhausted Sam moved in, wailed on her groggy adversary with her right fist. Blow after blow after blow rained down on the larger woman's face. She almost seemed to be grinning at her. Enraged, Sam lunged for a piece of broken glass on the floor from the smashed window frames they had fallen through, forced it deep into her neck.

To Sam's amazement, the disorientated, battered merc still tried meekly to throw punches, though by now the power and ferocity had vanished as the life drained from her. Lennox used all her weight to ram the glass in further. A second later, all movement had ceased. Game over.

Chapter 22

Miles rushed across open ground making for the nearest of the burnt oil drums, firing the remaining bullets in his Sig Sauer P365 at the oncoming vehicles. He managed to smash the windscreens of both, bringing them to a crashing halt. Whilst the occupants tried to escape glass and tin coffins, their now unarmed prey searched for deliverance. Atop the old cinders and ash within the drum, he discovered to his delight a H & K MP7A2 compact machine gun, along with two spare thirty-round magazines. Miles hoisted them upwards like a professional soldier and fired immediately in the general vicinity of any enemy standing, trying to make them search for cover. Then he shifted his aim to the new vehicles. Bodies were appearing fast now from all corners, exiting rapidly. He was just about to open fire again, when a sudden and unexpected shot rang out in the nearby distance. A burnt-out car on the other side of the square, which was well away from Miles himself and his current woes, nowhere near *any* of the hostiles he faced, was inexplicably holed with a loud bang.

Even with his current distractions Miles couldn't help but raise his eyebrows at such a strange development. 'Jeez, Sam!' he hissed into the microphone of his PTT. 'Put your glasses back on, will ya? That was a bit wayward. What you shooting at over there? There's nobody left alive,'

'Nuh-uh,' came an instant reply from an out of breath Lennox, who was at that time rushing back to aid her civvy spotter. 'Wasn't me.'

'Sorry!' Jenny called out. She worked the action on the rifle with some difficulty in order to load another round. 'I was just trying to help.'

'No, that's fine. Good. Keep it up. Only, don't point that thing anywhere near me,' quipped Miles.

The SUV's occupants had decamped in all the confusion and soon they began targeting Miles with sustained and accurate fire. Another shot ricocheted off the concrete well away from their location and this seemed to embolden the attackers. Eight fresh combatants were soon closing in fast. The situation had changed dramatically in such a short space of time and it now looked increasingly dire for Miles, as more bullets began to slice through the air all around him, zipping about like fireflies. He returned their fire somehow. Sent murderous, unbelievably accurate single shots and controlled bursts, of the kind usually only seen in combat vets. He hit one in his knee and another in his arm, darted across the compound the short distance to his car and took refuge behind it. Popped out almost immediately to catch them by surprise as they advanced and caught another in his side, before diving back behind cover to catch his breath.

'Sam! Don't mean to interrupt but it's getting a little hot down here and I could do with a little help?' he pleaded, sweat dripping from his brow.

The thin metal skin of the Audi pinged and zapped as round after round hit home and holed it like a cullender. It was miraculous that the bullets making it through had not wounded him and only a matter of time before they fired underneath the car itself, set it ablaze or worked their way around. So, Miles decided to risk all in a suicidal move and he launched himself at the entrance to the nearest unit. He reached the door even though he had no idea how he was still alive and he was soon safely inside, the brickwork around the entrance completely disintegrating in places under the weight of fire brought down upon it.

A grenade landed close, rolled to a stop at his feet. He picked it up without thought or delay and hurled it straight back, killing and maiming several of the fighters closing in for the kill. The others kept moving forwards however, relentless in their determination to end him. Miles was running out of options. They were so near that he heard their kit jangling as they ran and he knew his time had come. He could do nothing but face them head on. He inhaled deeply and then let out a resigned breath, prepared to die.

'Bang! Bang! Bang!'

Miles had stepped up to the opening, his MP7 ready to deal carnage in one final act of heroism. However, Sam Lennox had at last regained control of the sniper rifle and she downed the nearest attackers with three rapid single shots.

Miles had a reprieve. He gave thanks to the British Army and its high-quality training, as well as the extremely high calibre of its former employee. What a formidable woman she was.

The remainder of this desperate group of unknowns all bore wounds of some description. Many were calling out in pain and no longer a threat but others still had fight in them, were reaching for their weapons. Miles slotted all those reaching without an ounce of forgiveness. The remainder were granted clemency though, instructed to jump into the nearest SUV, to leave without delay or die on whatever piece of ground they occupied.

They chose survival. Left their weapons and comms behind and made a pitiful sight as they withdrew in pieces from a lone operator and his one-gun support. The least seriously wounded merc drove them away with some difficulty, leaving Miles and a string of corpses alone in the square. The silence was temporary, he knew that. And all the more deafening for it.

'Apologies for being late to that one,' Sam offered, as the parched and exhausted bait in the killing ground watched them go, scarcely able to believe he was still relatively unscathed. 'Had a spot of bother with a rather stubborn old grunt.'

'That so? Old grunt, eh? You can tell me all about it later. Any more of 'em Jen?' he asked.

'Yes. 'Fraid so,' she replied, straight away. 'I was just about to holler. There's a green estate of some description just appeared on the rise, coming your way at speed.'

'No rest for the not so wicked then, is it? Why not? Bring 'em on. We're taking on allcomers today,' Miles answered.

He watched the car career towards him and skid up close to the remaining SUV. The front doors opened swiftly and the passenger dived out, forward rolled into a firing position and sent flashes of hot metal hurtling in his direction.

Slick manoeuvre. Good skills. No wasted effort or time.

Miles had tried to conserve his ammo and dived for cover once again. The tanned and proficient female shooter was joined by her male counterpart almost immediately, who decamped on the driver's side of their vehicle. Miles only caught a flashing glimpse of his face, hair and body but he recognised him instantly as the murderer from the London train. His blood boiled and his lips curled as he came face to face at last with the guy who had so callously slayed the brother he would never get the chance to know.

The contract killers moved and ran at speed, exchanged several rounds with Miles until it was clear that nobody had a clear shot. When the firing had died down a little, the male assassin shouted out in a loud South American accent.

'Hola, Miles! Como estas, mi amigo? I was wondering if I see you again. Why you no step out into the open to greet me? We can have a little hablar, si? Sorry for your hermano, your brother. You know how these things go. Iss no personal. A job, is a job, no? We make the most of what skills we have.'

Miles raised his weapon intending to shut him up permanently but he could hardly see the guy as he dared to peak round the entrance to the unit. He needed to play for time.

'You didn't have to kill him. You'll pay for that!' he hollered back in frustration, trying to come up with something, his mind fogged by fury and swamped by too many thoughts rushing him all at once. 'You should have finished me back on that train, when you had the chance.'

That was better.

'Si, Miles, you iss correct. I no pay you close enough attention. Mi culpa. I have to answer for zat error in judgement. No to worry. You have granted a second bite of cherry, as you say? Esta todo bien. I'm here now.'

'Yes, I see that. Thanks for showing up. Tell me, what's it all for?' asked Miles, checking once again on the movements of both parties. 'I'm about to die, so do a lad a favour, won't you? Indulge me, seeing as you're so chatty? What's all this about?'

'Dinero. Why, *money*, of course. What else is there, for you and I?'

'No, I wasn't talking about... Beyond *that* I mean. You're risking way too much for just making some cash. Your neck's on the line. Death, or a lifetime in prison if caught, and there's the entire world chasing you. There *has* to be more to it. Why don't you grant my last request? Come on? We're nothing special. Why is it that we have to die?'

There was a slight hesitation as the assassin's partner started working her way around the bodies and wreckage to the right whilst the train murderer kept Miles engaged, flanking her kill.

'You know northing, do you?' the Latino suddenly blurted out, sounding almost surprised and deliberately distracting his foe. 'Nada. You are Jon Snow.'

'Know? What should I know?'

'Iss no for me to say. But seeing as you preguntar, *ask*, so nicely... You're *it*, Miles!'

'*It?* What does that mean?'

'Imbecil… You have no brain cell. It was *you* all this time. The target. We assumed it was your brother. We were, equivocado. Um, mistaken. It came as a nasty shock. Especially, as I had you in my sights, let you escape. We were on back foot. Changed everything. All our plans up in fumar. We readjust our aim since. You see, we think the job was done. I no leave otherwise.'

Miles was engrossed now. So much so, that he almost missed the sly female operative who had sneaked up on him to within an unhealthy distance, a position on his left from where she had a clear shot, or could toss a grenade.

Almost missed.

A sixth sense of impending doom made him glance in that direction. Though he knew not from whence it came, it most certainly saved his life. He scurried forwards and two rounds intended for his torso whistled past so close, that they actually shaved his jacket. He fired a solitary bullet in her direction in reply and in no time, the luckless would-be slayer dropped to the ground, blood oozing from her left eye and a decent portion of her head at the rear now missing.

The enraged Latino used the distraction this afforded him to launch an attack of his own. Miles was exposed by his evasive action and the killer's first bullet caught him high where his chest met his shoulder. The power of the blow made him swivel and most men would have been unable to correct the subsequent fall, powerless to save themselves from the inevitable follow-up.

However, Miles Dalton was not *most men*. Not now. He, by some miracle, succeeded in controlling his gun hand and fired from an impossible angle, holing the Hispanic agent in the gut just as he sent his second shot. Miles then hit the ground hard. The bullet missed and the wounded hitman fell to his knees, lifted his weapon one final time to finish the now helpless Miles off.

A solitary 7.62mm projectile once again crashed through skin, blood, bone and brain, taking everything with it, the suction created impossible to avoid. The assassin lurched sidewards, before dwindling to a motionless, silent heap and oozing copious quantities of the red stuff.

Wounded badly, Miles was nevertheless stunned to have survived this fight. He gazed up to see Sam exposing her head and shoulders deliberately, from behind one of the cars in the square, and the reason for her inaction and silence of late became immediately apparent. She'd spotted the extreme danger he was facing and left the safety of her concealed and elevated position in the factory. Which was *madness*. Sheer madness. She'd deliberately and knowingly exposed herself to colossal risk, unnecessarily putting her life on the line. For *him*.

Again.

Sam was now holding out her smoking gun like a Wild West gunslinger with his Remington 1875 Frontier pistol, having just survived the skirmish at the O.K. Coral.

'*That* was... sublime,' he stated, unable to think of anything else to say and sounding a little more like his old self. 'Absolutely lovin' your timing. I had begun to think I was done for and...'

'Heads up!' shrieked Jenny, still manning surveillance on overwatch, on Sam's orders. 'Get back into cover! Tangos! No, wait... Friendlies?! No... I don't know which. Two, no four, no *six*... *Multiple* vehicles approaching with sirens wailing. Police. Must be. They're almost on top of us!'

Sam cast her eyes around and then looked straight at Miles. 'Well, they have us with our pants down this time. There's no point moving now, not in this condition. Not from those kind of numbers. We may as well stay where we are. The game's up,' she admitted with a heavy heart, great concern evident in the way she spoke into the PTT. 'We're in the lap of the Gods now. I'm not certain there is such a thing as *Friendlies* anymore, Jenny. Not sure I know how to tell them apart from hostiles anyway. It's not right, but the lines are blurred. I only hope that we're about to welcome the decent kind. We're outgunned, out of choices. We *could* fight on, but that would only mean certain death. I'd rather trust to fate. It *ends* here. One way or another. Agreed?'

Miles slowly moved his head up and down. He held his ear for a moment, which was burning fiercely like you wouldn't believe. Then, he put his hand to his shoulder. He looked down at the masses of blood as he pulled it away, threw his weapon to the ground, walked out to an open area away from any bodies or debris and with great difficulty, dropped to his knees. He placed both of his hands on his head as best he could, his open wounds leaking like a sieve as the vehicles approached and the sirens continued to wail.

Sam Lennox also discarded her sidearm. She moved to stand over him, ripped her sleeve and packed his shoulder wound to stem the bleeding. Then, she held her badge aloft for all to see, as if it might stem the slaughter. An array of motors packed into the square in the blink of an eye, sending dust flying everywhere. Others arrived in no time and surrounded the entire factory. The whole place looked like a war zone.

'Jenny! Don't resist! Discard your weapons quickly and don't make any sudden moves,' instructed Sam. 'Give them no excuse to...'

'Err... Yep. Hadn't planned to,' Jenny replied, sounding bullish, mightily relieved and also very, very scared at the same time somehow.

Within seconds, Miles and Sam had more weapons trained upon them than they could count. It was abundantly clear without a shadow of a doubt that if the order was given now, they would all be sent to oblivion.

Chapter 23

A mass of heavily armed police officers kept their fully loaded weapons trained on Miles Dalton whilst the paramedics treated his wounds. The cops were taking no chances, despite the fact that he was badly wounded and had already been thoroughly searched, found to have no concealed items. The medics patched him up as best they could but declared vehemently that he absolutely *had* to attend hospital for further expert treatment, to the intense disappointment and clear disgust of several of the officers present. It was a duty of care issue however and despite the forceful representations of the units deployed, the healthcare professionals defiantly stuck to their guns. Miles bore a nasty open wound to his upper chest/shoulder region, with probable debris inside, including splintered bone and fabric. The chances of infection were acute unless treated promptly and correctly which meant administering plasma and antibiotics. He had also lost a lot of blood and required a transfusion. DCI Tom Darling, who was temporarily in command, did not object as forcefully as the rest, though he selected four of his own officers for the escort and dished out instructions with some relish. One officer was to travel in the awaiting ambulance, the rest in an unmarked car following closely behind. Another two of his team were instructed to place Detective Sergeant Samantha Lennox under immediate arrest, which caused some disquiet among the onlooking crowd. One of their own.

'Oh no you don't! *None* of us are going anywhere with you!' objected Lennox, powerfully shrugging off the attentions of the two males trying to grab her arms and cuff her, making quite the scene.

DCI Darling then roared some more commands but a powerfully strong voice of supreme authority cracked over him like thunder, and the mutterings of the assembled horde ceased almost immediately. All heads turned in unison to investigate the source and looked upon a smartly attired senior officer striding across from an official-looking car, which had just been let through the cordon that had been set up.

'What the *hell* is going on here?!' he raged, the excessive volume employed clearly intended to emphasise that *he* was now assuming command. 'Two of our senior detectives putting on such a show? Is this the way the Met conducts itself in public? What is the meaning of this?!'

Mitch Lovell, Deputy Head of MI5, was a guy used to being obeyed. He gazed at Sam with an intensity which demanded an answer forthwith. Lennox was uncertain whether she should lay everything on the line but she took a little confidence from the fact that her old friend, whom she had contacted and who now headed up the local firearms unit, was standing just behind Lovell, smiling slightly.

'No, sir. It most certainly is not the way we do business! The Met prides itself on professionalism at all times. What's happening? It's quite simple. I know I'm under arrest and will do as I'm instructed, though I have serious concerns over these officers. DCI Darling here is trying to take me and Miles Dalton into custody. Not gonna happen. Dalton is *my* witness, and that makes *me* responsible for his welfare. Put simply, I do not trust anybody at this present moment, for good reason. And I have expended far too much time and attention on Mr. Dalton, just to see him disappear now. I know I'm in cuffs and have no rights, that I have a lot of explaining to do, but he's not leaving my sight until I'm *certain* he is safe.'

Lovell eyed her up and down dubiously. He scratched his chin and stared into her eyes. 'I see. You'll have to do better than that, sergeant,' he stated, having thought it over. 'A serving officer with your experience and record refusing to trust her colleagues? Unheard of. What am I to make of this? Explain yourself.'

Lennox looked to Miles and then back to Lovell. 'I can only give you a fraction of the truth at present. It's big. Gigantic in fact. For now... During the course of my short but very eventful investigation, I have unearthed several factors that you need to know before you send me away with these people. Miles too. Factors which, when analysed in conjunction with further intel, led me to conclude that we have some rats in our ship. The Met is compromised, sir, I am certain of it. They are destroying it from within. MI5 also, though I do not know to what extent. There are officers, I know not how many, who are working for a shadowy underground organisation allying itself with foreign assets. They are extremely well-funded, supplied and operating on an SF level, using high-quality mercs and contract assassins to eliminate chosen targets on British soil. You *must* hear me out and err on the side of caution here! Or, I promise you, we will vanish in the night and the truth goes with us... I know how this sounds. I am not wet behind the ears, as you have just stated. They have already attempted to kill Miles and Jenny numerous times, as well as myself. Attempts so determined and organised, that they make this unknown group a real and present threat to this nation's security...'

'Stop!' ordered Lovell. 'I expected a starter and got the full three courses thrust in my face. That's about the boldest claim I've ever heard. I trust you can back up these outlandish allegations? And what *factors* have taken you to this monumental conclusion? Tell me that you have more than just theories and attempts on your lives? How are you linking this incident to such a serious danger to the U.K.? I'll need concrete proof and lots of it, if you are expecting me to act, you know that.'

Sam Lennox pushed her shoulders back and stood up straight and proud. 'You'll have your proof, sir. Just as soon as we are out of harm's way and able to interrogate a few systems, bank accounts, comms devices and the like.'

DCI Darling made to object but Lovell waved away his protest, anxious to hear more.

'Fair enough. In the meantime, I'm supposed to trust your word, am I? It's a lot to ask. I risk upsetting the rank and file, most of whom are still unsure of you I'm told. What is your issue with DCI Darling here?'

Sam eyed the DCI with contempt. 'He was Farley's choice, but he's under investigation at present. The boss respected him I know, but we have been hunted by trained teams with prior and up to date intel. They were able to track our movements and respond even before law enforcement. They *had* to have been tipped off and helped in some way. He is one of only two I can think of with the access and rank to achieve this.'

'So he is,' replied Mitch Lovell. 'Highly irregular set of circumstances and pretty weighty allegations, but then we have already lost a damned fine officer on this. I hope for your sake you can back them up, for nobody will want to work with you again if not. The genie is out of the bottle now regardless. I believe I can guess at where you are going with this. I'm not happy, Sam. However, you've made your play and I believe we have to let this run its course. In the interim period, I think it best if you and your friends surrender yourselves into my custody. I will personally guarantee your safety. Does that satisfy you? Unless, *I* am on your list of suspects too?'

Sam looked towards Miles again and smiled in relief, just as Jenny was walked over to them in cuffs. Then she returned her gaze to Lovell.

'No sir, that will do nicely. You are not involved. As far as I can tell, you're clean.'

Lovell instructed his own people to cuff them. 'I'm very glad to hear it. And just how do you know that?' he asked.

'Call it a hunch.'

DCI Darling attempted once again to protest but Mitch Lovell stood firm and the DCI and his men finally skulked away.

Sam insisted on accompanying Miles to the hospital in the ambulance. This request was denied on the basis that he was also a prisoner and at least one officer had to go with him, meaning there wasn't enough room for her *and* the paramedics. Lovell explained that although they were quite unusually held in detention by MI5, they were still detainees until such a time that they had been cleared of any wrongdoing. That they would be afforded no special treatment. Miles therefore travelled in cuffs with one of Lovell's sergeants in the ambulance, whilst the remainder of his force occupied the lead vehicle in order to clear the route via their blues and twos. Sam Lennox was escorted in another car to the rear, staffed by her old friend and three of his team. Miles was in mild pain thanks to the hefty wound to his shoulder and the respite afforded by the strong painkillers already administered on scene. The medic was happy with his vitals and made herself comfortable for the journey. The ambulance convoy raced through the city traffic but the sergeant escorting Miles appeared nervous, edgy. His finger never left the trigger guard on his MP5 machine gun and his eyes were darting about continuously, anxiously flicking to the windows and occupants in turn, as well as the cuffs on his prisoner's wrists.

Only around fifteen minutes into the drive, as they slowed to a virtual stop in order to negotiate a right turn at a roundabout, two deafening explosions erupted, almost throwing Miles off the gurney and giving him a heart attack.

They were followed by numerous single shots, then a series of bursts of automatic fire and more solo rounds. A small war had erupted outside the ambulance. More weapons opened up, then the rapid and loudly-bellowed orders of a commander, which were not quite loud enough for Miles to make out what was being said. His now finely tuned senses were fully awake however and he found himself vigilant and concentrating hard, the pain of before dissipating completely as a familiar sensation began running through his veins, like somebody was ringing a warning bell and pumping him full of an energy drink simultaneously.

He turned his head away from the window just in time to see the police sergeant put a bullet into the unfortunate paramedic, then turn his SIG MCX Carbine onto him. Miles somehow managed to sit up with phenomenal speed in the confined space. He rushed forwards and grabbed the muzzle of the gun, pushed it upwards with all his might, just as the first of the ammunition exited the barrel and several neat holes instantly punctured the roof of the emergency vehicle. It had remained stationary throughout the ambush, the driver presumably killed in the initial explosions and original contact. Having narrowly avoided death yet again, the still cuffed Miles realised he was in the fight of his life, facing an enemy who held every possible advantage. The guy was stocky, armed, uninjured, unincumbered and standing over him now with gravity fully on his side.

However, Miles was not fazed in the slightest. He *should* have been, he knew that, but he wasn't. He knew instinctively what to do. He twisted the gun and yanked it towards him forcefully, wrenching it from the officer's grasp and throwing him off-balance. The armed cop stumbled but immediately reached for his secondary weapon, a Glock 17 pistol housed in a tactical holster on his hip. Before he could locate it though, having released his hold on his own carbine, the incredibly rapid Miles had wrenched it free of the sling and clubbed him about the head with the butt of his own gun. On the third strike of the man's skull, it was a complete mess.

Miles immediately checked on both the driver and the medic. They were beyond help. The ambulance was static, going nowhere. He rummaged through the sergeant's pockets for the cuff keys but found only the officer's own, which were of no use. Still, he used them to restrain him with his own cuffs, just in case he lived. Then, he grabbed his pistol in his restrained hands, grateful that he was now at least able to defend himself, and approached the door, took hold of the handle. The gunfire had died down completely by now and an eerie silence had taken hold of the ambush site.

A little earlier, in the rear vehicle, Sam Lennox had also been both cuffed and unarmed. She began feeling quite claustrophobic as she was sat between two fairly hefty individuals whose generous frames and added gear rendered space in the middle at an absolute minimum. She was pretty certain that the woman to her left was enjoying the close proximity a little more than she ought, given the circumstances. She smirked knowingly at her and then scowled to make her objection clear, looked forwards out of the front windscreen as they followed the ambulance and the lead escort. Satisfied that nothing was amiss, she began talking to her old comrade from police college, who was up front in the passenger seat.

'You know, Alan, whatever happens from here, I owe you a beer, or several. I want you to know that I really appreciate you having my six on this. I've lost so many good comrades of late, in one way or another. It's nice to know I can count on someone.'

The firearms team commander turned his head slightly as he replied, eyes remaining focussed on the road ahead. 'Think nothing of it, Sam. I know your heart and your worth. You'd do the same for me. I'd put my house on you being on the level. Your boy will be fine with us. I heard what you said to Lovell though. You're in a world of pain. You'll need to have eyes in the back of your head from now on. It's heavy-duty stuff. How are you going to make it all stick?'

'Unknown,' replied Sam. 'Find the evidence, I suppose. I have *some*, but I need more before I can share it. Then, present the facts, fill in the blanks, and trust the process?'

'Ha! *Trust?* That's a dirty word these days. Only works if those in power are…'

Bang! Bang!

Two immensely accurate gunshots were fired at almost precisely the same time. The commander was hit in his forehead and died instantly. The driver simultaneously received a round to the face which ended his life. He jolted backwards then forwards, as his foot slipped off the brake, and they rolled forwards a little before coming to a halt.

Sam immediately roared, 'Ambush!'

She scanned outside the windows but could see nothing untoward, except for the fact that the rest of the escort was also not moving. Though, a couple of explosions soon sounded which were way too close for comfort and smoke and debris began to fly all around the vehicles ahead.

'Snipers!' she added. 'At least two, possibly more. They'll move in now to finish us off.'

The Trojan officers immediately reached for the handle of the doors and stepped out onto the road. They hadn't even cleared the car fully before they were mercilessly gunned down by a hail of bullets from all directions.

Gunfire then sounded from within the ambulance and Sam threw herself into the footwell, just as a black-clad figure approached the front of the car and let rip. Metal peppered the seating above and behind her but Lennox reached forwards and took hold of Alan's gun, sensing the lone gunman was now making his way around the vehicle to ensure for himself that the job was done, and the troublesome DS unalived. No survivors. As he reached the passenger window, Sam rose just a little, just enough, and fired two rounds into his chest and head. Point blank, or near enough.

With her hands bound she knew she would not be able to reload and had to make every shot count. She launched herself from the motor and hard-rolled on the road surface, wincing in pain, took stock of her surroundings. Once again, the scene before her was reminiscent of her time in Afghanistan. *Slightly*. Memories and training kicked in from out of nowhere, jolting her senses good and for some reason, causing her old wounds to fire up and scream out at her in agony.

Two more unknown assailants wearing balaclavas, just like the first guy she had dropped, were approaching the ambulance with weapons cocked and ready, barrels smoking. She put a bullet into each of them in rapid succession and then immediately trained her gun onto a third, who was responding to the sound of contact to the rear.

This attacker was fast and managed to get the drop on her, firing off a bullet which narrowly missed and grazed her right thigh. The distance was difficult for an accurate pistol shot for anyone other than a true artist but luckily for Sam, she was an expert marksman with most weapons and she took her time, aimed and squeezed the trigger gently. She hit the shooter centre mass, almost certainly rupturing his heart. An incredibly robust impact then flung her backwards and spun her around. She tumbled to the ground and landed awkwardly with a bone-shuddering bump.

'Not again!' she cried, exasperated, the weapon having fallen from her hands and unable to cushion her fall.

Struck in the side of her stomach, it was like a switch had been pressed inside her mind once more and she was all of a sudden returned to another world. A place of turban-wearing fighters carrying assault rifles. Of RPG's,

Improvised Explosive Devices and danger around every corner...

Sam was *lost*. Completely, utterly lost now. Could not function as a police officer at all and staring vacantly into space, in a violent, hell-like world all of her own. Her side was holed. Blood was pouring out of the through and through, but she barely registered what was happening. All she could see and sense was the incredible heat, the almighty thirst, and the tiny bits of sand which ladened the air and stuck in her throat, eyes and nostrils... The cries and screams of the dead and dying... The smell of cordite, burning flesh, rubber and fuel...

Lennox was a thousand miles away from where she needed to be. More bullets zinged off the road around her, some within inches of her head, but they all had zero effect on her state of mind. For all pain and sensations had evaporated now. All thought of Miles or anyone else. She was fighting a different battle, her brain and body shutting down in unison, just when she needed them most.

A solitary individual made his way menacingly over to where she lay, firing his weapon as he walked and getting closer and closer with each shot.

'Sam!'

A voice inside her mind broke through the haze somehow, pleading with her to awaken from her stupor.

'Sam! Get up, you waster! Up on line now! You *have* to save us!' it screamed in abject desperation.

But it was noise. Just noise. Added to all the rest. The Sam of old had disappeared, replaced by a shivering wreck useful to nobody. She stared up pathetically at the sole remaining warrior on the battlefield.

On the inner perimeter at least.

All was silent. Everyone in the immediate vicinity had either bugged out, or taken up permanent residence in the afterlife. Sam was about to join them. She was just waiting for the curtain to fall. For death to claim her.

Her would-be slayer moved to within six feet, having reloaded. He saw that she was badly wounded and unarmed, removed his face covering and stared down upon her with eyes of pure hatred.

'You! If ever there was a death deserved. You can't comprehend what it is you have done. Destroyed years and years of work, the careers of some great patriots. You are not fit to wipe their asses! You've handed our enemies the keys to the mansion. They will be victorious in any future conflict because of *you*. In one foul swoop, you have set us back to the stone age with your meddling. Congratulations, DS Lennox, I hope you are very proud of yourself. We won't stand a chance now. We'll be the whipping boy of Europe, clinging to the coat tails of tinpot nations, begging for scraps from their table…'

DCI James Darling was absolutely livid. His hands were shaking uncontrollably with rage but he pointed his pistol straight between Sam's eyes nevertheless, her refusal to answer him in any form only angering him further. His finger tensed on the trigger and…

At that precise moment, the doors to the ambulance flung open and Miles Dalton made his way out into hell. He immediately spotted Darling standing over his new friend with weapon poised and Miles acted without a second thought, emptied the entire contents of his magazine into his body, happy to take the consequences for himself should any more enemy remain alive, just so long as he saved the life of his friend, Sam Lennox.

Chapter 24

Mitch Lovell was now an extremely worried man. The Deputy Director of MI5 had despatched what he thought was a well-armed and capable escort team with Sam Lennox and Miles Dalton, to ensure they arrived safely at the hospital. The extremely shocking, devastating news that they had failed to deliver them at all, had very nearly floored him. To learn that they'd been ambushed in military style by an unknown squad of... Well, *who?!* Who had the audacity and capability to pull off something on that scale, at short notice? To be able to organise and strike so fast, probably with real-time knowledge of the hospital chosen, the route they would take etc? Details were coming in thick and fast but they were sketchy at best. He had therefore turned his small force around at high speed and was now racing to the incident site, fully expecting to find that his star witnesses in what was conceivably a domestic and international conspiracy of stupendous proportions, were either dead, having been butchered on *his* watch, or in the wind. Kidnapped by unknowns who were likely to be backed by foreign powers, if anything Sam Lennox had claimed was to be believed. Either of these scenarios he knew only too well would put his head firmly on the block. He already had the chief and others breathing down his neck, wanting immediate answers and assurances he could not provide. He quickly went over it all in his mind, what little he knew so far. A very brief radio transmission was made by the escort commander at the beginning of the ambush. It confirmed they were under attack, but little else. It was explained to Lovell by the Police Control Room operative that the officer in charge had simply stated there were, *multiple hostiles.* No numbers or descriptions were provided, which might have proven helpful. The second or so that remained of his life which could be heard, before his fingers moved off the transmit button, were crammed with explosions and gunfire. Then, *nothing*. No open channel. Complete radio silence. It was a spontaneous disaster of epic magnitude.

Mitch Lovell's team were armed and nearer than any similar force of locals, or the Met, so he had volunteered their services. They arrived on scene having fought their way through miles of stationary traffic to find nothing but complete anarchy. Blackened smoke was billowing out of the wreckages of several vehicles. Twisted metal, blood, debris and body parts were strewn across the road. Riddled corpses, most badly shot up or missing limbs, grotesquely disfigured and devoid of life, spoke to an extremely violent confrontation, heavy and light ordnance strikes. A junior officer alongside Lovell had turned and retched up the entire contents of his stomach. His furious and single-minded commander pushed on, understanding and believing for the very first time, that Sam Lennox may just have been telling the truth.

He became determined to discover the fate of his prize assets. The ambulance was badly damaged but relatively intact, the escort deceased. No sign of Miles Dalton. The escort vehicle carrying Sam was a complete mess, holed from every conceivable angle. Two bodies sat up front with seatbelts still buckled. There were two more in close proximity, both obviously slaughtered as they attempted to exit and engage the perpetrators. And there was a number of killed unknowns. Lovell brushed his fingers through his rapidly receding hairline and tried to piece together what had actually happened here.

Then, he saw it. Or rather, *him*.

James Darling. What was *he* doing here?!

The DCI's prostrate body was lying on the road face down ripped apart by small arms fire. In his rush to account for Sam Lennox, Lovell had walked right over him. He retraced his steps, turned him over, just to make certain. It was Darling alright. The proof he needed that Sam was correct in her suspicions. There was no possible explanation for his presence other than the fact that he was a part of the ambush squad. Presumably, in command. Which meant the lifeless traitor sprawled at his feet wasn't just *dirty*, he was up to his neck in *filth!*

Lovell's stomach turned and he swore under his breath. He seethed at the thought of such betrayal. And berated himself for not leading the escort personally, despite the pressure he was under to keep the higher-ups informed. The briefing of his bosses could and should have waited. Though, he would never in all his days have believed that whoever was behind this thing, would be so brazen as to launch an all-out attack in broad daylight in the heart of England. Not on this scale. It just wasn't done... And yet, here he was, staring down both barrels of a fully loaded and cocked shotgun. When the truth emerged of what occurred here, which would not take long, *he* would be the one facing the absolute mother beast of all enquiries. And at present, he had *very* few answers for the myriad questions about to be hurled in his direction.

The buck always stops at the top but those in such lofty positions had become quite adept of late at dodging those bullets. Wasn't that what deputies like him were for?

'Sir? Forgive the intrusion. There's nobody else left alive,' a female sergeant stated dutifully, her weapon like her ready to respond to any residual threat.

'And Dalton and Lennox?' he asked.

'Nothing. Gone.'

'Yes, I know *that*, sergeant. Gone *where* though? Right, set a perimeter. You know the drill. As soon as the local plod show up, I want crowd control in place, nobody within a hundred yards, screens up, the works...'

'Sir.'

Lovell cast his eye around once again and caught sight of a small trail of blood. It was different from the rest in that it came from beyond Sam's car, led *away* from the devastation.

'Hold! As you were. You, plus two others, with me right now!'

The firearms team joined him rapidly. He drew his weapon and together they followed the blood. After a short while it was clear that it led to a small row of shops, at the side of which was a walkway up to some units at the rear. Performing drills ingrained into them all through years of training, they worked their way up to an open garage door. Lovell took the lead and eventually rounded the brickwork to find Sam Lennox lying on the ground, with Miles Dalton kneeling over her. He was injured himself but he was applying pressure to the front and back of her torso as best he could, whilst she squirmed in pain. She looked far paler than she ought. To be fair, they *both* looked as though they had been dragged through the fires of hell and back.

'Nice of you to join us. I'd put my hands up in the air for you again, but I daren't relieve the pressure on her stomach,' said Miles, staring at the guns pointing straight at his head, unaware of who he could trust right now and fully expecting to be culled.

Lovell's eyes moved slowly down to Sam Lennox. 'You can relax now. I think we are *finally* on the same page. I can only apologise and hope you can forgive this blind old fool? I should have believed you earlier. You going to make it?'

Lennox smiled weakly, answered him in an uncharacteristically feeble tone. 'Me? 'Tis but a scratch, as the old timers used to say.'

She tried to laugh but ended up coughing and screwing up her face with the resulting agony. '...I've had worse,' she forced out. 'And you weren't to know.'

Lovell put away his weapon and turned to his officers. 'Stand down. Form a protective cordon around this unit. Get an ambulance in here right now. Don't let *anyone* else through, only the medics. And they are to be watched like a hawk. Not to be left alone with them. If the King himself should show up here demanding entry, I want you to politely turn him away with my compliments. Knighthood be damned.'

Miles and Sam spent the next seventy-two hours in hospital receiving all kinds of treatments. Miles was then released into police custody. Lennox needed way longer to recuperate but in true Sam style, she promptly discharged herself as soon as Miles came to say goodbye, ignoring all medical advice and protestations, joined him in detention at the high security Paddington Green police station. They were held separately from other prisoners and watched over by a special detail selected personally for the task by Mitch Lovell. Jennifer Pearce soon joined them in captivity and all food was brought in by associates of the Deputy Head of MI5, purchased from independent, rotated suppliers at the very last minute. Lovell was obsessed with their safety now. For the present at least, he had been granted complete autonomy by the Prime Minister and he was using it. No visitors were allowed. No access to television, radio or internet. All electronic devices had been confiscated and about the only thing they *were* granted access to, was the station's very limited library.

It wasn't long however before they were seen. Lovell was under increasing pressure to unravel what had gone on and why. Who *exactly* was involved. He needed to brief all those in power of the very real threats which had suddenly appeared right on their doorstep. There were numerous twitchy figures in Whitehall and beyond as a result. The whole of London in particular felt like the inside of a giant melting pot, atop the flames. So, as soon as he felt they were up to it, Lovell assembled the three fugitives in a small interview room. He told everyone else to leave and then explained that he was recording the conversation solely due to the fact that he had a memory like a sieve. That they had no lawyers present at this time and had not yet been cautioned. And that although they could be interviewed and charged at a later date, they were there of their own free will and *this* was their only opportunity to tell their version of events *off* the record.

Understandably, he was met with complete silence. Which just wouldn't do.

'Okay, then I'll start things off,' he stated, looking at each of them in turn. 'We've discovered a vast conspiracy here, as you suggested we might. Round one to you. We're uncertain how deep this thing runs, but all indications are that it's like the Mariana Trench. Seismic. From what little we know so far, I expect there to be hundreds, possibly thousands of arrests worldwide before we're through. Sackings, resignations, prosecutions and suicides... You've opened up an entire casket full of worms.'

Sam, Jenny and Miles still did not respond.

'I'm not wired, if that's your concern, so talk to me!' Lovell yelled, his patience running thin. 'Help me to make sense of all of this?'

'Sense? We *can't*. Not completely. We're still figuring out the details for ourselves,' Sam answered, honestly.

'Then, maybe I can assist some? Let's start with what you *do* know. The Met? Was it Darling, or Elizabeth Barker, the Chief Constable?' he asked.

'You tell me.'

Lovell wasn't impressed with that reply from Lennox but he soon relented and began the discussion he knew he had to have.

'Right. It was *both*. We went to work the moment I left you. Specialists I chose myself. They were extremely well hidden but we discovered regular payments to offshore accounts set up in their spouse's names. Family too. I suppose greed got the better of them. Homes were searched and burner phones recovered. There's enough there to tie them to some very unsavoury characters. Names and addresses. Social media accounts. Enough for successful prosecutions at least. Though, Darling of course, got off lightly.'

'I wouldn't call being turned into human macaroni *getting off lightly?*' said Jenny.

'*I* would. There's nothing more despicable than a corrupt cop,' Sam stated.

She meant it too.

'Quite. In that, we are in complete agreement. You know, throughout all of this, you've proven yourself immensely capable. I want you to know that I'll always have a spot open for you at MI5, once you've recovered.'

Miles smiled at Lennox, seriously impressed. 'None finer,' he said, winking at her. 'Congrats. You really deserve it.'

'Thanks. But you may change your mind on that, sir, once you hear it all. Jack Walters I'm afraid, was also in it up to his eyeballs. I was a little economical with the truth. I had to take him out. I had no choice. It was him or me. Plus, he tried to kill Miles,' said Sam.

Lovell put his hand into his pocket and took out a cough sweet, unwrapped it and popped it into his mouth, began sucking away. 'Figured as much. This whole thing is never going to make sense unless you explain what you know. You have to open up. Come on? It's time, surely? What was this all over? Why am I dealing with multinational hit squads and a trail of corpses?'

Sam looked down at her feet for a second or two, then lifted her head and stated softly, 'Okay, I'll try. Here goes nothing...'

It all began with James Dalton, Miles' father. A young guy setting out on a career with the army. A scientist. He had a vision. He dreamt of producing an entire force comprised exclusively of genetically enhanced supersoldiers. Fully funded and resourced, sanctioned by the U.K. government. Plus, our American allies. Only, somewhere along the line, the dream turned into a nightmare. James Dalton forgot who he was. The mild-mannered family man morphed into a monster... Maybe that's a tad overdramatic and I'm sorry, Miles... He sired a love child. No, in fact, he had *two*. He took a young lover on the base, whom he kept secret from his wife. When this woman died in childbirth, he, for whatever reason, acted shamefully. He came clean to his missus partially, but he took only *one* of the children home. That bit I can never get my head around. The other baby remained a secret and went into care. We know now that the child he took was his obsession, possibly due to the guilt and shame he must have felt for abandoning the other. Miles grew up without knowing any of this. Not until the day his long-lost twin brother was gunned down right in front of his eyes.'

Mitch Lovell crushed the sweet in his teeth and swallowed it. 'The other child. With you so far. Continue, please?'

Sam gave a little cough and took a sip of water. 'Jason Murphy was the first victim on the train. Also, the first fatality that we know of in this country. Major James Dalton, their father, had been injured at work in a freak accident before they were born. The wounds he received somehow altered his DNA sequencing. It is my belief that all of a sudden, he discovered that he could think clearer, run faster, jump further... Became fitter, stronger than any man, able to run a marathon, reactions off the scale. The mutation it caused became the catalyst that catapulted his hitherto unremarkable work, right into orbit. Breakthroughs of extraordinary consequence were now possible. They were suddenly very real, achievable and imminent. And the entire world was on the brink of... Well, nobody knows quite what. War? A new Arms Race?'

Problem was, *only* James Dalton's blood would suffice. He was unique, the only source. And he had precious few of the sought after enzymes, genes or whatever. No more than anybody else in the world in fact. There was nobody with that special blend they needed to produce the required material... Except for one other.'

'What?!' Miles exclaimed, turning to look at Sam in the same way as Jenny. Both were unaware of what she meant and now inviting an explanation.

'That's why we are here. Your father, the not so good major, realised to his dismay that his beloved son's blood was the same, or far superior to his own.'

'No!' objected Miles. 'That's...!'

'It's *true*. It's the only explanation. He tested them all. Used his own as a base comparator, but it was *yours* he was working with. That's why he didn't take your brother. The *real* reason. Jason wasn't like you. Heaven knows why. He'd already tested you both at birth. *Two* samples, remember? In *every* video. Not three.'

'But I...?'

Miles fell completely silent then, cut his own sentence short as his mouth fell wide open.

'Go on? Finish what you were going to say?' Jenny encouraged him.

He shook his head, ashamed. 'I can't do it. My poor brother. I don't want to be confronted with this. It's awful. To think, *I* was the cause of... As a child I had diabetes. Or at least I *thought* I did. I was injected with insulin, gave samples of blood regularly, so they could be sent away for analysis. They said it was acute. I often fell ill afterwards. In my later years though, not long before my father's death, I was suddenly given the all clear. I was astounded but they said that it sometimes happens, and I believed them. That some bodies counteract it of their own accord. I couldn't care less. I was just relieved to be free of all those needles.'

'You were the second subject to be experimented upon, Miles. That's what the Latino hitman was trying to tell you when he said, *you're it.*'

'*It?*' said Miles, not thinking straight and seeking confirmation as his brain was swamped all of a sudden.

'Yes,' answered Sam. 'The host. The world's only living supersoldier. Call it what you will. The fruit of their research. Genetically superior to any other living being on this earth. Our very own Superman... Your skills and attributes are there for all to see. And all that, with *zero* training. Imagine what great feats you might achieve if you harnessed those powers and developed them some more. What you could be capable of. It's my contention that your father had a final breakthrough, around six to eight months ago, just before his death. The accident in the lab he mentioned. Told very few but produced a serum of sorts. I think he left a sample of that with your mother. And that *she* gave it to Jason. Maybe he tried it on himself, but it was never going to work, not on him. It was created for *you*. And due to unforeseen events, you were injected with it on that train. That's why you reacted so badly afterwards. And it's why you suddenly developed increased abilities. Why you are alive today.'

Miles felt physically sick. He turned to Jenny. 'Can you believe all of this? It's crazy!'

'No, I...'

'She knows.'

All eyes turned to Sam Lennox once again.

'What do you mean by that?' asked Lovell.

Lennox nodded once at Jenny. 'Are *you* going to tell him, or am I?'

Jenny remained silent, so she continued.

'She isn't who she says she is, Miles. Jenny Pearce doesn't work at a pharmaceutical company. She's never even met Sir Nicholas Johnson. She's a freelance journalist, looking for a scoop. She just wanted a good story. Admit it.'

Jenny's face spoke a thousand words and Miles turned away from her in disgust.

'Don't? I never meant...' Jenny began, then sank back in her chair, sobbing.

'...Can't hide it any longer. She's right. In the beginning, that's all it was. A story. All I ever wanted. Your brother was my fiancé and I loved him dearly, truly I did. It was *me* who drove *him* away though, not the other way around. I kept pestering him about his father, as soon as he confided in me that he'd sought him out. He had mentioned little details about his research and I'd begun piecing things together.'

'Oh for...!' began Miles, his thoughts running away with him. 'I can't believe what I'm hearing! It was *you!* You're to blame! You're probably what led to word escaping of what he was doing. He was butchered and my entire life was ruined because of your interference, your insatiable quest for fame and glory!'

Sam Lennox stepped in-between them. 'Now then Miles, you have no way of knowing any of that for certain. There were others in that lab, or on that base, who could have spoken out. And whatever her motives back then, *she* was the one who stuck around when you needed her most, defended you bravely, with her life on the line.'

Silence descended on that room like a heavy mist. A poisonous gas.

Mitch Lovell broke it, piping up with, 'So, Jason was killed because the murderer thought *he* was the *special one?*

Only, it wasn't Jason, it was you, Miles. Which now places you in serious peril.'

'Huh! You don't say?' said Miles, not impressed in the slightest with the learned spy's deductive reasoning skills.

'And Major James Dalton?' said Lovell.

'Murdered, we think, by the Americans perhaps. They were furious with him for destroying their lab and they had real motive, with him sharing his research. Possibly to the highest bidder, as far as they could tell. Though, the real culprits are to be confirmed.'

'His wife?'

'Still out there somewhere. I'm assuming she disappeared presumably to protect her sons, one of which she had only recently learned of. She probably believed that *whoever* killed their father, would come for her, or them, next.'

'But, why target only one son?' asked Lovell. 'Why only Jason?'

Sam took a deep breath and grimaced in pain as she let it out slowly. 'I think the mother reached out to the babe she lost, possibly her husband's wishes. She may have been followed when she met up with Jason. May have sent him to warn Miles, unaware that they had been made. These forces in play now were searching for an elite warrior, remember. One son was a hardened criminal who looked the part, tough and resilient, handy with his fists. A mechanic whose lifestyle was a little on the edge. They tried to take him out in his local. The assassin on the train succeeded. He caught a fleeting glimpse of the other lad and probably did not realise who he was. A computer nerd. No offence, Miles. Looks like nothing. His best friend hasn't seen the light of day for a decade.'

Miles' jaw dropped again but he remained silent.

'Besides, who's to say that once they dealt with Jason, they didn't plan to return for Miles? Though, I'm not certain they actually knew for sure that he even existed at that point, not until he showed up on that train and they made further enquiries. They probably weren't looking for him. It was possibly early days for their own investigation, for we don't know exactly when they found out the truth about the major and his discovery, do we?'

'And your best guess? Was there a leak at the major's end?'

'Either that, or an increasingly pushy journalist rattled too many cages, roused the sleeping lion.'

Chapter 25

'There's still so many things about this whole situation that puzzle me but I guess chief amongst them all is the U.K. assassin. Operative? What are we calling him? This, *Owen James*. Obviously, we know his background now and we have linked him to various factions, though we are still no clearer to establishing exactly who he was working for on this occasion, when he tried to take you all out?' Mitch Lovell stated.

'How can that be? Seriously? Did you not interrogate the phone he had in his possession?' asked Sam Lennox, amazed by that embarrassing statement and also somewhat disappointed.

Lovell shook his head. 'We never had the chance. Hard to believe I know, but the body and the phone disappeared before we could examine them thoroughly. Don't ask me how that was allowed to happen, because I am livid about it. But it *did*. The arms of this beast we face are long and many it seems. Having uncovered its existence and exposed its activities, all you have succeeded in doing so far, is to give us all the world's greatest neck ache. We're all of us suddenly unsure who we can rely on, where the next knife will strike, questioning everything and anyone. I want to chop off its head as quickly as possible. Strike it down so it will never rise again. But tell me, where *exactly* do I begin?'

'That's easy. At the very top. Sir Nicholas Johnson,' Sam answered boldly, noting the immediate looks of confusion which greeted her response.

'There was no hesitation there at all, was there? You sound mightily convinced. I can see it, but how can you be so certain?' Lovell eventually added.

'The voice I heard on Owen James' phone. It was him, I'm *sure* of it. I couldn't place it before, what with all the confusion. To be perfectly honest, I've had quite a lot on my mind. However, the nagging doubt about Jenny and her alleged profession, has brought it back to me. Honestly, you need to arrest him right now, obtain the proof you require. Don't give him chance to escape. Take him down and the others will fall. If you let me go free, I'll do it for you?' she begged.

Miles and Jenny were in full agreement despite her injuries, but Mitch Lovell was having none of it. 'Nice try, sergeant,' he said, 'you are going nowhere. The three of you are hot potatoes right now. You're all sitting ducks out there in the real world, until we put this entire thing to bed and remove them all from power. You've already seen what they can do. You wouldn't last five minutes if I do as you ask. Besides, you're all shot up and can barely walk unaided, so what do you think you are going to do if he has company and tries to resist? No, I'm afraid you're all going to have to trust *me* for a change. Wait here and enjoy the peace and quiet. Read some more. I'll obtain a warrant and command the unit myself. We'll bring him in for questioning and search his houses, belongings, financial records, electronics, the whole caboodle... That's it for now. Get some rest. You look as if you need it. You can remain together in the large cell if you wish. As soon as I have any news, I'll be back to update you all.'

It was late in the evening when a clearly agitated Mitch Lovell finally returned. He had them escorted back into the interview room without delay.

'Well?' asked Miles, before he had even taken a seat.

The Deputy Head of MI5 looked into the eyes of his expectant audience. Three lost souls, including two of the most capable soldiers in the country. Possibly the world. And all three of them now looked like abandoned puppies.

'We were too late,' he stated.

'I *knew* it!' raged Sam Lennox. 'I warned you he would run!'

'Yes, you did. I'm not sure we would have been quick enough anyway. I know you had no reason to believe that he *knew* you were on to him, but he must have been tipped off by somebody. It was like he waited until we made our move. Had eyes on us all the time. Believe me, I had all assets in play on this one. He was in London as late as this morning. Confirmed by satellite and ANPR cameras. We raided his mansion and the two houses he owns in the city that we know of. He and his immediate family appear to have left in a hurry. Strange, that he waited so long. Perhaps he believed we would not act. There were clothes strewn everywhere at his estate but the servants were saying nothing. They'll talk eventually I'm sure, though by that time it will be too late.'

'What the hell does that mean?!' asked Jenny, alarmed like her associates that the big fish might slip the hook, as they always seem to do.

'Do you have no idea where he has gone?' questioned Miles.

'I didn't say that. We know *precisely* where he is heading. We're just powerless to stop him. He has a holiday retreat near Cuba. As you know, we have no extradition treaty with them. We can't touch him.'

'No!' roared Sam Lennox again, almost bursting her stitches. 'He *can't* be allowed to get away with it!'

'That's life, Sam. He's a fugitive now though. He won't be able to return home ever again. He's hardly got away with it?' replied Lovell.

'It's not enough. Not for him. Not for all he has done. What about Edward Farley, and the others he and his henchmen have butchered? There *has* to be some justice! A bullet between the eyes, or a lengthy prison sentence is the least he deserves.'

'I know, sergeant. I agree with you. We'll keep tabs on him and should he so much as set one toe in a friendly country, we'll swoop down from a great height… There *is* a little good news I can share with you all.'

Miles' head lifted a little and his ears pricked up. 'Thank heaven for that. What then?'

Lovell for some reason beckoned them all in close, as if he was afraid someone was eavesdropping. 'I… I had the tech teams beavering away whilst I was out of the office. They came up trumps for me. Took some doing mind. Sir Nicholas owns many motors, as you can imagine. Leases a lot too. We trawled the systems for sightings of any that are used frequently, then targeted hits on the speed camera just up the road from his estate. A Bentley triggered the system doing forty in a thirty-mile-an-hour zone. This gave us the registration number. We then traced the movements of this vehicle over the past six months. Added to that, he only uses one of three regular chauffeurs, so we were able to crosscheck with their phones and shifts.'

'Should give you a good picture of what was going on. And?' said Miles. 'I mean, how?'

'All mobile phones communicate with Satellites regularly, just to let them know they can receive and to check for updates. We tracked this data. Though most criminals are wary of this and know how to evade detection, the hired help usually do not consider themselves targets and we find they are often less discreet… We have Sir Nicholas and his driver travelling quite regularly and to no set pattern, to an underground car park in the centre of London.'

'A car park? Hardly a damning revelation. What of it?' asked Jenny.

'A totally unregistered Lexus LS leaves that facility five to ten minutes later every single time.'

'He switched cars!' rasped Lennox.

'Yes. Again, it took some doing but we figured he didn't go far. The security cameras at the Savoy Hotel capture his arrival via the trades entrance. He is joined by an assortment of high flyers on each occasion, in vehicles they would not normally use. We're talking police, bankers, entrepreneurs, directors of utility companies, oil firms, judges and the like. *Highly* influential people. Profiteers. Those most certainly in a position to orchestrate murder and mayhem.'

'We've *got* them!' hissed Miles, triumphantly.

'Not so fast. All except Sir Nicholas,' Sam corrected him.

Mitch Lovell placed a hand on her shoulder. 'Patience. Rome wasn't built in a day. Take the win, Sam. The Chief Constable was one of those seen. She visited only once, but it's enough to tie her to the group. It's over for her, and the rest. If I know Elizabeth Barker at all, she'll sing like a canary if a deal is offered. And she'll have kept an insurance policy or two for just this scenario. We'll have the entire network then… But why don't you finish what you started?'

'Sir?'

'Your explanation. It was incomplete. Why was this group of wealthy individuals prepared to risk *everything* to terminate James Dalton and his siblings? Even with all you have said, I don't buy the fact that they were prepared to ruin all they had created. I need a motive beyond what I've heard?'

Sam fell silent as she thought of what to say. Then, she whispered calmly, '*Greed*. Just basic gluttony. It all boils down to *that* at the end of the day, as it often does. This research project Miles' father was embarked upon, it has been in operation for decades.'

'Go on.'

'Okay. It began small, as all such fishing expedition do. The British only. Then we involved our allies. The rewards for success were total and complete; uncontested dominance of the battlefield. So great in fact, that the purse strings of every government were cut loose for once. *Mountains* of funding meant that the contracts to supply every experimental drug along the way, were enormous. Never ending. And the secrecy required dictated that only a few select organisations were used to obtain them. All sworn to confidentiality of course and threatened with charges of treason should they divulge anything at all. A virtual monopoly meant they could charge what they liked for their products, had been handed a license to print money in effect. The success of Johnson's Pharmaceutical you'll find is almost entirely due to the green ops it was conducting for successive U.K. governments. And I don't believe they were alone and stopped there.'

'Really?' asked Lovell, enjoying seeing the imaginings of her mind take flight.

Sam was on a roll now and her eyes were alive.

'No... Failure to keep our secrets in this case, was actually very good for business. The word was leaked to all and sundry where the drugs were being sourced and Johnson's began to sell to our prospective enemies too. Anyone who could pay in fact. That's why they were able to call upon international teams of agents, no questions asked. South America? Russia? Asia? If anything went wrong, they had plausible deniability and those in power would be only too quick to pin the blame on the Russians, Koreans, Cubans or Chinese say. Just so long as James Dalton did not succeed in creating an advanced warrior, and the world learning of it, the gravy train would continue to run and thrive, and Sir Nicholas and his cronies would reap the plentiful rewards year after year... And then along came Miles.'

'Nearly there,' said Lovell. 'What about his father? His death?'

'Getting too close for comfort. Journalists had begun sniffing around.'

Miles glared at Jenny but her head was lowered and she was avoiding eye contact.

'So, the killers, they weren't government assets but mercs working for Johnson and his band of deathdealers?' said Lovell.

'As far as I can tell, yes. Muddy waters though. Owen James was British but I don't think the establishment was pulling his strings. I'd like to oversee the search for evidence if I may, sir?' asked Lennox.

Lovell nodded his agreement. 'Welcome to the team. I'll square it with whoever. It's the least we can do. When do you want to start?'

Sam Lennox looked at him as if he'd gone mad. 'Why right now!'

'Don't be stupid, Sam. It's late and you need some rest. There's a detail outside. They'll take you to a hotel and guard your door. Leave with them right now and only if you feel up to it, come back in the morning and get to work.'

'Yes, sir. Gladly,' answered Sam.

'And DS Lennox?'

'Sir?'

'Time to face the music. You and I have to talk about what happened out there in full. Don't imagine that I am blind, or a soft touch. I know you are hiding something from me and I'm not going to rest until I find out what it is. I can't have loose cannons on my squad. You have an issue, anything at all, and you square it away, you hear me?'

'Understood. We'll talk soon. It's all in hand.'

She stood up and Miles did likewise. They hugged briefly, given their injuries, then Sam said, 'This is goodbye then. I'd like to stay in touch after this but I'm not sure that will be possible. We've been through a lot together and you'll be a wanted man now for the rest of your days. You know that don't you?'

Miles simply stared back at her blankly. Of course he knew it.

'Take care of yourself,' she murmured.

'I'll do my best. Thanks for everything. And good luck at MI5. They're lucky to have you.'

Sam turned then to address Jenny. 'I can't forgive what you have done. Being a journalist and lying about it was pretty low. I hope you were not the cause of all of this, for I don't know how you would live yourself. I wouldn't sleep too good if it were me. I *can* acknowledge the loyalty and bravery you showed afterwards. For that, I'll always be grateful.'

Jeny had tears in her eyes. 'I'm so sorry. For my actions before we met. You're alright, for a copper. A little intense, but alright. Goodbye, DS Lennox. I'm sure I'll be told to keep my mouth shut and my ink dry. No major scoop for me. However, you've provided plenty in the way of inspiration for a kick-ass female heroin and there's a little idea I've been kicking around inside my head for a story.'

'Ha, ha... A novelist, eh? Well, I'm sure it will be a bestseller. Glad to have been of service.'

Lennox left the room and Lovell turned to Jenny. 'You can leave now too,' he said, more by the way of an order, than an invitation.

She rose swiftly and placed her hand on Miles', who drew his away rapidly and refused to look her in the eye.

'I deserve that. You have to believe me that I never *meant* to place your father in danger. If any harm came to him because of me, I'll regret that to the end of my days. I've grown quite fond of you in the time we had. You're unlike anyone else I know. Looks sure can be deceiving. I've never met anyone so strong and... Well, I'm sorry to you also, that's all. Can't change what happened and there's nothing else I can say to right the wrong.'

She turned away, weeping.

Miles did not flinch as the door closed.

Mitch Lovell took something small and black out of his pocket. 'A very strange thing happened to me as I returned to the station. The desk sergeant approached me and gave me this.'

'What is it?' asked Miles.

'Now, that's not quite becoming of your burgeoning reputation. I would have thought a computer bod like yourself would have recognised it? It's a USB drive, silly. When asked where it came from, the desk sergeant simply stated that a small boy had been approached by somebody in the park, paid fifty pounds to deliver it. The lad gave your name and vanished. Said it was for you, and you alone. We checked the cameras but that park has many exits and we have nothing to show for it. The sender is therefore a mystery at present. I *did* think of interrogating it myself. Had planned to in fact. Given all you have done for us, all you have sacrificed, I'm prepared though on this occasion to keep it between us for a little while. Just long enough to let you view it alone. On the strict understanding that you must inform me if there is *anything* contained on it that I should know?'

Miles gave his agreement willingly and Lovell called an officer into the room. She was carrying a laptop that was already in use. She set it down on the table, closed every programme she had open so that the home screen popped up, inserted the USB stick and left swiftly.

'All yours,' said Lovell, once the door closed fully. 'If you access anything else, we'll know about it and you will be charged.'

Mitch Lovell then left the room also.

Chapter 26

All kinds of thoughts were swirling around inside Miles' head as he stared at the screen and the file named simply, *M.A.D.* The USB drive was completely empty otherwise. His fingers hovered over the laptop for a good few seconds before he finally sucked in a few deep breaths and tapped it twice. The icon expanded in no time and a full-length picture appeared. The image which presented itself was of a woman he knew as well as anybody. Like no other in fact. Respected and cherished, trusted, loved and missed terribly. Deeply. Despite all that had occurred. The one person who knew the workings of his mind before even *he* did, who had nurtured him through good times and bad, counselled him and supported him always…

His darling mother had vanished several months prior however, failed to explain why. She'd not contacted him in all of that time. Not when his thoughts had run away with him and his worst fears were realised. *Others*, yes, but not him. She was absent from his life as it was being ripped apart, as his entire world came crashing down around him. After he had lost his father in such horrendous circumstances and was struggling to deal with his immense grief, she had abandoned him and left him to fend off the demons alone. When he'd needed her most and he had nobody else to turn to, she was conspicuous by her absence, nowhere to be seen…

Okay, given all he had subsequently learned, maybe he was being a little harsh on her?

A tad overdramatic, or simplistic? She may well have done her very best for him, in the unique set of extraordinary circumstances she faced. Believed *that* in her heart and soul at least. Done what she thought was right at the time.

And she probably *did*, in her own unique way, try her best to warn and protect him, by sending Jason to seek him out.

Still, Miles was mightily confused. As to how he should feel towards her. Right now, right this instant, in the cold light of day and after the heat of battle, having heard the magnitude of what he was embroiled in, he still found it extremely difficult to look beyond the abandonment issue. She should *never* have left him. Not in a million years. He wouldn't have deserted *his* son, he knew that much. It wasn't what loving parents were supposed to do.

But then, who was he to judge?

On the screen, Sarah Lennox was sat at a table, on a balcony somewhere, presumably a hotel or apartment in a very hot country. The sun was shining brightly making her squint and she was sweating a little, so it was a pretty safe bet that she was probably *not* in the U.K. Though, the camera had been positioned so that the backdrop was nothing but a blank wall, making an accurate determination of her exact whereabouts nigh on impossible. By design no doubt. She shuffled about in her chair awkwardly, clearly uncomfortable, as if she hardly seemed to know where to begin. Looked extremely nervous, like she'd practised this speech over and over again in front of a mirror, but knew in her heart of hearts that it was never going to suffice, would come up short each and every time.

After what seemed like an age, her lips began to move.

'Hello, Miles,' she began, in that soft voice of hers which had calmed his fears so many times in the past. He thought it strange that even as a fully grown adult, one who had suffered and achieved more than most, the everyday sounds she made could *still* move him to tears.

'I'm so, so very sorry that it has come to this. You must be... I've been updated and know what has happened. I've e-mailed this through as a matter of urgency, in the hope it will

reach you in time. It was a risk worth taking. I'm going to try my best to explain a few things if I can, because I know I owe you that much. I expect you're feeling very sorry for yourself right about now? With good reason. You no doubt feel betrayed and alone at this point? Well, I can't say that I blame you at all.'

'Hmph! You can say that again!' he hissed.

'Well then, let's grab the bull by the horns, shall we? To begin with, I had to leave. I had no choice. There was no other way. Your father made me promise to protect you. You see, I had something in my possession and was told to deliver it to you, should anything happen to him. I just couldn't do it though. To do so, would have been to place you directly in harm's way. I'd never forgive myself. It is the one and only time I failed him.'

You have to know that I did not realise the true extent of what we were facing in the beginning. Not until it was too late. If I had, I promise you I would have acted sooner.'

When I learned of all James had done, his fears, the changes in him, of Jason and that woman... He was my husband, Miles! Your father. However, despite the fact that I loved him dearly, I swear to you now, that had I have known he was placing us in danger this way, I would have walked away with you and we would have never come back... I came close to doing that several times.'

Secrets, lies and deceit, such was my marriage. But a military man must hold some secrets. At least, that's what I told myself. Of late though, he became convinced that factions beyond the norm were going to kidnap him, or worse. And then he made some kind of discovery. I have never understood exactly what. I did as I was told. Our lives changed dramatically from then on. Though he hid it from you, his nerves were totally shot. He began seeing and hearing things, voices in the shadows, threats everywhere he turned... I never wanted to get involved but this was the only way I could see to protect you both. The file he gave me, the package, it was meant as insurance only. It was never supposed to see the light of day and nobody was supposed to know of its existence. I moved us back to England to keep that secret. So nobody would know and we would never have to use it. You had nothing holding you there in the U.S. No friends or girlfriend. And I believed we would be safe so you did not need to be told.'

The very moment we arrived here however; I knew it would not be far enough. I prayed and hoped but not long afterwards, I was followed, I'm certain. I managed to find Jason and warn him. Left the stuff with him. Told him I worked with your father but that I knew your mother too. Told him about you. I had to be quick and couldn't get involved in a lengthy discussion at that stage, thought we'd have time to... Never mind. I tried to explain that it was too dangerous and it should never be used, asked him to find you and warn you to be careful with it. He was to let you know that your mother was alive and it needed to be stashed away. I'd already come to understand that the only way to shield you both was to leave. They knew all about me and my whereabouts but I was hoping you would not be targeted if I drew them away.'

Miles swallowed a huge lump in his throat. He felt really guilty all of a sudden. How could he remain angry at the one person who had sacrificed everything in an attempt to keep him from harm?

On the video, his mother continued.

'I would have disappeared forever, Miles. If I thought it would keep you both alive. Now I know better. It proved all to be in vain. They found him somehow. Jason. And ultimately, they found you. Whether we hastened that, I'll never know. I hope not. I believe it was only a matter of time, thanks to your father. Jason died doing my bidding. I have to live with that. I just had to reach out to you one final time.

My heart is broken already and it will never mend, for I fear I've lost both of you now.'

Though you may hate me, you have to be told why I did what I did.'

I'm not proud of any of it. I tried my best but your father only confided in me so much. Love is blind, it's true. By the time I understood fully what he had become, the damage was already extensive and could not be reversed. I stayed in the marriage because of you. It's what we did back then. You were and are the very best of me, my whole world. I've watched in horror at recent events, saw the news and received some inside information of my own, from old friends who thought they were helping with their silence. I do know that you are not safe there, Miles! Anywhere. You are not out of the woods just yet. And that is the second reason for this message.'

Miles sat up straight, his interest piqued.

'The truth is out now. I'm so sorry I never saw it before. You're a fly in a bottle. A lab rat. Everyone knows what you are. Make no mistake, be it us, our enemies, or our friends, they will all want a piece of you from hereon. If what I suspect is true, you are the answer to a thousand prayers... No, it's more accurate to say, the cause of a million nightmares.'

They will come at you in droves, to prod, poke and push you around, until you are completely destroyed by it all. They will test and operate on you to within an inch of your life. Then wake you up and start all over again, until they get what they want. And even if you play nicely and do all they ask of you, there are enemy forces engaged already who will never allow that to happen. Allies too. You are no doubt already top of their kill lists. There will be no place to hide, for nowhere will be beyond their reach.'

That lump in his throat had returned, only now it was the size of a golf ball and affecting his breathing.

'You are an intelligent man, Miles. You know all I say is true. It is only aired now because you have to acknowledge it. I wasn't there for you before. I think perhaps that I can be here for you now. If you let me. I have access to funds. Lots and lots of funds your father liberated for us. My plan is for the pair of us to vanish again. Only, to make a better job of it this time. To that end, I have arranged transport, papers, everything we need. I have a destination in mind but obviously will not divulge that to anyone. Drastic times call for drastic measures and it involves many sacrifices; new country, friends, surgery perhaps, learning new languages...'

Well, that's it. That's all I have to say. It's your decision to make. All I am offering is a way out of the impossible situation you find yourself in, because of the actions of others. I am giving it to you now. Be brave enough to grasp it. I will watch from afar. The day of your release, I will observe and give you three days to decide. If you are agreeable, simply place a vase of red roses in your front window at home. I will take care of the rest. A few of your father's old comrades are still loyal and prepared to help us, though they will not be told everything.'

Take care, my son. If I don't hear from you, remember always that I love you deeply.'

Miles ended the playback and ejected the USB. He threw it immediately onto the floor and then stamped on it with all his weight numerous times, until all that was left was totally useless fragments of plastic and metal.

Mitch Lovell heard the noise he made and entered the room swiftly. He gazed down at the smashed device and balled his fists in fury, cursed his earlier leniency and stupidity.

'I really wish you hadn't done that,' he stated.

On the tropical isle of Cayo Esquivel, Sir Nicholas Johnson was relaxing by the pool in his luxurious hideaway. He drained the remnants of his Louis X111 Cognac and then called out to his wife to bring him another.

No reply was forthcoming, which was strange.

He then hollered for the servants. Still nothing could be heard. He was not used to being ignored. He called out to his sons and daughters but his cries were again unheeded and his legendary quick temper flared. Eventually, in a huff, he stormed into the building with the empty glass, walked through the French windows and the lounge, into the hall.

A distinct but muffled cry caught his attention there. It was coming from the understairs cupboard and sounded very much like someone, someone who was gagged, trying their best to scream for help. He placed the glass down quickly on a table and rushed to open the door.

'Ah-ah! I wouldn't do that if I were you,' a deep throaty growl of a voice warned him ominously, from somewhere to his rear.

Sir Nicholas stopped in his tracks just shy of the closet and remained perfectly still.

'After all, they are safely locked away at present and unable to see anything. You release them now and they become *witnesses*. Which means there would be a price to pay in the final reckoning. A very messy, unnecessary price, if you get my drift?'

The elderly knight of the realm didn't know what to do but he sensed correctly that the lone stranger was armed and *extremely* dangerous. Could feel it in the way he had just narrowly avoided soiling his swimshorts. He therefore held his hands way up high to demonstrate his willingness to comply.

'That's more like it.'

'If... If it's money you want, just take it. All of it. There's a safe in the lounge, behind the painting above the fire surround. Enough cash and jewels in there to make you rich beyond your wildest dreams. Only, leave me alone and my family unharmed.'

The stranger in the room spoke again, as Sir Nicholas tried to turn around.

'No! You stay right where you are. Face that door and stand still. We need to get one thing perfectly clear; I've come for payment. However, it's not just your money I'm after.'

Johnson was sweating now, aware that he was about to die.

'What then?' he blurted out, though he was fearful of the answer.

'Yours is a blood debt, I'm afraid. You're not long for this world, Jonno me ol' mate. You should make peace now with whatever God you worship, though your sort are more likely to head downwards I think, rather than upwards.'

'Hardly an angel yourself!' the peer of the realm cried out, almost in tears. 'I'll *treble* whatever you are being paid. What do you say?'

'That's mighty generous of you. I already know about your safe though. And besides, this one is personal. Business too. But personal. *Combined*, if you will.'

'I... I don't understand?'

'It's not so late, is it? Just time to explain it to you then, I suppose... You have somehow evaded capture and prosecution, having offended against a conglomerate of some very powerful states, including Great Britain. That has raised more than a few toupees amongst the elite. Questions are being asked at extremely high levels, by many in the corridors of power. There *are* those who are convinced that you ratted them out. Squealed your rather large posterior off in fact. They are not *pleased*, Nicky boy. A little put out. Justice is likely to arrive at their doors any day now, with a huge slice of vengeance thrown in for good measure. They are determined to tie up any loose ends before it does. And here *you* are, enjoying the sun in paradise, without a care in the world, whilst *they* contemplate a prison cell and how to avoid dropping the soap in the showers. Not good optics, is it?'

'But I have said nothing!' Sir Nicholas protested. 'I never would!'

'I believe you, ol' chum. It matters not though,' the gunman stated, raising his suppressed pistol. 'Because of you, a very good mate of mine was slotted. One of the best. I've had waterworks at home because of it. My daughter is inconsolable and no longer talking to me. That's the *personal* side of things.'

'James? You're speaking of him? That was just business, that's all.'

'Yeah? So is this.'

Phut! Phut!

The former SBS officer stepped nonchalantly over the corpse and turned in the direction of the safe. Rude not to. Seeing as he was there.

Thank you for reading this novel. I love hearing what people think so please review it and help spread the word.

M J Webb

Also by this author;

12+ Fantasy genre – The Jake West Trilogy.

Jake West – 'The Keeper of the Stones'

Jake West – 'Warriors of the Heynai'

Jake West – 'The Estian Alliance'

18+ Adult Thriller – *'A Child of Szabo'*

18+ Adult Fantasy – *'Realm of Ruin'*

Available online now at Amazon

Printed in Great Britain
by Amazon